A Fracture

Alison Baillie

www.bloodhoundbooks.com

Print ISBN 978-1-912986-12-5

To Akira, Magnus and Robin

Chapter 1

Someone's watching

Wildenwil, Switzerland – Thursday 12 November, 2015

Olivia watched as the children ran down the lane towards the village, their school bags bobbing on their backs. As they disappeared into the shadow of the winter trees, she waved and turned back to the farmhouse, looking forward to a peaceful cup of coffee. She loved this moment of morning calm after the mad rush of breakfast when Christian and the children had gone.

As she passed the post box by the gate, a flash of white paper caught her eye. Strange. The postman didn't come until later. She pulled the note out, glanced at it, and froze. The handwritten words leapt out at her:

How can you sleep at night after what you did in Edinburgh?

Her heart started to race. Who could have written it? Nobody here in Switzerland knew what had happened, why she'd had to leave Scotland.

Behind her, a rustle in the trees. She swung round, but the woods were still, and the narrow lane winding up to the peaks was deserted. Apart from a hawk floating silently in the morning sky, there was no sign of life.

A shudder ran through her. For the past few days, she'd been sure someone was watching, that eyes were following her. She'd dismissed it as imagination, but now there was this note. Did somebody out there know her secret?

Feeling numb, she walked back to the kitchen and sat at the scrubbed wooden table, her head in her hands. The words of the note kept echoing through her brain.

She'd thought she was safe, that she'd managed to escape from her past. For the past eleven years, she'd led an idyllic life in this small Swiss village, in her beautiful farmhouse, with her lovely family. Christian had been such a source of strength, taking care of her and adopting Julian. The births of Marc and Lara had completed her happiness, but this note threatened to ruin everything.

The wooden walls of the farmhouse were closing in on her. She had to get out. At the kitchen door, Bella, the St Bernard dog, stood wagging her tail hopefully. She was supposedly Julian's pet, given to him when he first came to Switzerland, one of the bribes to encourage him to leave everything he'd known in Edinburgh. Now he was a teenager he wasn't interested in her anymore, and Bella was all hers. Her best friend.

Olivia fastened Bella's collar, fondling her silky ears, and stepped outside into the crisp mountain air. It was a magical November morning, with jewel-bright colours and long shadows from the low winter sun. Below her house, the forest snaked its way over the hillside and into the valley where Lake Zug sparkled in the distance.

Trying to shake off the dark shadow of the note, she put Bella into the back of her car and drove up the winding lane towards the Wildenberg Peaks, which loomed in dark spikes against the pure blue sky. Hardly anyone used this back road, only a few farmers struggling to survive on the harsh mountain slopes, so as she passed the farmhouse belonging to their nearest neighbours, the Kolbs, she was surprised to see an unfamiliar car behind her. From the number plate she could see it was from another canton, one often used to register hire cars. Gripping the steering wheel more tightly, she increased her speed and was relieved to see the other car continue towards the pass when they reached the foot of the funicular railway.

She parked the car and as the historic railway creaked its way up the imposing cliffs, she felt the tension ebbing away. As they reached the top, her spirits lifted. The lakes and forests of central Switzerland were spread out beneath her and, far in the distance, the snow-covered Alps glittered in the winter sun. Although she'd lived in Switzerland for more than ten years, the beauty of the landscape still took her breath away.

Below her, nestling in a clearing in the forest, she could see their farmhouse, and beyond it the village of Wildenwil, where her two younger children, Marc and Lara, were at school. When she'd first arrived in Switzerland, Wildenwil had been a sleepy farming village, but now there were new houses being built in every direction. Because it was so close to the town of Zug, a magnet for international business because of its low taxes, the village was now becoming popular with foreigners too.

She and Julian had been the only non-Swiss in the village when they'd first arrived. That had been one of its attractions, allowing her to hide away in a different country and culture, far away from the horrors of the past. Her integration had been made easier because she could already speak German, and she'd quickly mastered the tricky local dialect.

She walked along the ridge with Bella padding beside her, the light breeze blowing through her hair. After a few hundred yards, they reached a wooden bridge over a torrent of water crashing down the cliffs. She put Bella on her lead. The path was narrow and dangerous here and Bella's eyesight wasn't as good as it had been.

Leaning over the balustrade, she saw the dramatic waterfall and, in the shadows beside it, the creepy outline of the Grand Wildenbach Hotel. It was a four-storey Gothic building with turrets, arches and enclosed balconies. It had once been a famous stop on the European Grand Tour, visited by aristocrats and literary figures, but had long been abandoned and fallen into disrepair. Village gossip said it had been bought earlier in the year and was being extensively renovated, but as it was hidden behind the high wall and tall trees of the overgrown grounds, it was difficult to know what was going on.

Olivia looked at her watch. She'd have to hurry to get back for lunch. There were no school dinners for primary age children in her village so Marc and Lara came home for lunch every day. Although it was so different from what she'd been used to in Scotland, she now loved having her children home for the long lunch break, so they could eat together and have a chat before afternoon school.

Once again, she and Bella were alone in the funicular as it rocked down to the foot of the crags, but as she was driving home, she caught sight of a car in her rear-view mirror. The same one as before.

Her heart pounding, she slowed down, trying to identify the driver, but could see nothing but a dark silhouette. Who could be following her? Despite the bright sunshine, the familiar landscape became sinister. She drove to the farmhouse as quickly as she could, ran into the kitchen, slammed the door behind her and leant against it, her breath coming in painful gasps.

When her pulse rate had returned to normal, she heated the spaghetti for lunch. Marc and Lara would be back soon, so she had to calm herself. Julian went to the Kantonsschule, the high school in Zug where Christian was Head of the English department, so they ate lunch in the cafeteria there.

The door slammed as Marc and Lara rushed in, throwing their school bags down and declaring they were starving. Listening to their happy chatter as they ate, Olivia pushed thoughts of the note and car to the back of her mind as everything seemed so normal.

After lunch, Reto Kolb, the youngest of the five sons from the farm up the road, called in for Marc and a few minutes later Sandra, Reto's little sister, came for Lara. As usual, Olivia waved as they set off down the lane and forced herself to remain calm. Switzerland was safe and it was normal for young children to walk to school without adults.

Olivia was glad Sandra called for Lara every morning and after lunch. She was a year older than Lara, and much taller and sturdier. As the youngest of a large farming family, Sandra had to be able to look after herself. Although she was only eight, she helped on the farm and could often be seen bringing cows in from the meadow, or helping to gather the cut grass on the steep mountain slopes. Lara seemed much younger than Sandra, small and slight like Olivia, and she still enjoyed playing with her toys.

Olivia went back into the house and, after clearing the lunch things, made some Schinkengipfeli – the typically Swiss ham pastries everybody loved. Bella was lying in front of the wood-burning stove, curled up with Shadow, the long-haired grey cat who'd walked into their home one evening and never left, always sleeping in the warmest corner of the house.

When her pastries were in the oven, Olivia sat at the kitchen door in the winter sunshine with her Kindle, reading the latest Ian Rankin novel. He was her favourite author and, although she hadn't been back to Scotland since she'd left eleven years before, she loved walking the Georgian Edinburgh streets with his detective, Rebus. But today she couldn't concentrate; her mind kept wandering back to the strange car and note.

She told herself to forget them and take advantage of this time to herself. Up until the month before, she'd never had a minute to call her own. As well as looking after the family, she'd cared for Zita, Christian's old aunt, who'd lived in a tiny wooden chalet next to their house. She'd been a cantankerous old woman, looking and sounding like a witch from a fairy tale, with thin grey hair and a hooked nose. Olivia had sometimes resented having to go to her three times a day, taking her meals, washing her and getting her ready for bed. Now Zita was gone, it was a relief for everyone because she'd been in considerable pain at the end, but Olivia missed her. She'd liked the feeling of helping and being needed and now, sometimes, her life felt a little empty.

The shadows were lengthening and the air was starting to chill, when she looked at her watch. Lara and Sandra were late. The boys had football training after school, so she wasn't expecting them until later, but Lara should be back by now. The cloud of unease that had been hanging over her all day intensified. She tried to calm her fears by convincing herself that because the weather was so mild, the girls were playing on their way home from school, but the disquiet lingered on.

As the evening sun was sinking behind the alp, reflecting pink on the mountains beyond the lake, she began to panic. As soon as the sun set, it would get dark very quickly. She fixed her eyes on the corner of the lane where it vanished into the darkness of the trees, but there was no sign of life.

She was just about to get into the car to go and look for the girls when she saw two figures emerging from the shadows, and sighed with relief. They were back.

Then she saw a ball being kicked between them and realised it wasn't the girls, but Marc and Reto.

Shaking with fear, she ran towards them and reached Marc as he was waving goodbye to his friend. She put her arms out to hug him but he pushed her away, looking round to check that Reto hadn't witnessed the embarrassing scene.

Olivia smiled, forcing herself to remain calm. 'Hi, have you had a good afternoon?' Trying to keep the anxiety out of her voice, she added, as casually as she could, 'Have you seen Lara and Sandra?'

'No, we had football training.'

'You didn't see them after school?'

'We were down at the field and didn't come back past the school. I'm hungry. What's for tea?' Marc walked towards the kitchen, oblivious to the look on his mother's face.

Olivia looked at her watch again – nearly five o'clock. She ran back to the car and was just putting the key into the ignition when she noticed a movement in the shadows at the corner of the lane. A small figure appeared. Olivia let out the breath she hadn't realised she'd been holding and got out of the car, her hands shaking with relief. They were safe.

She was running down the lane, when panic gripped her again. There was only one figure making its way through the gathering dusk. Where was the other girl?

The dark silhouette trudged up the lane, head down, dragging her feet. As it came nearer, Olivia could make out a red jacket.

Feeling a surge of guilty relief, she recognised it as Lara's. She was safe.

Olivia ran to her daughter and swept her up into her arms. 'Darling, what's happened? Where's Sandra?' Kissing her damp cheeks, she looked over Lara's shoulder and down the road. It was deserted.

Lara clung on to her, sobbing loudly. 'Sandra's not my friend anymore. She wouldn't play with me at school. She says she's got a new friend.' She gulped back her tears. 'And after school I couldn't find her. I looked everywhere and I couldn't find her. I looked for Marc too. But he wasn't there.' She let out a wail. 'Mummy, I was scared.'

Olivia held her daughter close, rocking her in her arms. She was annoyed with Sandra. However badly they'd fallen out, she should never have left Lara alone.

She carried her daughter into the kitchen and drew the curtains. The room was cosy, filled with the smell of baking, and the single standard light cast a soft glow over the wooden table in the corner.

A burst of laughter came from the small television room next to the kitchen; Olivia guessed Marc was watching cartoons. Setting her daughter down at the table, she poured a glass of milk. Lara sipped it, her lip trembling. 'I want Sandra to be my friend again. She said I was a baby and she didn't want to play with me anymore.'

Olivia held her close. She knew what it was like to be rejected by other children and wished she could protect her daughter from this. 'Do you want to go through and watch television with Marc?'

'No, I want to play with my ponies.' Lara reached into the box under the corner bench where she kept some of her old toys. She'd loved My Little Pony when she was younger, but hadn't played with them for years. Olivia helped to bring them out and watched as Lara arranged them in a row, combing their long, colourful manes and tails, her blonde hair falling over her face.

Chapter 2

Sandra is missing

Wildenwil – Thursday 12 November, 2015

A vehicle screeched to a halt in front of the house and the kitchen door crashed open. It was Hans Kolb, the farmer from up the road. 'Have you seen Sandra?' He was a very shy man but his panic made him rush in, his weather-beaten face creased with fear. He was a typical Alpine farmer, short and wiry, wearing the traditional tasselled hat.

Olivia shook her head. 'Isn't she home yet?' The relief she'd felt earlier dissolved. 'Lara came home alone. They seem to have had some kind of argument.' Olivia nodded towards Lara whose head was down, avoiding the farmer's eye. Olivia lowered herself to her daughter's level. 'Lara, this is important. Tell us everything you remember. When did you last see Sandra?'

'I don't want to talk about it.' Lara pushed her mother away, keeping her eyes on her toys.

'Lara, darling, we don't know where Sandra is. You have to help us find her, and the best way you can do that is by telling us everything you remember about this afternoon.' Olivia put her arms round her daughter. Sometimes Lara seemed quite mature, but at this moment Olivia realised she was still very young.

Lara looked up, her face tear-stained. One of her plaits had come undone. 'She said she's not my friend anymore. She's got a new friend.'

Olivia held her tight, trying to keep her voice as steady as possible. 'Perhaps she went to play with her new friend. Do you know her name?' Olivia looked over her daughter's head and saw the confusion on Hans's face.

'She didn't tell me. She just said she was a better friend than me.' Lara's bottom lip trembled and she buried her head in her mother's shoulder.

The farmer moved towards the door. 'I'm going to phone Frau Fisch to see if she knows anything about it.'

'Good idea. She might know who the new friend is.' Olivia stood up and put her hand on his arm. 'There's a class list with phone numbers. Shall I phone to see if anybody knows anything?'

'Vreni is phoning the girls. Could you try the boys? You never know, maybe she's got herself a boyfriend.' He gave a forced laugh, seeming to grasp at any explanation.

Olivia hesitated. Hans and Vreni were neighbours and their children were friends, but they'd never been close. Despite this, she felt a sudden urge to put her arms round the farmer.

Drawing back the curtain, she saw the darkness had fallen quickly and it was totally black outside, with only a few pinpricks of light far in the distance. 'Perhaps she'll be back at the house? Please let me know if you hear anything. I'm sure we'll find her soon.' She hoped her words sounded more convincing to him than they did to her.

As Hans was moving towards the door, there was a sound outside. Olivia was relieved. Christian was home. He'd know what to do in a situation like this.

The door swung open and Julian crashed into the kitchen and took off his helmet, shaking his long dark hair. 'I was late for school again today. That heap of junk is absolutely useless. I'll have to get a better moped or I'll be in real trouble.'

Olivia kept her voice steady. 'We'll talk about that later. This is important – have you seen Sandra? She hasn't come home from school.'

'Sandra?' He made a show of thinking. 'Not since this morning, when I was trying to get that thing started. You do realise I must have reliable transport.'

Olivia shot Hans an apologetic glance, and was about to say something to Julian, but realised another argument wouldn't help. Were all teenagers so self-centred?

Hans left quickly and had just driven away when the beam of headlights appeared outside the window and another car drew up. Christian was back. Olivia ran to the door and hugged her husband, relieved to see him. Christian was so dependable and safe.

He seemed to sense her mood immediately. 'Is something the matter, Livy?'

'It's Sandra. She's missing. She didn't come home from school.'

'I saw Hans's pickup. That explains it; he was driving like a maniac.' Christian indicated Lara with his eyes. She usually rushed into her father's arms when he arrived, but today she remained hunched over her toys. 'She's okay?' he asked softly.

Olivia nodded and explained what had happened. Christian stopped taking his coat off. 'I'm going out. I've got to help.'

Olivia put her hand on his arm. 'Wait for a while. I'm going to help phone round the class. Perhaps she's with one of them. There's soup on the stove and Schinkengipfeli. If you do have to go out, you should eat something first.'

Olivia went into the study and, picking up the telephone, worked her way down the list. Nobody knew anything. Boys were called to the phone, questions were asked, but none of them said anything useful. The calls got progressively shorter as she tired of explaining what had happened.

The last time she put the phone down, it rang immediately.

'Any news?' It was Hans. Olivia told him about the blank she'd drawn. The farmer's voice was husky with fear. 'Nobody has seen her. I'm calling the police.' The line went dead.

Olivia ran to the kitchen and told Christian what Hans had said. Christian immediately stood up from the table. 'I'm going out to look.'

'It's dark. We should leave it to the police.'

'I've got to do something. I can't just sit here. What if it were Lara who was missing? I have to go.'

Olivia nodded and followed him to the door. Bella stood up stiffly from her bed by the stove and looked hopeful, thinking it might be time for another walk, but Christian ignored her. Olivia realised Christian was right; they couldn't just sit around and do nothing when Sandra could be lost in the darkness, lying injured or, Olivia shuddered, even worse. What if somebody had taken her? She thought of the strange car she'd seen that morning. Could that have something to do with Sandra's disappearance?

Christian lifted Lara. Her thin arms and legs clung round him and she held him tight as he kissed her. Marc got up from the table, blond and stocky, his father's little mini-me. Christian tousled his head. 'I'm just going out for a while. You look after your mum and Lara.' Marc nodded solemnly and Christian turned quickly away.

After the door had closed behind him, Olivia tried to keep things as normal as possible and asked about homework. Julian had already disappeared upstairs, supposedly to do his. Marc, as usual, said he'd finished his at school, and Lara looked anxiously into her schoolbag. She couldn't remember. Olivia took the bag away – homework didn't matter tonight. Lara clutched one of her ponies tightly in her hand. Olivia knew how she felt. She wanted to hold Lara and Marc and never let them go.

They went through to the television room and sat together on the sofa with a fleecy blanket over them. Bella lay on Olivia's feet, a warm, comforting presence, and Shadow stretched out along the back of the sofa, purring loudly. Even Marc cuddled up to one side as they let Lara choose the DVD. He sat and fiddled with his Game Boy while they watched her favourite, *Rise of the Guardians*. Olivia sat between her two younger children, stroking their hair, filled with an overwhelming feeling of love.

Later than usual, she took them up to bed and was relieved when they both fell asleep quickly, Lara surrounded by her soft toys and Marc wearing his favourite blue and white Scotland football strip.

Olivia sat down in the kitchen. Only the standard light behind her was lit and she watched the window, wishing Christian would come home. Usually she felt safe when she was at home alone with the children, but this evening, she couldn't relax.

Feeling the note in her pocket, she thought of the strange car following her. Did the driver have something to do with Sandra's disappearance? Had he been watching her? Was there somebody out there?

A terrifying thought came to her. Olivia felt ashamed even considering it, but she was sure anybody would agree that Lara was an exceptionally beautiful child – small, golden-haired, with large dark eyes and fine features. Sandra was a lovely girl, but there was no denying the fact that she was a plain child – solid, sturdy, with ruddy cheeks, chapped lips and the neglected appearance of the youngest child of a large poor family. Olivia pushed the thought away but it forced itself back. Had Sandra been abducted by mistake? Was it Lara they really wanted? Maybe the car had been following her?

No, she was imagining things. Sandra would be found. She'd just gone to a new friend's house and been caught out by the early nightfall. Luckily the mild weather would mean she'd be able to survive until morning light. The thought of Sandra alone and frightened outside horrified her, but she had to cling on to the hope that she'd soon be found.

The wind blew round the house and through the trees. There was a creaking sound and the snap of branches. Were those footsteps she could hear? She held her breath as she strained to hear noises in the black void outside the window. There were many times she'd felt alone and frightened in her thirty-nine years, but she'd never experienced terror like this before, fear for her children's safety.

Chapter 3

The search

Wildenwil – Friday 13 November, 2015

Olivia opened her eyes with a start. Was someone moving in the house? She lay rigid, straining to hear any sounds. Christian was lying next to her, breathing gently. He'd come in late and slid into bed beside her. She'd been longing for him to come home, but he didn't have any news of Sandra.

The Swiss Alert system for missing children, which instantly sends text messages to every police force, railway station and airport in Switzerland, had been activated, but the search of the area with sniffer dogs had been called off until the morning. The operation would be resumed at first light, when the helicopters would join the search.

Christian had immediately fallen into a deep sleep, but Olivia had to get up to check the doors again. The old floorboards creaked and the shadows were sinister and unfamiliar. As she crept along the wooden corridors to check on her two youngest, every dark doorway and corner seemed threatening.

Her heart thumping, she peeped into Lara's room and by the light of the corridor could see her bed filled with soft toys, a teddy barricade against her fears. In the next room, Marc was flushed, his duvet thrown off. She pulled the covers over him gently, smiling as he protected himself with the magic powers of his Scotland strip.

As she was getting back into bed, Christian stirred. 'You must sleep, Livy. We must hold it together for the children. It won't help anyone if we fall apart. We must make everything as normal as possible.'

Eventually she fell asleep, and when she woke, it was already light. In the first moment of half-waking, she knew something terrible had happened, but couldn't remember what. Then she remembered. Sandra was missing.

She jumped out of bed and ran along the corridor, looking in panic into the children's rooms. They were empty. A momentary feeling of terror, and then she heard voices and breakfast sounds downstairs. The smell of coffee and toast should have been comforting, but it was a mockery, like the incredible beauty of the bright morning sunshine through the narrow bedroom window.

She tried to think positively. Perhaps Sandra was home? Maybe she'd slept in one of the stone huts dotted over the hillside and was now sitting in the back of a police car having a warm drink. Olivia clung to this image, hoping against hope it was true.

She washed her face and went downstairs. Christian was standing by the table packing his briefcase. 'I'm taking Marc and Lara to school this morning, and you can come with me too, Julian.' Her eldest child hated the fact that his stepfather taught at the school where he was a student, but this morning he was happy to get a lift into Zug.

Olivia forced herself to put on a bright smile. 'I'll come and collect you at lunchtime,' she said, looking at her two younger children, 'and we'll have bridie.' This traditional Scottish pasty was their favourite.

She kissed Christian as he moved towards the door. He was right; they had to keep everything as normal as possible for the children. With a flurry of jackets and school bags, they disappeared through the door and the kitchen was silent.

Olivia automatically cleared the breakfast things, fed Bella who was sitting by the door looking up with soulful eyes, and noticed it was nearly eight o'clock – time for the news. She switched on the radio, holding her breath, praying she'd hear something positive. But it was a vain hope. The main story was of an eight-year-old girl, missing on her way home from school in central Switzerland, adding that the search had been resumed at first light.

Overhead, Olivia heard the sound of a helicopter and opened the kitchen door. The view was as idyllic as ever, the valley sparkling in the bright autumn light. Looking up into the blue sky, she couldn't see anything. With Bella padding at her heels, she walked round the outside of the farmhouse, checking the garage and the shed, under the table in their sitting area, behind the leafless bushes and the gaunt winter trees. She couldn't imagine Sandra being there, but she had to do something.

There was nothing to see, so she went back into the house and searched every room, looking under beds, into cupboards, behind curtains and sofas. She knew in her heart Sandra wouldn't be there, but she clung to the hope that she might find her asleep, her sturdy legs sticking out from a hiding place.

Taking the key for Zita's small chalet from the back of the kitchen door, she made a wider tour of the land around the house. Zita's house was dark, the clammy interior filled with cobwebs. Olivia looked around, but it was obvious that nobody had been in the house since Zita had died. She shivered and locked the door behind her. Despite the sunshine and the crisp autumn air, the long shadows from the low sun gave the familiar scene an eerie stillness.

The quiet was broken by the sound of voices. Over the brow of the hill above her, a group of dark figures, silhouetted against the skyline, moved steadily across the tussocky grass. The search parties were out.

A sound behind her made her spin round, but she couldn't see anything in the gloom at the edge of the forest. A branch moved. The fear she'd pushed away the night before returned. Was there a gang out there stealing children? Did they want Lara? The feeling of terror was so strong she wanted to jump into her car and park outside the school, watching, keeping her children safe.

Olivia tried to calm herself. Christian always said she read too many books, had too much imagination. She tried to think rationally; Sandra had probably just wandered off. Even as she said this to herself, she didn't believe it. Sandra wouldn't do that. She'd lived her whole life on the farm and wouldn't move far from her daily route down to the village. Tears came to her eyes. She just wanted Sandra to be found safe so all their lives could go back to their normal, peaceful routine.

Gravel crunched as a police car drew into the yard. She walked towards it as two policemen stepped out. Olivia recognised the older one, Ruedi Wiesli, one of Christian's old school friends and a member of the gym group he trained with every week in the school hall.

He was the one who spoke first. 'We've just come to check your outbuildings, if that's all right with you. You'll have heard that a young girl has gone missing.'

'Yes, Sandra Kolb. We've looked everywhere, but I know you have to check. Is there any news?'

The younger policeman shook his head and looked down at a list. 'You're Frau Olivia Keller? From England?' She nodded. Usually she said she was from Scotland, but this was no time for national distinctions. 'Your German is excellent.'

'Thank you.' Olivia was used to compliments because so many of the expats down in Zug could hardly speak any German, even after years in Switzerland.

The officers looked in the same places she'd searched a short while before, including Zita's chalet. As she watched them, there was a crackle behind her. The hairs on the back of her neck stood up as she looked round. Although the forest was dark and silent, she was sure there were eyes watching her.

The police officers finished their search and came over. 'When did you last see Sandra Kolb?'

Olivia explained that Sandra was her daughter's best friend, and how they always walked to and from school together. 'The last time I saw her was after lunch yesterday when she came to collect Lara as usual.' In her mind's eye, Olivia saw them walking down the lane – when her world had been normal.

The younger policeman took notes. 'We'd like to speak to your daughter. Do we have your permission to question her at school? You can, of course, be there if you wish, but we'd like to talk to all her classmates and the teacher will be present. We want to keep everything as low-key as possible.'

Olivia nodded and then plucked up the courage to ask the question that had been haunting her. 'Is there a possibility that Sandra's been abducted? Are the other children in danger?'

Ruedi Wiesli spoke calmly, as if he were repeating a script. 'At the moment, there is no evidence of abduction, but we have to keep an open mind.' He looked tired; he'd probably been up searching all night. 'Have you noticed anything unusual in the neighbourhood recently?'

Olivia paused, wondering whether to say anything.

The younger officer noticed her hesitation. 'Anything at all out of the ordinary, please tell us. The slightest thing could help us find Sandra.'

Olivia took a deep breath and told them about the car she'd seen the day before. She couldn't remember the exact registration number but she knew it was AI, from Appenzell, a mountain canton in the east of Switzerland where hire cars were often registered. 'It was going towards the village. Are there CCTV cameras? They'd show any strange car and the exact number plate.'

'There's a camera at the Raiffeisen bank, but unfortunately it's directed towards the cash machine and we doubt there'll be any useful footage on it. We will, of course, look at it. Is there anything else that struck you as unusual?'

Olivia hesitated again. She didn't want to come across as a hysterical mother, but she told them about her feeling of being watched. The policeman noted it down, writing seriously, although Olivia wondered if they were just humouring her. 'Every piece of evidence is important to us, no matter how trivial it may seem. Of course, there are search parties out at the moment, and journalists are beginning to gather in the village so you will see some strangers.'

Olivia watched as the police officers drove away, holding tightly on to Bella's collar. She hadn't told them about the note. It had arrived before Sandra's disappearance, so it wasn't relevant. And she didn't want anyone asking questions about what had happened and why she'd fled from Scotland.

Chapter 4

Marie

Marie packed her books into her cotton bag as slowly as she could, waiting for the other girls to leave the classroom. She didn't look up as they ran out of the room, laughing and chattering.

Mrs Elkin was at the front desk, tidying her things away. 'Hurry up, Marie. I've got a meeting soon so I'll have to lock up in a minute. Have you got everything you need?' Marie nodded. The teacher hesitated for a moment and then picked up a brightly coloured book from her desk. 'Would you like to take this book too? It's brand new, just come in. You read so quickly I thought you'd like it first.'

Marie took the book and smiled at her teacher. Mrs Elkin was always nice to her and even tried to protect her from the other girls' nastiness. But she wasn't always around. Marie thanked her quietly and left the classroom, bowing her head to the crucifix by the door as her mother said she should.

She slowly approached the front door of the old Victorian school and looked cautiously out over the concrete playground. She could see her mother, wearing her usual drab brown coat and clutching a large shopping bag, standing on the other side of the wall, a little further away from the gate than the group of chattering mums. The coast seemed to be clear, so she stepped out into the pale afternoon sunlight.

'Oh, there you are, Swotty Pants. You'd better hurry up. You're keeping your granny waiting. She needs to get home to knit you another school jumper.' Victoria Sutton stepped out in front of her from the side of the door, her shiny black ponytail bouncing, her perfect school uniform looking as if she'd put it on brand new that morning. Marie tried to sidle past without catching her eye. Victoria was the worst of her tormentors in the class, pretty and full of confidence. Marie couldn't believe she was only eight, the same age as her. But her father was rich and she went to singing and dancing classes. She said she was going to be a film star when she grew up and Marie could believe her.

Keeping her eyes down, Marie walked as quickly as she could towards the gate. Victoria followed her, muttering in her ear, 'Be a good little girl and go straight home and hold Granny's hand tightly.' Marie flushed. She didn't mind the taunts so much for herself – she was used to them – but she didn't want her mother to hear. Therese was older than the other mums, but she didn't look like a granny. She was kind and did everything she could for her. Victoria was just mean.

She ran the last few steps and, taking her mother's hand, looked up at her soft, kind face. Therese's hair was grey and wispy, but her deep-set brown eyes were filled with love. She brought her to school every morning and back again after lunch, and was always waiting for her when she came out. Marie looked over her shoulder. She was afraid Victoria might make a comment, but was relieved to see the other girl was standing with her back to her, laughing with a group of her friends.

'Nice day at school, dear?' her mother asked, in her soft Scottish tones. Marie nodded. She didn't want her mother to know how the other girls teased her. She'd once suggested that perhaps she could get her uniform from a shop, rather than Therese making all her clothes herself, but the pain and disappointment in her mother's face had made her wish she'd never said anything. She knew they didn't have much money, but her mother tried to make sure she always had everything she needed for school.

'Mrs Elkin gave me a new book today. Nobody else has read it.' Marie rustled in her bag so she could show it to her mother.

'That's nice, but I thought we'd go to the library today. Your father is home early.' She felt her mother's hand grip her more tightly and her pace quicken as they hurried away from the school. She didn't need any more explanation. Their small flat was peaceful when her father was out, but when he was at home, she and her mother were on edge, not knowing what would trigger one of his violent mood swings.

The cold east wind blew off the sea and along the white Regency crescents as they walked towards the rocky promontory that separated Scarborough's north and south bays. The outline of the ruined eleventh-century castle was silhouetted against the azure sky between the grand terraces. The library was not far from the castle – in the old town perched on higher ground between the bays – and it was Marie's favourite place. Ever since Mrs Elkin had told Therese about the library, and she'd realised it was free, they went after school several times a week.

They climbed the steps of the library and pushed the heavy wooden door. The air was warm and smelled of books. The librarian smiled in recognition, and while her mother went off to choose another hospital romance, Marie ran towards the children's room. She felt a thrill of excitement as she looked at the Recently Returned shelf and saw a Secret Seven book she hadn't read. Taking it down, she sat at the small table, looking at the cover and savouring the moment of anticipation. She loved Enid Blyton's books, especially the Secret Seven. She liked to imagine she was in a gang like Peter and Janet. It would be wonderful to have a brother or sister like them – or a friend. In all the books she read the children had friends, but she only had her mother.

She didn't have any friends in her class. Perhaps if she stayed at school over lunchtime she would, but she was the only person in her class who went home for dinner. She wished she could carry a shiny plastic lunchbox like the others, but she'd never mentioned it to her mother. She knew without asking that she wouldn't be able to get one, and it would only hurt her mother if she suggested it.

Marie had learned to be careful about what she said. Her mother got upset if she asked for anything that might be expensive, and her father got annoyed and exasperated by almost everything. She couldn't predict what would set him off on one of his rants, so she tried to say as little as possible to him.

He seemed to hate the school, her teachers and everything that happened there. He wasn't pleased that Mrs Elkin encouraged her, telling her quietly that she was the best at reading and writing in the class. Marie was glad Mrs Elkin was her teacher again this year, although her father didn't like her at all, calling her 'that interfering busybody'.

One occasion he'd been especially annoyed was when she'd had to draw a family tree for homework. During supper she'd asked about their family because she knew nothing about her parents. She knew they'd come from Scotland, but she'd never been there herself and didn't seem to have any grandparents, aunts and uncles, or cousins. In the books she read, people always had fun with their relatives, but she didn't have anyone.

Her father had exploded. 'That nosy cow! What's it to do with her?' Then he'd sneered, 'She's always saying what a great imagination you've got, so do something useful with it – make something up.' She'd gone to her attic room and invented the most wonderful range of relatives in Scotland. She just wished it could have been true.

She was sitting, lost in the first chapter of the book, when Therese came in. 'We'd better go so your father can get his tea on time. But first I want to pop into the church and light a candle. Princess Diana has had another little boy and I want to thank God for her blessing.' She smiled fondly at her daughter. 'And for mine.'

Marie was used to this. Her mother always lit a candle to give thanks for her daughter, who she called her little miracle. The church was very important to Therese, and Father Dominic seemed to be her only friend. Apart from the cleaning she did at the betting shop beneath their flat, the only place she ever went to was church. Marie went too, every Sunday, and her first communion the previous spring had been one of the most exciting days of her life. Her mother had spent many evenings making her a beautiful white dress, not as flashy as the shop-bought ones Victoria and the other girls had, but as she received the first sacrament, she'd felt very proud.

The church wasn't far from the library so they walked there quickly in the gathering gloom. A cold breeze was blowing off the sea and Marie shivered as they hurried through the dark streets.

They pushed open the heavy door of the church and dipped their fingers in the holy water. Marie could see her mother relax in the tall shadowy church, with the evening light shining through the stained-glass windows, the flickering candles and the heavy smell of incense. As her mother lowered her head and prayed, Marie felt pleased. She wanted beyond anything for her mother to be happy. In the past, her father had gone to church as often as her mother, but now his visits were very rare.

After lighting the candle, they walked back to their flat above the betting shop opposite Peasholm Park. They climbed the narrow stairs and heard muttered swearing above the low hum of the television news. Frank McGuigan was sitting in front of the small box television waving his fist in anger at scenes from the miners' strike.

He turned and glared at the women. Although Marie didn't know exactly how old he was, she knew he was ten years older than his wife, so she'd worked out that he must be over sixty. He looked even older with his gnarled features and grey stubble.

'Where've you been, Therese? I've been waiting for my tea.' He glared at Marie. 'You haven't been talking to that interfering teacher woman again, have you?'

Therese shook her head. 'We went to the church,' she said, and hurried to the kitchenette, appearing a moment later with a plate of ham, which she set in front of her husband. Therese returned with another two plates and they all sat down at the plastic-covered table. The one dim ceiling light in the centre of the room accentuated the cheerless utilitarian furniture.

Frank turned to Marie. 'What's the homework tonight, Einstein?'

'Just reading,' she answered quietly.

'Just reading?' He gave a sneering smile. 'Shouldn't you have a little arithmetic?' Marie knew what was coming next. 'Little Miss Clever Clogs had ten sums for homework – and not one of them was right!' Her father gave a humourless laugh and she lowered her eyes. When they'd first learned take-away sums at school, she'd had ten sums for homework and made the same mistake in all of them, so they were all wrong. Her father had been so delighted when he found out that he mentioned it at every opportunity.

Therese tried to change the subject. 'You know Charles and Diana have had another little boy. Did they show a picture on the news?'

'Parasites. They should do an honest day's work like us.' Frank shovelled the rest of his food into his mouth. Marie ate slowly, finding it difficult to swallow, the tension in the air forcing her throat to close. She wondered what work her father actually did. The story was that they'd come to Scarborough from Scotland to find a better job, but his work seemed irregular and they never had much money.

He moved back to his chair in front of the television and picked up a newspaper. He was studying the horseracing form, something Marie knew he prided himself on knowing a lot about. She stood up and pushed her chair back from the table. She couldn't eat any more. Frank barked at her, 'Where are you going with that plate? You clear it. Food is expensive so make sure you eat it.'

He turned back to the paper and she tried to swallow another mouthful, but the blockage in her throat made it impossible. Therese moved quietly behind her and picked up her plate, indicating the steep stairs up to the attic room with her eyes. Marie nodded gratefully and crept away.

Her bedroom was the only one on the top floor, very narrow with sloping eaves and only space for a single bed. She perched on the edge of it and opened her Secret Seven book. Her heartbeat slowed and her breathing became more even. She disappeared into the world of Peter and Janet and the rest of the gang, a world where she had friends who solved mysteries. The biggest mystery she wanted to solve was why her father was always so angry, and what she'd done to make him hate her so much.

Chapter 5

A body is found

The Christmas lights had been put up in the village and the first Advent candles flickered in the windows. Olivia was baking Christmas biscuits. Usually their spicy smell filled her with anticipation for the coming season, but this year she felt in limbo, unable to look forward to anything.

Sandra was still missing. It was more than three weeks since she'd disappeared, but despite a huge national and international search, there was no sign of her. CCTV footage had been checked, not only in Zug, but also in Zürich and all the main stations and airports. There had been appeals on television and in the newspapers. A school photo of Sandra had been enhanced, put on posters, and published in every newspaper in Switzerland and many abroad. Everywhere you looked, her shy smile gazed out at you.

Ruedi Wiesli, Christian's old school friend, wasn't at the centre of the operation as he was just a local policeman, but he'd told Christian most of the investigation centred on Sandra's family. Hans and Sandra's older brothers had all been questioned, and their house and grounds searched with infrared lights and sniffer dogs, but no trace of Sandra had been found.

Olivia had gone to visit Vreni the day after the disappearance. The Kolbs' farmhouse had always seemed shabby and rundown, but the kitchen was even more disorganised than she remembered. Vreni walked among the piles of plates, beer cans and scattered clothes in a robotic haze. She was obviously under very strong medication. Olivia wasn't surprised. How could any mother come to terms with what had happened?

Olivia had found a place for the tray of biscuits she'd brought, but Vreni hardly seemed to notice and didn't offer a cup of tea or a glass of water. Olivia hadn't known what to say. She offered to help in any way she could, but her voice sounded insincere even to her. She genuinely meant it, but just the fact that her daughter was safe seemed to be unspoken gloating. Afterwards she'd hurried from the house, hating the way she'd handled it but not knowing how to act in that awful situation. When she'd returned the next day, Vreni hadn't answered the door, although Olivia could tell she was there.

Next Sunday was 6 December. It was tradition in the village for two men to dress up as Samichlaus and his black-clad companion, Schmutzli, and wait with a donkey in a hut in the forest. Samichlaus was like a traditional jovial Santa Claus from an old-fashioned Christmas card, but Schmutzli was a frightening figure. He carried a wooden broom made of twigs and a sack, which folklore said he used to carry away naughty children. In the past he'd been used as a threat to keep children well-behaved, but now they just had to learn a rhyme and say they'd been good to get a present of a little sack of nuts and mandarins.

Every year, the children walked through the woods to the hut. It was a lovely tradition but this year Lara didn't want to go. Olivia wasn't surprised. Lara had always gone with Sandra and the fact that she wasn't there would make it unbearable. The whole atmosphere was strange, as the warm weather had continued into December. There was no snow, and spring flowers were growing in the garden. Everything seemed wrong and out of kilter.

Olivia looked at her watch. Just about time to go and collect Lara and Marc. She hadn't let them go anywhere alone since Sandra's disappearance. Lara accepted it. She was still quiet and subdued, missing her best friend and hating the strangeness of everything. Marc had protested that his mother didn't have to watch every football practice or take him to and from his scout meetings, but she hadn't given way. She didn't know when she'd ever be able to let her children go anywhere alone again.

She was taking the trays of biscuits from the oven when the kitchen door crashed open and Julian strode in. He was growing up so quickly, tall and handsome. Olivia waited for the usual complaints. He was so moody she often felt she was treading on eggshells.

But he was smiling. 'Guess what? I've got a job!'

Olivia put the tray down and reached up to hug him. 'That's fantastic!' She breathed a sigh of relief. Christian had been on at him for months to find a little job instead of asking for money all the time, for a new moped or computer games. According to Julian, he was undoubtedly the most disadvantaged child in the school and was also discriminated against in the family compared to Marc and Lara. Christian would reply by describing how he had helped on the farm when he was young, getting up at five to look after the cows before he went to school. Julian just shrugged. 'More fool you. You wouldn't catch me doing anything like that.'

'What sort of job is it?' Olivia wondered what would satisfy Julian. She'd suggested he apply for a job on the till at the Migros supermarket in Zug when they were looking for extra staff for Saturday and late-night shopping, but that had provoked a diatribe about how students were exploited in such jobs, and anyway it would be impossible as he'd got so much schoolwork to do.

'Translation work for one of the financial companies in Zug. I met this guy and he said they were looking for someone like me with perfect English and German. It's well paid, too.' He grinned and took a small bundle of notes out of his pocket.

Alarm bells rang for Olivia. 'What sort of man was this? Where did you meet him?'

'I was just looking at computer games in the Media Shop and we got talking. When he found out I was bilingual, we went for a coffee and he offered me a job.'

'Just like that? This sounds weird to me. Strange men don't just come up to you and offer you a job without any kind of test.'

Immediately, Sandra came into her head. One of the theories was that she'd been stolen by child traffickers. Julian wasn't a child but he was a very attractive young man, with his long dark hair, high cheekbones and long, slender limbs. Perhaps he was just the sort some men would like?

Julian stared at her in amazement. 'Typical. Always on at me to get a job and then, when I get one, you can't be pleased for me. You can't believe I can get anything better than slave labour at a bloody supermarket.'

He reached into his pocket and drew out a card. 'Look, here's the company, totally legit, UK-based, with offices in Zug. And he did give me a test. I had to translate a press release there and then, and he said it was excellent.'

Olivia looked at the card. It was a thick, expensive-looking one with engraved writing. PGM Phoenix Global Management. There was a Zug post box number, but no name or telephone number.'

'What's his name? How can you contact him? There's no number on this card. I think we should meet him before you agree to work for him.'

Julian snatched back the card. 'Stop treating me like a child. You've got your precious babies you won't let out of your sight, but I'm able to look after myself.'

Olivia gulped. She shouldn't let him speak to her like that, but she didn't want to alienate him completely. Julian spoke slowly as if she was a bit slow on the uptake. 'His name is Patrick and he's a director of this company. His main office is in London, but he also has an office and a flat in Zug, where he comes regularly. He's very smart, well-educated, classy. I have his mobile number on my phone. And incidentally, he's getting me a new iPhone. He says I need the latest one for my work.' He took his older model out of his pocket and looked at it with distaste.

'Julian, of course I'm thrilled for you. It's just with everything that's going on we have to be careful. When are you next seeing him? I'd like to meet him.' Olivia gave what she hoped was an encouraging smile.

'He's off to London tonight and he's going to contact me when he comes back. He'll send me some stuff he wants translated into German this week.'

'I hope this isn't all going to be too much. You've got your schoolwork to think about.'

'Mum, listen to yourself. For weeks, you and Chris have been on at me about getting a job. I get a job, a really good one, but you're still not pleased. What do I have to do to keep you happy?' He grabbed a handful of biscuits and Olivia heard him running up the stairs to his room, slamming the door behind him.

Olivia looked at her watch again. She should have set off ten minutes ago to collect Marc and Lara. She'd be late. What if something happened to them? What if they started walking up the road? She grabbed her keys and rushed out to the car, her heart thumping. This was awful. Was life ever going to be normal again?

When she arrived at the school playground, they were sitting together on the edge of the ping-pong table, swinging their legs. She slammed on the brakes and ran over to them, kissing them, although Marc tried to push her away. Popping the children into the car, she drove the short way down to the Spar supermarket. She'd meant to go before picking them up but there hadn't been time. Most people who lived in Wildenwil did their main shopping down at the big supermarkets in Zug, but she liked supporting the local shop.

Taking Marc and Lara with her, she grabbed a small basket and was running round, picking up essentials, when she noticed a woman staring at her. She was tall with dishevelled grey hair, wearing a long dark coat. She looked vaguely familiar. Olivia thought she must have seen her in the village before, but she didn't look like one of the glossy incomers who might pop in for something they'd forgotten. Olivia had also seen some strangers she'd thought were from the hotel – a couple in traditional Tibetan robes and an exotic woman with magenta hair – but this woman looked too ordinary to be part of that community.

Drawing the children close to her, Olivia went to the checkout and exchanged the normal pleasantries with the assistant at the till.

As she started to pack her shopping, Olivia looked up and saw the woman peering round the end of the aisle, a look of hatred in her deep-set eyes.

Ushering the children out, Olivia hurried back to the car. Once again, she felt she was being watched. And she still had no idea who could have written the note in her letterbox. She should have told Christian about it, or maybe even the police, but it was too late now.

The car was approaching the house when the silence of the countryside was broken by the sound of sirens in the distance. Above her, she could hear a helicopter. Parking quickly, she grabbed the children and ran into the house, locking the door behind her. What was happening? Olivia pulled her children close to her. There was danger all around and she had to protect them.

Her heart rate had returned to normal and they were sitting at the table when Christian came in, his face grim. Hanging his jacket on the hook he indicated with his head that Olivia should come over. She approached him, apprehensive about what he was going to say, pleased the children were absorbed in a cartoon on the kitchen's small television. Christian moved his head nearer to hers. 'They've found a body.'

Chapter 6

The birth certificate

Scarborough – October 1993

'Please let me go. It's such an honour to represent Scarborough in our twin town and Miss Williams says she's never known anyone who can speak German so well without having been to the country.' Marie looked across the table at her parents. The whole meal she'd been plucking up enough courage to mention the trip to Osterode am Harz – the opportunity to go abroad for the first time.

Frank McGuigan put his fork down, his mouth grim. 'You'd do better concentrating on your secretarial. You'll be getting a job in England so what's the use of foreign languages?'

'Miss Williams says languages are the key to the future and that I should go to study them at university.'

Her father stiffened. Marie could feel his pent-up anger. 'That Anne Williams should get on with her job and stop interfering in our lives. What does she know about real life, stuck in that school?' Although they'd lived in Yorkshire for nearly twenty years, his Scottish accent was still so strong that people often struggled to understand him.

Marie looked at her mother. Therese never openly disagreed with her husband, but was often more open to new ideas. This time, however, she looked anxiously towards Frank and shook her head. 'Marie, you know your father and I have always supported you, going to the Girls' Grammar, and all the uniform and books, but we can't afford a trip like that. And university would be out of the question on our pension.'

Marie lowered her eyes. Her parents were old, really old in comparison to the other parents at school. They'd been well into their forties, in fact, her father must have been over fifty, when she was born. Throughout her childhood, she'd always been told things were too expensive or a waste of money, and she'd learnt not to ask for anything. She didn't want to upset her parents, but because this was so important, she made one last attempt. 'But there would be a grant. Miss Williams said she would arrange it.'

Frank stood up, slamming his hand down on the table. 'That's enough. There's no more discussion. I don't want to hear the name Williams again. I don't need nobody's charity.'

Marie pushed her chair back and managed to hold back her tears until she reached the front door. Ignoring her mother's voice behind her, she went down the stairs and out into the street. It was a grey day, the heavy clouds leeching all colour from the surroundings and matching her mood.

Still blinking back tears, she crossed the road and went through the ornate gates into Peasholm Park. This beautiful park had been her refuge over the years. It was a place of mystery and fantasy. She could explore the overgrown paths of Peasholm Glen, with bridges twisting over the water between the majestic old trees, by the pagodas and other oriental buildings. It must have been very exotic in 1912 Edwardian England when the park was opened, and Marie could let her imagination run free.

As she walked by the lake, the tears finally fell. Her parents were so protective of her. She'd been their miracle, born after many years of praying to St Jude for a child, and she understood in some ways that they wanted to keep her safe, separate from the rest of the world. Her mother said she'd always been small, born too early, fragile and prone to infection, so she'd never played with other children. Her parents never had any visitors, didn't seem to have any friends or relatives and, although they spoke nostalgically about growing up in Edinburgh and read *The Sunday Post* every weekend, they'd never once been to Scotland on a visit.

In fact, Marie had never been anywhere. When other girls at school talked about their holidays abroad, she kept quiet. Her family would never be able to afford to go away and Therese was always saying how lucky they were to live in a town where other people came for their holidays. It was true, Scarborough was beautiful – Marie loved the long beach and the grey North Sea waves – but she wanted to see more of the world.

The library had been her escape; the imposing building with a wonderful smell of dark wooden shelves, and books had been her haven. She consumed stories of every kind, discovering a world with greater horizons. She read about exploration in Africa, intrepid Victorian ladies setting off on travels all over the globe, romances, friendship – all things she craved in her everyday life. Her teachers said she had a real talent for languages, and she wondered if one reason she loved them so much was because they were the key to the outside world, a world far away from Scarborough.

She'd always tried to keep her parents happy. It was easier with her mother, whose unconditional love had surrounded Marie all her life. Therese scrimped and saved, buying the cheapest meat scraps and battered vegetables from the Market Hall, going to Boyes Department Store to the offcuts table in the fabrics department to make her clothes. Therese's life revolved around Marie and the church. But she was scared of almost everything and wanted to protect her daughter from the world she saw as dangerous, frightening and evil. Marie loved and respected her mother, but she was seventeen and felt the love suffocating her.

It was much more difficult to please her father. Although she'd spent her whole life trying to do things to make him proud or happy, she'd never succeeded. Over the years he'd become more embittered, angry and unpredictable. Now she tried to avoid saying anything to him at all.

Walking out of the park, Marie climbed the gentle slope up Columbus Ravine and into the cemetery. She often wandered between the old gravestones, reading the worn inscriptions, seeing the children who'd died, the families of brothers who'd all been killed in strange places during the world wars. She crossed herself. It reminded her to be grateful for what she had, to respect her parents and the sacrifices they'd made for her. At the regular confessions in the church, she'd tried to get absolution for her lack of gratitude and unworthy thoughts, but Father Dominic, the old Irish priest who'd christened her and seen her grow up, didn't seem to listen. He just told her what a good girl she was and such a credit to her parents.

She walked back down the hill and towards the sea. The North Bay in Scarborough was a long stretch of pale sand, with the wide expanse of the grey North Sea beyond. The long prom was deserted apart from a few joggers and dog walkers. This part of Scarborough was very different from the South Bay, with its tourist shops and games arcades.

She'd always liked the sea. Walking with the cold salt wind blowing her hair, she felt she could escape the claustrophobia of her mother's love. Over the sea, she saw another world, a world she wanted to experience too.

The air was darkening as she walked slowly home. The trip to Osterode am Harz was such a wonderful opportunity. It was a small town in the middle of nowhere in Lower Saxony, but Marie was intrigued by the pictures of the half-timbered houses and the wildness of the Harz National Park nearby. And afterwards she wanted to go to university and become a teacher like Miss Williams. She wanted to change lives like her teacher had, to inspire girls to appreciate the literature and culture of foreign lands.

She'd been delighted when her parents had got a new television and she could take the old one up to her room and watch foreign films with subtitles as her father sneered at game shows below. Watching them, she felt she had a new identity. One where she could be herself, not the daughter her parents wanted her to be.

The streetlights had come on as Marie opened the main door and walked slowly up the stairs. She didn't know what would greet her – a chilly silence or maybe her parents would just carry on as if nothing had happened, as they often did. She took her coat off and was surprised the television was turned off. Her parents watched her as she came into the living room.

They looked at each other as if they had agreed something, but didn't know how to start. It was her mother who spoke. 'Sit down, Marie. We've got something to tell you.' She sat on the edge of the hard chair by the dining table and waited.

'We've been talking and we've decided that now is the time to tell you.' Therese looked at her husband, who was pursing his lips with fury. Therese continued. 'You've been a wonderful daughter to us, the best we could wish for, but there's something you have to know.' Marie was holding her breath.

Her mother took out a folded piece of paper. 'This is your birth certificate.'

Marie took it. She'd never seen it before, had never needed it. She looked down and saw her birthday, 10 July 1976, the place was Edinburgh, and the name… the name was Lucy Olivia Sheridan.

She gasped. 'What…?' She looked further. Under 'Mother' it said Geraldine Elizabeth Sheridan. The space for 'Father' was blank. She looked up at Therese.

'We always knew we had to tell you one day,' her mother started, 'but we just put the day off. We didn't want to lose you.'

Marie was numb. She'd never felt part of her parents and, when she was about ten, had even asked her mother if she was adopted. Therese had reassured her that she wasn't. She'd never asked again.

'We'd always wanted a baby, Marie, and the good Lord never blessed us with one until you came along.' Therese crossed herself. 'We wanted to adopt but they told us we were too old. Then we met wee Geraldine. She was pregnant and frightened, and we did a deal. The Lord moves in mysterious ways.'

Frank took up the story, his voice gravelly. 'We're telling you now because you're just the age she was then, and you're turning out like her – arrogant and ungrateful.'

Marie flinched, as if she'd been physically slapped. She'd tried so hard to be a good daughter. Frank leant forward and spat the words out. 'She was a wee hoor, hung out with hippies and druggies. When she fell pregnant, she just wanted rid of the baby. She'd left it too late to do anything wicked, but she said she couldn't tell her parents and didn't know what to do. When we offered to take you, she jumped at the chance.'

Tears were running down Therese's face. 'St Jude had answered our prayers.'

Marie looked from one to the other. She had so many questions, she didn't know where to start. 'Where is she, my mother?'

'We don't know, that was part of the deal. We gave her all our savings, but she had to give you up. She registered your birth but we had to promise to change your name, take you away and never contact her again. We didn't want any of they social workers involved so we just made it unofficial like.'

Thoughts raced round Marie's head. In some ways, it all made sense, but she couldn't believe her parents could have entered into a transaction like this, which was, she was almost certain, illegal.

Therese sobbed more loudly. 'You won't hold this against us, will you, Marie? The reason we didn't tell you was because we were afraid of losing you.'

Marie looked at her parents with a sense of detachment. Now she knew why she'd never had anything in common with them. She didn't want to cause them pain, but she was going to get a passport and go to Germany. And then she was going to university. And when she went to university, she was going to become Lucy Sheridan. She'd always hated the name Marie, and now she knew why.

Chapter 7

Christmas Eve

Olivia stood in the living room putting decorations on the perfectly shaped tree Christian had found. As was the custom on Christmas Eve, Christian had taken the children out for a walk while she put the tree up and decorated it. According to tradition, the tree and the presents underneath were brought on Christmas Eve by the Christkindli – the Christ child.

When they were very young, the children had gasped with genuine surprise and wonder when they came in and saw the tree with its real candles and the presents underneath. Even now they loved this traditional start to the Christmas celebrations.

As Olivia put the tasteful red and silver baubles on the branches, a wave of grief washed over her. What would they be doing at the Kolbs' farm up the hill? The thought of the family sitting with the empty place at the table was too sad to bear.

It had been six weeks since Sandra had disappeared and no real progress seemed to have been made in the enquiry. A couple of weeks earlier, there seemed to have been a breakthrough when a body was found at the foot of the Wildenberg Peaks. Everyone's first thought was that it was Sandra's.

When she heard the news, Olivia had felt a strange mixture of horror and relief. She didn't want it to be Sandra, but she wanted to know what had happened to her. For Vreni and Hans, not knowing must be the worst thing. Perhaps finding Sandra's body would allow them to get some closure.

But it hadn't turned out like that. The body was quickly established as male and a few days later his identity was released. It was a young Englishman called Jeff Simons, an analyst working for one of the international companies in Zug. He'd fallen from the top of the cliff.

A note in his pocket confirmed it was suicide. Work colleagues said he was a quiet loner, who seemed to have difficulty adjusting to living and working in a foreign country.

Ruedi Wiesli said the note had mentioned children being harmed, so the police had originally suspected a connection to Sandra's disappearance. However, a search by dogs and forensics had failed to find any evidence of Sandra being in his car, which had been abandoned in the car park at the foot of the peaks, or in the studio apartment he'd rented in Zug.

Every detail of his life had been thoroughly investigated. His computer had been analysed, and every website he'd visited or email he'd deleted was followed up, but there was no evidence of any connection to Sandra. After a few weeks the body had been released and returned to England, and so what seemed to be the most significant lead into Sandra's disappearance had come to nothing.

Olivia put the final bauble on a branch. The tree was quite plain by British standards, with a few simple ornaments and real candles, but Olivia loved it. British Christmases held no happy memories for her and the flickering candlelight in the glow of the log-burning stove created a warm and cosy atmosphere.

Bella rubbed herself against Olivia's legs. The old dog had set off with Christian and the children, but had wandered back alone a short while later. She'd been getting weaker in the last few weeks and her old legs were shaky. *Please don't let Bella be ill*, Olivia thought, stroking her soft fur. Bella was one of the few constants in her life at this time, when everything around her seemed to be in upheaval.

She moved over to check the final touches on the table. Christmas Eve had always been a big celebration in Christian's family, but things had changed from when she first arrived. Christian's parents, who'd always been kind to her, had both passed away, his father dying very quickly after his wife's death from cancer. The family liked to think that after nearly sixty years together they couldn't bear to live apart and their deaths were a peaceful release from their lives of hard work. Now Zita was gone too. She'd always enjoyed her Christmas dinner, although she'd sat at the corner of the table, eating steadily, oblivious to everything going on around her. This was the first year her chair would be empty.

Rolf, Christian's much older brother, was coming this evening. After many years abroad with an international children's charity, he'd come back and was living in an isolated smallholding further up the valley. Nobody knew exactly what had happened on his last posting, but he seemed to have suffered a breakdown of some kind. Olivia could understand that. He must have seen awful things in his years in war zones, dealing with child refugees and victims of conflicts.

He obviously hadn't wanted to talk about it, so nobody really knew what had happened, not wanting to press him. Now he lived quietly in a tumbled-down collection of farm buildings higher up the Alp. These were usually only used in summer, when the cows were taken up to the high pastures, but Rolf was living there alone throughout the winter, following his new hobby of raising old breeds of sheep in danger of extinction.

Marlene, the middle sister, would also be there. She'd always come home for Christmas, from her high-powered legal job working for the Swiss government in Berne, but it was only after her parents' death that she'd felt comfortable bringing her partner, Sibylle. She'd fitted into the family immediately and the children loved her.

Olivia looked at her watch and checked the window. Although there was no snow, the area around the farmhouse still looked magical, the trees festooned with little lights shining in the night. There was no movement or sign of life, and despite the beauty, she felt a sudden sense of panic. Christian and the children should be back by now. They were out in the woods, going off the beaten track. Would Christian be able to watch Marc and Lara every minute of the time? Who might be lurking out there in the darkness?

It was nearly six o'clock, when the others were due to arrive. Usually Christian and the children would come back long before the guests so they could have some family time together looking at the tree.

Julian clattered down the stairs. He, of course, was far too sophisticated to go for the traditional walk in the woods. He looked at the tree and smiled. 'Very nice.' Olivia listened for the sarcasm in his voice and then felt annoyed with herself. Since his new job, he was a lot more pleasant.

There was a sound outside. She hoped it was Christian and the children, but realised it was a car parking. The door was flung open and Marlene and Sibylle swept in, laughing and smothering Olivia in kisses. They put their extravagantly large number of beautifully wrapped presents under the tree and removed their coats and boots.

'Lord, I need a drink,' Marlene said, as she walked towards the kitchen. 'The traffic on the autobahn was crazy.'

'But it was all made worthwhile by the sweet little lights in your village. So simple and retro,' Sibylle added. The women looked at each other and laughed. Olivia wondered if they were making fun of her village's Christmas decoration efforts. They were simple, with stars and angels, and were the same every year, but she liked them. Her face must have reflected her thoughts.

'Heavens, don't think we were mocking! Have you seen Berne's pretentious, modern minimalist lights? Cost a fortune and everybody hates them.' Marlene came back from the kitchen with two large glasses of wine. 'Can I get you anything while I'm at it, Livy?'

Olivia shook her head. She couldn't relax until everyone was safely back and the Fondue Chinoise was on the table. Families had different traditions for Christmas Eve but in Christian's family it was always this fondue. Olivia loved its simplicity. She just had to make the salad and sauces, put out the thinly sliced meats and the fondue dish of bubbling bouillon soup, and then everyone cooked their own food. It was an easy option.

But where were Christian and the children? Olivia was looking at her watch again, when a sound outside raised her hopes. She was disappointed when she realised it was a bike being propped up by the door. Rolf came in, removing his helmet and scarf, and gave her a dry kiss on the cheek. She hadn't seen him for a few weeks and was shocked by how thin he looked. She knew he did a lot of running and cycling, but wondered how well he was eating. She smiled to herself. Christian always said she tried to mother everybody.

Marlene was preparing the gin and tonic, which Julian had apparently asked for. Olivia wondered where he'd picked up that drinking habit; she hadn't thought he'd gone beyond a supermarket beer with his pals.

Standing in the glow of the fire, the room lit only by the flickering candles, Marlene, Sibylle and Julian raised their glasses, making a tableau like an old-fashioned Christmas card. Rolf joined them, holding a glass of mineral water. He'd stopped drinking alcohol, saying he'd seen its effect on too many expats during his travels. He'd also become a vegan, but after quizzing Olivia on the contents of the bouillon, had agreed to cook raw vegetables in his small separate bowl. He was so different from what he used to be like – a hard drinker, the life and soul of the party, full of stories about the places he'd visited and the characters he'd met. Now it was difficult to get him to say anything at all and Olivia was just relieved he'd agreed to come at all.

She did a last check in the kitchen and saw that everything was ready. In the living room, Julian was roaring with laughter. Olivia went to the window again, her stomach tight with fear. Where were they? Christian must know everyone would be here by now.

Then in the darkness of the forest she saw bobbing torches. Opening the door, she ran out into the cold dark air, her heart pounding with relief.

Lara ran towards her, laughing. 'Mummy, Daddy got lost! It was *so* funny.'

Marc joined her. 'But he kept pretending he wasn't. He said he'd been walking through the forests since he was a boy and knew every tree!'

Christian joined them. 'And so I do. I knew exactly where we were all the time.'

'Except we were going round in circles.' Marc and Lara laughed in delight. Olivia hugged her children, her heart bursting with relief. 'Come in. Look what's happened while you've been out.' Marc and Lara ran into the living room, gasping with joy at the sight of the candlelit tree, knowing it was in their interest to play along with the fantasy. Then they noticed Marlene and Sibylle and threw themselves into their arms, shrieking with delight.

After they sat at the table, Christian said a quick grace – a nod to parental tradition because none of them were at all religious – and they started eating. The conversation was light, mostly Marlene and Sibylle telling tales of the outrageous mix of artists, musicians and actors they knew in Berne.

The wine was flowing, and Olivia allowed herself to relax and have a glass. She managed to push aside the feeling of dread that seemed to hang over her all the time and enjoy the celebration.

Sibylle raised her glass. 'Time for another toast, I think.' She looked towards Julian. 'To our young entrepreneur. Congratulations on getting a job in international finance. What's the point in living next to the financial cesspit that is Zug if you don't get a bite of the action yourself?'

Everyone raised and chinked their glasses, including Christian, who added, 'You'd better not forget your schoolwork, now you're an international businessman. I've heard reports your marks are slipping.' He said it in a playful tone, but it was obvious he meant it.

Olivia stiffened. Why did Christian have to bring this up now? She looked across at her son, willing him not to reply. No such luck as Julian held his glass tighter and stared at his stepfather, his tone, though light, loaded with sarcasm. 'It's bad enough having you teaching at the same school, without you gossiping about me. My marks may have slipped in useless subjects like Latin, but haven't you heard that my Economics marks have greatly improved?' He took another slug of wine. 'I'm going to concentrate on subjects that are important for my future now.'

There was a shocked silence, until Sibylle broke the tension with a scream of laughter. 'Julian, my dear boy. Good for you!'

Christian moved as if to say something, but Marlene turned to him. 'Don't be such a stuffed shirt, Chris. You should be so proud to have brought up a young man who can be so articulate and stand up for himself.' She turned to Julian and raised her glass again. 'Well said, my boy.'

Julian smirked across at Christian, and Marc and Lara, who'd been watching the scene with round shocked eyes, giggled, clearly pleased to be party to this adult exchange.

Olivia turned to Rolf, looking for some way to lighten the tension in the air. 'Tell us more about your sheep, Rolf. The project sounds fascinating.'

Rolf caught on immediately and produced some leaflets and pictures from his rucksack. 'These are the Valais Blacknose sheep.' He held up a photo. The sheep were lovely, with long fleeces like an Old English Sheepdog and faces so black you could hardly see the features.

'Oh, they're so cute.' Lara's eyes opened wider. 'Have you got any lambs yet?'

Rolf smiled. 'Not yet, but that's the idea. I want to breed lots of them.' He looked round the table. 'There are so few of these beautiful creatures left that they're officially classified as an endangered species. A few other enthusiasts and I are starting an intensive breeding programme in the hope that the numbers increase. I've rented some buildings up on the Alp, have a ram and several ewes, and hope that by the spring we'll have lots of lovely little lambs. It's ideal there because they're used to snow and high altitudes, but have a low resistance to human diseases, so they'll be away from passing traffic.'

'But I can come and see them?' Lara looked up hopefully at her uncle.

'Once they're strong enough to go out into the meadows you certainly can. The lambs are beautiful, like little cuddly toys.' Rolf looked fondly at the pictures before folding them up and putting them back in his rucksack.

Olivia stood up from the table, relieved the tension had been dissipated. 'I think we need a little break before dessert. Let's go and unwrap some of the presents.'

Marc and Lara leapt up excitedly and ran over to the tree, pulling out some parcels and looking at the labels. The adults moved towards the sofa and Sibylle perched on the arm next to Marlene. Marc was just about to hand over the first present when the house phone rang.

'Who'd phone at this time on Christmas Eve?' Christian looked irritated. Olivia moved towards the phone. 'Don't answer it, Livy.'

Olivia hesitated. 'It must be something important to phone now.'

'All right, I'll go.' Christian moved to the hall. Everyone pretended to be interested in the presents, but Olivia could see they were all straining to hear the conversation.

Christian came back in, his face drawn. 'That was Wiesli. Another girl has gone missing.'

Chapter 8

Stevie

'Livy, Livy, wake up.' Olivia opened her eyes, blinking in the darkness of the bedroom. Her cheeks were damp with tears.

Christian was shaking her gently. 'Were you having a nightmare? You were shouting and thrashing about.'

Olivia tried to catch the fragments of her dream. She'd felt petrified with fear, running but unable to move her legs, reaching out to grasp Lara, who'd dissolved in her hands; the distorted face of Frank, the man she'd thought was her father, hovered behind her, and she'd heard his bitter mocking laugh. She sat up in bed and the images melted away, leaving her with a feeling of empty grief.

Christian put his arms round her. 'I'll get you a cup of tea.' He went out of the bedroom, leaving Olivia with her fears. Ever since Christmas Eve, when Ruedi Wiesli had phoned to warn them that another girl had gone missing, Olivia had been unable to relax. She and Christian had tried to keep things normal for the family, but life felt unreal to her.

She kept thinking of Sandra and Ruth Frick, the other girl who'd disappeared. At first, the newspapers had been quick to link her case to Sandra's, but the police had played that down. Ruth had disappeared from a foster family on the other side of the mountains, in canton Zürich, and had a long history of running away. She'd lived in a succession of foster homes and was a troubled child, alternately picked up and rejected by her drug-addict mother.

The police's theory was that she'd run away again on Christmas Eve, possibly after an argument with her foster family. Her birth mother had disappeared at the same time, and, according to Wiesli, the police believed the two were together and were concentrating their search in the city of Zürich.

Despite this, Olivia couldn't stop thinking about the missing girls and, although she tried to maintain a veneer of normality and calm, underneath she felt danger for her children all around.

She became obsessed with the investigation. She searched the Internet for cases of missing children, trying to work out where Sandra could be. Was she imprisoned in a cellar, frightened and abused by a monstrous paedophile? Had she been captured by child traffickers, spirited off to a distant land and become a longed-for adopted child? Was she appearing in sick films and images on Darknet, the secret deep web of the Internet? She'd read about a group of aristocratic paedophiles in Belgium who had weekend parties abusing and sometimes killing children. Was Sandra part of something like that? Or was she dead, lying alone and cold in a crevice of the mountains? Wiesli had said the longer she was missing, the more likely it was she was no longer alive.

Tearing herself away from the computer, she went down to the Spar. On the window there was a large poster of Sandra, and also a smaller picture of Ruth. She found herself blinking back tears. There was no way to escape her fears. She walked round the aisles in a daze, filling her basket automatically.

Her thoughts were interrupted by a voice calling her name. 'Frau Keller. Can you come and help us? There's a gentleman here who doesn't speak German.' Olivia moved along the aisle and saw a thin figure wearing a baker boy cap standing at the checkout. He turned and she recognised him.

It was Stevie Dawber, singer of the legendary Tarantulas. She'd heard gossip that he'd moved into the area a few months ago with Priska Preisig, his Swiss beauty-queen wife, but Olivia had never seen either of them in the village. Now here he was, in the Spar, wearing a leather jacket and with a thin grey ponytail peeking out from the back of his cap.

He smiled at Olivia. 'Ah, you speak English. Thank you for coming to my rescue, fair maiden.' He lowered his head and for a moment Olivia thought he was going to kiss her hand. He didn't, merely looked into his wallet, and raised his eyes to hers. 'I'm very much afraid I can't pay for my shopping. I've tried to use my credit card, but they don't accept it here.' He pointed down to his basket, which was filled with sweets, chocolate biscuits, little fruit gum bears and other children's sweets.

Olivia raised her eyebrows in surprise. 'Is this your basket?'

Stevie coughed and blushed beneath his tan. 'Hmm, yes. Some of my favourites.'

Olivia took out her purse. 'I'll pay for them and you can pay me back later.'

Stevie clutched her hand. 'Thank you so much. I'll certainly do that, as soon as I get some cash.' He smiled sheepishly. 'Don't often need it now.'

She took out her purse and paid for his purchases along with her own. As she walked towards her car, Stevie followed her. 'Wait for me. I'll just pop down to the bank and get some money from the machine and then, please, let me buy you a coffee.' He indicated to the bakery opposite, which also served as the village café.

Olivia nodded. She hadn't got anything else to do until she picked the children up, and she'd always liked the Tarantulas when she was young. Their heyday had been in the seventies and eighties, but they'd brought a few records out in the nineties and Stevie had even had a short-lived solo career. Olivia remembered the glam rock photos of the band. Stevie had been the singer, with long, flowing blond hair and a Regency jacket. In later years he'd taken to wearing a hat, so she guessed his long golden locks were thinning.

Stevie ran back from the bank with a bundle of notes in his hand and led Olivia across the road to the café. As he passed the counter, he pointed to a cream cake and took a seat at the furthest back table. The waitress brought the cake and took their coffee orders.

Olivia had wondered what they'd talk about, but Stevie was very easy to talk to. He wasn't at all as she'd imagined and there was something about him that made her feel comfortable. 'So how do you like living in Wildenwil? I've seen your house from a distance. It looks amazing.'

Stevie wiped some cream from the corner of his mouth and smiled grimly. 'Oh, it's amazing all right. Have you not seen the glossy mags? We've been in them all. It's a designer marvel and as uncomfortable as hell.' He slurped his coffee.

Olivia wasn't sure what to say. 'Yes, sometimes the most modern places aren't always the cosiest.'

'Priska employed all the best architects and she's a really talented interior designer, but she's finding it difficult to fit me into the concept. I'm afraid I make the place look untidy.' He smiled again. 'Oh, don't worry, I'm not talking behind her back. We discuss this,' he took another gulp of coffee, 'all the time. I'm afraid I'm not quite up to scratch for the perfect house.'

'But she married you. I'd have thought your rather…' Olivia hesitated, looking for the right words, 'alternative image was one of your attractions.'

Stevie shook his head and smiled. 'Thanks. That was then. Like all women, she tried to change me after we got married.'

Olivia thought of herself. She'd spent her whole married life trying to fit in, to become a perfect Swiss wife, and had certainly not tried to change Christian. 'Maybe I'm not very typical, but that isn't the case with my marriage.'

'Ah, my dear girl. Why didn't I meet someone like you?' He looked at Olivia and laughed. 'Don't take me too seriously. It's so refreshing, speaking to someone who understands a bit of banter. Do you know, we've been in this house for five months and you're the first person from the village I've spoken to? What's it like living here?'

Olivia looked down at her coffee. 'I used to think it was paradise – beautiful countryside, lovely safe schools, wholesome family values. But the girls disappearing has changed everything.'

Stevie hit his forehead. 'Of course, I'm sorry, so crass. I did hear about that, of course, but it hasn't been reported much in the British press and I can't read the local papers. One of the girls was from here, wasn't she?'

'Yes, she was a friend of my daughter's.' Tears pricked behind her eyes as they did every time she spoke about Sandra.

'Oh, I'm sorry.' Stevie looked over towards her with sympathetic eyes. 'How awful for your daughter.'

Olivia nodded and told him how Sandra had vanished when she should have been coming home with her daughter.

'What about the other missing girl? I haven't heard much about her.' Stevie leant forward, keeping his eyes on Olivia's face.

'Poor Ruth disappeared on Christmas Eve. That was so awful, the timing, just when everyone was trying to be positive. But the police don't seem to think the two cases are connected. They were both living on farms only twenty kilometres apart, but on different sides of the mountains. Ruth is older, eleven, but she's small and looks younger. She was being fostered and had run away before, so the police believe she's taken off again. They're trying to find her birth mother, thinking she might have gone back to her.' Olivia's voice faltered again. Had Ruth made it? Would it work out this time, the triumph of hope over experience? Like Sandra, Ruth seemed to have disappeared completely, not appearing on any CCTV. Appeals to motorists had led to a few coming forward, but there were no real leads.

Thinking of the girls, Olivia asked, 'Have you got any children?'

Stevie's face fell. 'Loads of them apparently, but I don't see any of them. All their mothers are far too sensible to let them have anything to do with me.' He lowered his eyes. 'I was a terrible father and I don't really deserve to see any of them, but I do miss them.' He gave a wistful sigh. 'Or the idea of them, I suppose.'

Olivia looked at him with sympathy. Here he was, a household name, loads of money, but seemed so lonely. Stevie caught her glance. 'Don't feel sorry for me. It's mostly my own fault, and I'm really lucky Priska's taken me in hand. I'd probably be dead if it wasn't for her. I'm her project – and she's succeeding. I'm healthier, off the drugs, go into the torture chamber – the gym she's installed – and she's a good person.' He said these words as if he was convincing himself and then quickly changed the subject.

'Hey, you live here and I bet you know all the local gossip. What's with the creepy house of horrors by the waterfall? I hear somebody's doing it up.'

Olivia realised that he wanted to talk about something else and told him what she knew. 'It's called the Grand Wildenbach Hotel. It was originally built in the eighteenth century next to a thermal spring. People came from all over Europe to sample the waters, which were supposed to have great healing powers. But it became really famous when it was rebuilt after a fire in the 1860s in that amazing Gothic style. It became part of the Grand Tour for British aristocrats as they travelled round Europe. It was also supposed to be an especially creative place, and famous poets and novelists like Byron, Goethe, Thomas Mann and Robert Louis Stevenson all stayed there and found inspiration for their works.' Stevie nodded, seeming to be fascinated by every detail.

'However, holiday fashions changed and when a small earthquake closed the spring up, it was the end of it as a hotel. I thought it was frightening when I first arrived – so creepy and often in the shadow of the mountains. The children used to make up all kinds of horror stories about it.'

'But I've heard somebody's doing it up and is going to reopen it. Is that true?'

Olivia nodded. 'Yes, a woman's bought it. I've seen her once or twice in the Spar. She's difficult to miss – very dramatic, big flowing clothes, wild red hair. Apparently, she was originally from this area but went abroad and made some money. It must have been a lot because the hotel was totally derelict and must be costing a fortune to renovate. There seem to be quite a few people living there already because I've seen strangers in the Spar who must come from there – a Tibetan couple and other exotic foreigners…' As she said this, Olivia wondered again whether the strange woman she'd seen a few days earlier was part of this community, but she doubted it. She looked much too ordinary.

Stevie beamed. 'Wow, you know everything. I'll definitely come to you when I need some local information.'

Olivia looked at her watch and jumped up. 'I've got to go and collect the kids now.'

Stevie grasped her arm. 'Olivia, we must do this again. You've no idea how wonderful it's been for me to talk to you, to speak to someone English. Please, let's meet up again.'

'I'd love to.'

'On Friday then. Here at ten. Can you make it?'

Olivia nodded. She'd enjoyed the conversation and realised with a sense of shock that she'd been laughing and hadn't thought of Sandra for at least twenty minutes.

Meeting a pop star was exciting, and that afternoon, she spent several hours on the Internet finding out everything she could about Stevie Dawber.

Chapter 9

Aurelia

Wildenwil – Friday 15 January, 2016

Olivia opened the shutters. There was a spectacular scarlet sunrise over the mountains, and the fields were white and sparkling in the morning light. The snow had come at last. She tried to push the aftermath of her nightmare away; her nights were always disturbed by dark images of the missing girls and childhood memories.

She went downstairs and was making toast and hot chocolate when Christian looked up from the table. 'Livy, I've got an idea to run past you. Please think about it.'

Olivia wondered what was coming. Christian had been very preoccupied the last few days. One of the teachers in his department had been off sick since Christmas and had been signed off with burnout and depression.

'You know Jolanda is unlikely to be back this term. With the exams coming up we really need a reliable replacement but we haven't been able to find anyone. I thought you could take over her classes, just until Easter?'

Olivia gasped. 'I'm not an English teacher!'

'But you taught German. You need the same principles to teach English as a foreign language. You're an excellent, qualified teacher.' He laughed. 'And we're desperate!'

Olivia thought of the time she'd been teaching in Edinburgh. She'd met Christian when he'd come to her school as a language assistant and he'd been really supportive when she'd been struggling with some of her classes. But there were lots of things about that time she wanted to blank from her mind, and teaching was one of them. She didn't say this to Christian, though. 'That's really nice of you to have confidence in me. But I don't think I can at the moment. The children are still so young and come home for lunch.'

'We could work out hours so that you weren't away over lunchtime too much. And Ruedi Wiesli's wife is organising a lunch club for children whose mothers are working. The mothers take it in turn to provide lunch. It's a great idea.'

It was a good idea, and Olivia thought she could get involved in the rota later, but it wasn't the right time. She was thinking about what to say when Christian put his arms round her. 'Livy, you need to do something. You're alone all the time and brooding about the missing girls too much. You were great with Zita, but now she's gone you need something else to keep you occupied.'

Olivia nodded. It was true. She enjoyed helping people and felt complete when she was needed. But teaching was impossible. She had to look after the children, keep them safe.

Christian pulled his jacket on. 'I'll take the children to school. Think about it. It could be fun for you.' Olivia didn't think it sounded fun at all, but smiled and kissed him on the cheek before hugging Marc and Lara. She put her arms out to Julian, but he ran quickly past her.

She was just relishing the morning calm when she remembered that it was Friday – the day she was meeting Stevie. She was looking forward to it. She took Bella out for a quick walk and then went down the winding lane to the village. Most of the village was picturesque, with half-timbered houses and an onion-roofed church. However, the row of shops, with the bank, post office and Spar, were ugly concrete buildings, set back from the street with car parking space in front. They'd obviously been built when this style was considered modern and controls were not so strict.

She still had half an hour before she'd arranged to meet Stevie so she went to the Spar and had a quick chat with the cashiers, her main source of village gossip, before going across the road to the warmth of the café. She was early, so she sat at a table at the back and ordered a coffee. There were newspapers in a rack so she picked up a copy of the *Blick*, Switzerland's most popular tabloid newspaper, and read the latest headlines. Nothing about Sandra or Ruth.

Stevie had said he'd be there at ten, but when he didn't come Olivia wasn't surprised. She hadn't expected him to be as punctual as the Swiss are, but when it reached half past she wondered whether to order another coffee or leave. She wished they'd exchanged numbers when they'd met.

A shadow blocked the light from the window. She looked up. It wasn't Stevie, but the flamboyant magenta-haired woman she'd assumed was from the Grand Wildenbach Hotel. The older woman smiled and said in English, 'May I sit down?'

Olivia nodded, moving her bag from the seat beside her. The woman extended her hand and looked at her with a gaze so intense Olivia had to lower her eyes. 'My name's Aurelia. I've been wanting to speak to you for some time so when I saw you sitting alone, I took my chance. You're English, aren't you?'

Olivia hesitated. This time she did say she was Scottish and introduced herself. She wanted to know more about this extraordinary woman with her mass of wild red hair, her huge exotic caftan and her penetrating eyes. She was sure she came from the hotel, but checked by asking, 'Have you recently moved to the area?'

'I have. I've moved into the Wildenbach Hotel with some members of my group. We're in the process of renovating this wonderful old building and are going to make it a centre for our community.'

'That's wonderful news. It's been allowed to decay for too long, and there's so much history associated with the building.'

Aurelia nodded. 'It's not only because of the building, which is wonderful, but also the location. It's in a magical place at the crossing of ley lines, so it has great geobiological force.'

Olivia was intrigued. 'Really? I've vaguely heard of ley lines, but I'm not sure exactly what they are.'

'A ley line is an energy line that connects vortices – high-energy spots on the Earth. Switzerland has many of them, which is why the mountains are so inspirational. They often come to the surface where there are thermal springs, like at the hotel. Zermatt, Leukerbad and Engstlenalp are all other places in Switzerland where the ley lines cross.'

Olivia nodded. Although she felt sceptical about such New Age things, she too had sensed something magical in those areas.

Aurelia gave her another penetrating stare. 'Earth vortices are like the chakras in the human body. Our community has travelled far in the world, but it was only when my dear husband, our inspirational leader, died that I came back to Switzerland and realised that this place where I was born is so powerful.'

Olivia nodded again. She'd heard of chakras too, but had never really been interested in this esoteric stuff. At the same time, she was drawn to the magnetism and passion in the older woman. 'I don't know much about all that, but it sounds interesting.'

Aurelia sat up straighter and held her arms out towards Olivia. 'Your aura is very interesting. It shows you have great spirituality.' She looked into her eyes. 'But there is something blocking your happiness, something preventing you from fully developing your inner self.'

A shiver ran down Olivia's back. Of course, she couldn't feel happy now with the girls missing, but what could this woman mean? It was getting too weird.

Aurelia seemed to sense her hesitation and moved closer. 'I feel a strong connection to you.' She laid her hand on Olivia's. 'You're a solitary person, but we all need to have the support of friends. Our souls cannot flourish alone.'

Olivia shrank back in her seat. This was too much, too close, physically and emotionally. Aurelia extended her plump hands and placed them on each side of Olivia's face. 'I would love to get to know you better because I feel something is troubling you.

Until you acknowledge the root of your pain, you will never be truly happy.'

Olivia straightened, trying to avoid her touch. There was something hypnotic about the older woman, but at the same time she was disturbing.

Aurelia stood up, sweeping her huge colourful poncho round her ample figure. 'Please come and visit us in the hotel very soon. I know we will see each other again, when you are ready to talk. And if you are ever in trouble, I will always be here for you.'

With a final smile, she swept out of the café, moving remarkably gracefully for such a large woman. Olivia stayed in her seat, unsettled by the encounter. At university she'd met people who believed in all sorts of esoteric things – Tarot cards, astrology, pendulum needles, numbers – but she'd never met anyone as intense as Aurelia. Perhaps she should go and visit her one day, and get a chance to look around the house.

A clock struck behind her and she realised it was time to meet Lara and Marc from school. What a strange morning. She was disappointed Stevie hadn't turned up but meeting Aurelia had been interesting. Her life, which had seemed so ordinary, was changing.

Chapter 10

Patrick

Wildenwil – Monday 25 January, 2016

The late afternoon sun cast long shadows over the melting remnants of snow as the sky turned pink. Olivia scraped the cake mixture from the bowl into a tin. She could hear the sounds of Marc and Lara playing in the next room. They were safe. She'd collected them from school as usual, and she should have felt calm.

But she didn't. Anxiety still flowed through her, seeping into every corner of her life. In her dreams, she kept seeing Sandra and had a strong feeling that Sandra was out there somewhere. The police seemed to be getting nowhere. There had been some reports of girls who looked similar to Sandra in various countries, with talk of international child-smuggling rings. Volunteers with trained sniffer dogs had joined the locals searching the woods and rocks in the area, remembering how a member of the public had found the body of a missing girl in Appenzell some years before, but there was no trace of Sandra.

The papers were bored with the story and had gone on to the next bit of click-bait. Olivia heard that Vreni had been admitted to a psychiatric clinic and the Kolb family kept themselves to themselves even more than before. Some fingers had been pointed at Sandra's older brothers, who were heavy drinkers and often in trouble, with mutterings about most murders being committed by a family member. This made Olivia even sadder, imagining the hurt of such accusations on top of the agony of losing Sandra.

The case of Ruth, the little girl who'd disappeared on Christmas Eve, had never captured the public or journalistic imagination in the same way. She seemed such a poor wee soul. Ironically, this case seemed to make people more inclined to forget about Sandra, or suspect her family were, in fact, involved.

Olivia had to keep her preoccupation with the missing girls to herself because Christian was getting impatient with her obsession and kept telling her to get a grip of herself, for the sake of the family. He was stressed and overworked because of Jolanda's illness and was disappointed that Olivia wouldn't consider taking any of her classes. He was having to work even longer hours and had to teach many of the students himself.

Even the children were getting back to normal. Lara had gone through an insecure phase, needier and reverting to babyhood, but now she was more like her old self. She'd even said she didn't want to be taken to school and collected every day because it made her feel like a baby. Olivia had reluctantly allowed Marc to come back from football training alone, now the days were getting longer and lighter, but she couldn't let Lara out of her sight.

The sound of a moped outside made her look at her watch. Julian was back at a reasonable time for once. He opened the door, pulling off his helmet. The first thing she noticed was his hair. It was cut in a rather trendy hipster style, short at the sides but with a longer bit flopping over one eye. He hadn't had his hair cut for ages, and she had to admit she'd liked it shoulder-length. He'd looked like one of the romantic pop stars from the seventies and eighties, the sort of music she liked listening to. Christian had hated the long hair, of course, and had used it as another reason to criticise his stepson.

'Hi, Mum.' Julian was smiling. It was lovely to see him in a good mood. 'What do you think? Smart, eh? Even Chris might approve.'

Olivia jumped up and gave him a hug. 'It's really smart. Any particular reason for the change of image?' She wondered if it might be to attract one of the girls in his class. There were some really pretty ones and she'd wondered for a while when he'd start being interested in them.

'Patrick is back in town and he suggested it. He said it fits in better with our clientele. And he's ordered me a smart suit.'

Olivia felt a twinge of concern. With everything going on, she'd almost forgotten about Julian and his job. Why was this man so interested in her son?

'Julian, you can't accept gifts like that from a man we know nothing about. You're sixteen, still at school. What does he want from you?'

Julian drew away. 'I might have known you'd find something negative in it. Can't you imagine someone would see some talent in me, some potential? Patrick says I'm exactly what his company needs and he wants to encourage me and get me involved as early as possible.' Julian looked at her defiantly. 'And I'm seventeen next month, or has that slipped your memory?'

'Of course, I remember. But that isn't the point. Who is this Patrick? I looked his company up on the Internet and couldn't find anything.'

'Mum, this isn't like those detective books you're always reading, you know. His is the sort of company that doesn't need to advertise and the sort of clients he deals with don't want publicity.'

'Which suggests there's something suspicious about it. A legitimate firm wouldn't need to be secret.'

Julian raised his beautiful arched eyebrows. 'I realise you don't know anything about international finance, but you've lived near Zug for long enough to know that this anonymity is part of its appeal. It's like numbered accounts in Swiss private banks – it's legal, but confidentiality is of the utmost importance.'

Olivia began to bluster. 'It seems very suspicious to me. Why is this Patrick so interested in you? For all we know he could be a dirty old man.'

'Mum, Patrick's not old, he's about your age. Okay, yes, old.'

Olivia laughed, some of her tension released.

'He's intelligent, well-educated, sophisticated, well-travelled. He went to university in the UK and then did an MBA in the States, at Yale. And he has chosen me, sees worth and potential in me. You and Chris just seem to want to put me down all the time.' He turned towards the stairs.

'Jules, of course I know you're intelligent and talented. I'd just like to meet him, especially now as he's beginning to groom you.' She bit her lip. She hadn't meant to say that, she'd only been thinking of the haircut and clothes, but the connotations of what she said had revealed her underlying fears.

Her son stared at her. 'I can't believe you said that. That's exactly why I don't want you to meet him. I'm not a child and I don't need all my friends to be vetted.'

He began to go up the stairs to his room, but stopped and turned again. 'I won't be in for dinner tomorrow evening as Patrick and I are going out with some clients.' Without waiting for a reply, Julian continued upstairs to his bedroom.

Olivia sat down at the table and put her head in her hands. She'd handled that so badly. She wanted to be fair to Julian, to be pleased for him, but she couldn't help hearing alarm bells. She was still sitting in the same position when Christian came in.

'You okay?'

Olivia looked up. 'It's Julian…'

Christian's jaw tightened. 'Has he been upsetting you again? That boy…'

'It's not really his fault. Actually, we ought to be pleased, I suppose.'

Christian looked exasperated. 'Come on, spit it out. I've had a long, hard day and I'm in no mood to play guessing games.'

Olivia straightened up and put a bright smile she didn't feel on her face. 'The good news is he's had a haircut.'

'About time too,' Christian muttered.

Olivia stilled him with her hand and told him what had happened.

Christian sat down next to her. 'It does all sound a bit odd. I'm going to speak to him and say we have to know more about this man. He could be any kind of pervert.'

'But I told you what happened when I suggested it.'

'Listen, we're the adults here. He's the child. While he's under this roof, he lives according to our rules.'

For years, Olivia had felt caught between her husband and her son. She'd thought Christian would be a good role model for her son growing up without a father, but since Julian had become a teenager there had been constant conflict.

She raised her eyes to her husband. 'Don't cause a fight tonight, please. What about if you followed him tomorrow? See where he goes and what kind of person this Patrick is...' Her voice trailed away as she saw the expression on her husband's face.

'Livy, I know you're worried, but that's a really stupid idea. I'm going to talk to him and find out what's going on.' Christian made his way to the stairs while Olivia set the table. Dinner was overdue, and as often happened when there was conflict, she sought to resolve it with food.

Angry voices floated down the stairs as she dished out the casserole, pretending not to hear. The television blared from the other room and Olivia was pleased that Lara and Marc seemed oblivious to what was going on.

There was a crash from upstairs and Julian flew down the stairs, pulling on his jacket. 'That's it! I can't stand it here a moment longer. I'm going where I'm treated with a little respect.'

He grabbed his helmet and went out of the door. Olivia ran after him, but he leapt onto his moped and roared off into the darkening night.

She ran back into the house. 'Christian, go after him. I'll stay here with the children.'

Christian walked down the stairs, rubbing his shoulder. 'He hit me, the little bastard. I'm not going after him. He'll come back when he's hungry.' He sat down at the table. 'Now let's have something to eat.'

Julian didn't come back. They sat down to a strained dinner where even the children kept quiet, sensing the tension in the air. Olivia constantly tried Julian's phone, but it went straight to voicemail.

After dinner, when the dishes were cleared away and the children had gone up to bed, Olivia turned to Christian. 'Please go out and look for him. He could be anywhere, lying injured.'

'Look, he's sixteen and if he wants to go off in a stupid adolescent huff he can. He's probably at one of his friends' houses.'

'But wouldn't he phone to let us know? He'll know I'll be worried.'

'That boy thinks of nobody but himself. He'll either be waiting until we go to bed to creep in, pleased with having caused a fuss, or he'll turn up tomorrow.'

Olivia put her head in her hands. Her lovely little boy. He'd been such an adorable child, with dark inquisitive eyes interested in everything. She was proud of him, coming to Switzerland without being able to speak a word of German, doing so well at school that he passed the entrance exam for the prestigious Kantonsschule. He was difficult now, but she hoped it was just a stage he was going through.

Maybe Christian was right and Julian was safe with a friend. She tried to believe that, but as she heard the wind swirl round the house and looked out at the inky darkness of the starless night, she couldn't help thinking of the two missing girls.

She started to prepare things for the morning, pretending she was busy. Christian wasn't fooled. 'Come up to bed and stop messing about. He'll be okay.'

She was just about to climb the stairs when she heard her phone beep. A message from Julian. '*Sorry, Mum. I'm fine. Staying the night at Patrick's.*'

She felt her hand trembling as she clumsily typed in a message. '*Thanks for letting me know. See you tomorrow.*' There was a lot more she could have said, all her fears about Patrick coming to mind again, but she didn't want to ruin the fact that Julian had sent a message, and the things she was afraid of couldn't be said in a text.

She was surprised when a reply came immediately. '*Patrick said I had to! He wants to meet you tomorrow.*' Olivia felt her heart beat. Violently. Who was this mysterious Patrick?

Chapter 11

Lucy

St Andrews, Scotland – June 1998

'Guy Montgomery asked you out to dinner? You've got to go!' Fiona leapt onto her bed, seeming more excited than Lucy herself.

Lucy shook her long blonde hair. 'I don't really know him. I don't know why he's asked *me* out!'

Fiona shook her head in exasperation. 'Because you're beautiful, intelligent and, now you've got rid of that plonker, David, free to run wild. University is supposed to be fun and you've spent far too much time in the library. Guy Montgomery, the sexiest man on legs, and dinner at the Grange! What's not to like?'

Lucy looked out of the high window over the Royal and Ancient Golf Course to the sea crashing on the West Sands. She wasn't the slightest bit interested in golf, but she loved this view. She'd chosen the University of St Andrews on the basis of pictures – of the harbour and sea, and the old ivy-clad buildings – but she'd never been here until she arrived on that first day of Freshers' Week nearly four years ago. As she'd approached St Andrews, she'd seen the outline of the old cathedral, castle and college buildings, and fallen in love with the town.

She was so lucky to have a room on the corner of the imposing red stone Hamilton Hall, the best student residence for girls. She'd also fallen on her feet with her roommate. They'd been put in a shared room when they'd started in the first year, and since then Fiona McCormick had been her best friend and guide. They'd stayed together ever since, even sharing a room in their fourth year so they could continue to enjoy the view and didn't have to go into one of the dark single rooms overlooking the well.

Lucy smiled at her friend. They were so different, but since that random pairing in the first year, they'd grown really close. Fiona had laughed at her at first, saying she was 'as green as grass', but despite being so different, they'd got on immediately. Fiona was lively and vivacious, with wild, curly red hair. She came from an air force family, so she'd lived in different countries, gone to different schools. Although she'd attracted a lot of male attention in the first year and had a few flings, she'd calmed down when she decided her relationship with her boyfriend from home, Rob, was the most important thing. She was getting married in the summer, as soon as she graduated.

Lucy had been thrilled when Fiona had asked her to be one of her bridesmaids, and they'd already had a weekend in Edinburgh with the other bridesmaids, having dresses fitted and exploring the pubs on Rose Street. Lucy had felt so naive compared to the more sophisticated students when she'd first come to St Andrews, and knew she was lucky to have Fiona as her friend. At first, her roommate had tried to persuade her to go to dances and socials, but Lucy had had it drummed into her by her parents that she was at university to study, and she spent as much time as possible in the library. She also didn't have the money to go out. Her bursary covered the place in the hall of residence, but her parents couldn't give her anything extra, and the little bit of money she earned cleaning the church in the holidays didn't go far.

In order to stop Fiona matchmaking, Lucy had invented David, her 'boyfriend from home'. As she embellished the story, he became real to her. She explained he could never visit her and wrote very few letters because he was in the army – special forces in Kosovo – and was not allowed to have much contact.

Unfortunately, the relationship had recently had to be broken off because Fiona was becoming insistent that David should come to her wedding. Lucy had had a period of mourning for the loss of her 'boyfriend', but now Fiona had decided it was time for her to come out of her shell.

Fiona was practically jumping up and down with excitement at the prospect of her shy friend going on a date. Lucy twirled a finger in her hair. 'He is really good-looking, but I don't know anything about him. What would we talk about?'

Fiona looked aghast. 'Don't worry about the talking, Lucy. Think of driving in his beautiful Alfa Romeo, being seen out with the most desirable man in St Andrews and getting a slap-up meal at the Grange instead of the same old hall food!'

Lucy hesitated, but her friend carried on. 'Look, the first two years here you were a nun because of being faithful to David, and despite his derring-do in the Balkans or wherever he was, he was a dead loss as a boyfriend. Then you were stuck in the back of beyond in Germany during your year abroad and since you came back you've never emerged from the library. What's the use of a first class degree if you haven't lived?'

Lucy had to laugh. 'It was actually in the library that Guy Montgomery approached me, so if you think he's a catch, studying there does have some advantages.'

'He must have been really keen. He'd never go to the library unless he thought it was the only place he could find you! You've got to go, Lucy. Instead of reading all those chick lit novels you love so much, you can live the plot yourself: beautiful, innocent Lucy captures the heart of playboy Guy and reforms him!'

Lucy laughed. 'You should be writing novels instead of studying Medieval History.' She thought about Guy Montgomery. She had to admit she'd noticed him since the first year – his long limbs, his floppy black hair and dark eyes, his easy confidence. He hung around with a smart set, who all seemed to have cars and plenty of money. She'd never thought he would even notice someone like her. 'It can't do any harm, can it?'

'Harm!' Fiona screamed. 'You'll have a ball! And I want to hear all about it!'

Lucy nodded, getting caught up in her friend's excitement.

'Right, that's settled. Now the next big decision is what are you going to wear?' Fiona opened their wardrobe and Lucy allowed herself to be carried away by her friend's enthusiasm and dream about her perfect date.

When Guy arrived that evening and escorted her down the steps of Hamilton Hall into his red Alfa, Lucy felt great. He greeted her with a wide smile and as he accelerated away from the kerb, she could feel envious watching eyes from the windows.

It was nearly eight when they drove into the car park of the Grange Inn. It was a beautiful converted seventeenth-century country house, with the dining room a fusion of old and modern. The white tablecloth, the sparkling glasses, the flowers on the table – it was perfect. Lucy began to feel as if she was in a film, a mixture of all her fantasies.

Guy knew exactly what to order; they had white wine with the scallops, and as they ate them he looked across the table into her eyes. 'I remember the first time I ever saw you, Lucy. You were walking across the old quad, the wind blowing your hair. I thought then you were the most beautiful girl I'd ever seen, and watching you opposite me now, I realise it's true.'

Lucy sipped her wine, feeling excitement welling up inside her as Guy continued. 'I used to wait for you then, but you never seemed to be anywhere, didn't go to the Union Bar or any of the dances. Then I heard you had a boyfriend, a soldier. But he's not on the scene anymore, I hope?' Guy raised one dark eyebrow and smiled.

Lucy felt herself blushing and shook her head. She was surprised this story had spread as far as Guy Montgomery. She'd only invented David to keep Fiona quiet. She was at university to study, and her mother had given her such terrible warnings about the dangers of male students.

She put all those thoughts behind her as the main course arrived. Guy had ordered medium-rare steaks with a full-bodied Beaujolais. As she toyed with the meat, Guy asked her about herself. 'I want to know everything about you.'

Lucy didn't want to say too much. Her childhood wasn't interesting for someone like him. She tried to make her year out in Brandenburg sound more exciting than it actually was, by emphasising its proximity to Berlin and exaggerating the funny incidents at her translation agency in post-reunification East Germany.

Guy seemed fascinated. He laughed at all her stories and as he encouraged her to tell him more, Lucy felt witty and attractive. She finished her glass of wine. How stupid she'd been to listen to all her mother's warnings about men.

With the dessert, Guy ordered a glass of sweet Marsala. Lucy had never had a dessert wine before, but discovered she really liked it. Guy was watching her across the table. 'When you're not in the library, what do you like doing?'

When Lucy told him how she'd always loved reading he seemed really interested. He asked which books she'd especially enjoyed. She mentioned some of her favourites, and he said he was going to read them because he wanted to be able to discuss them with her.

Lucy's heart leapt. Guy Montgomery was asking her for recommendations on what to read and wanted to discuss books with her! That meant he wanted to see her again. All those people who'd suggested he was a playboy were wrong; he was sensitive, thoughtful and polite, and he'd been watching her all these years. She thought of the romcom books she'd read. They were full of stories where somebody seemed to be a playboy, but he was just waiting for the right girl and fell in love with her innocence and purity. Lucy stood up feeling slightly shaky and when she looked in the mirror in the bathroom, she saw her eyes were sparkling.

As they left the restaurant, the sky was just beginning to darken although it was nearly eleven. The evenings were light and long in St Andrews in June. Guy opened the door of his car and Lucy slipped onto the leather seat. 'That was a wonderful evening,' Guy breathed, turning towards Lucy and brushing her mouth with his lips. 'I'd like to drive you to see my favourite view.'

They turned out of the car park and up the hill. The darkness had almost fully fallen when Guy turned the car off the main road onto a rutted woodland track. Lucy wasn't sure where they were going until they emerged from the trees and saw the lights of St Andrews spread out beneath them. The first stars were appearing in the azure sky and Lucy felt as if she were floating.

Guy put his arm round her and kissed her again. Lucy was surprised how good it felt. A warmth spread through her. She'd always been scared of getting too close to a man, but she felt her body responding and arching towards his. When Guy kissed her harder and his hand wandered to her blouse and unbuttoned it, she only hesitated for a second. His hand on her breast sent a surge of electricity through her. This was nice; what had she been so frightened of all these years? 'Mm, Lucy, you're lovely.' Guy pulled a handle and the seat fell back as he slid his hand inside the waistband of her skirt.

Lucy froze. What was happening? She'd been floating on a cloud of alcohol and sensation, but now she felt confused. How had she got herself into this situation? She liked Guy, really liked him, but she didn't know what to do. Would he be able to tell she was so inexperienced? She didn't want to disappoint him.

He pulled her clothes down and pressed himself into her. A pain unlike anything she'd ever experienced before shot through her. She tried to speak, but all that came out were strangled sobs.

Guy lifted himself off her, using a white hanky to clean himself. He noticed a smear of blood and looked at her with a shocked expression. 'You're not a virgin, are you?'

Lucy gulped and nodded. She felt dirty, humiliated, sore. Was this what all the fuss was about? She'd imagined her marriage night and visualised a beautiful experience. The reality was so very different.

'Why didn't you tell me?' Guy looked stunned. 'But you've had a boyfriend. I never…' He lowered his eyes. 'I've never been with a virgin before.'

Lucy pulled her clothes up. 'Please take me back to Hamilton.'

Guy started the car and reversed quickly back onto the track. They drove through the darkened streets in silence, down the cobbles of North Street and drew up in front of Hamilton Hall. Luckily the pubs were still open so there were very few people about as Lucy gingerly raised herself up out of the car and ran up the steps, hoping she wouldn't meet anyone. She managed to reach the lift and leant against the wall, trying to catch her breath as she went up to her floor.

She dived into the bathroom and caught sight of herself in the mirror. Her makeup was smeared and her eyes were huge and frightened on her pale face. She ripped off her crumpled clothes and went under the shower, scrubbing herself raw, trying to wash away what had happened. She thought of Therese. She'd always warned her of the dangers of men, told her to keep herself pure for marriage. Lucy flushed with humiliation. How had she allowed herself to get into this situation? She'd always pretended she was so good, but now she knew she wasn't.

Chapter 12

Final exams

St Andrews – June 1998

Lucy crept into their shared bedroom and felt relieved it was in darkness. Fiona had gone out to a concert and fortunately wasn't back yet. She slipped between her sheets and pulled the covers over her head, pretending to be asleep when Fiona came in. Her roommate tried to wake her up, obviously dying to question her about what had happened, but when Lucy refused to move, she gave up.

The next morning, Fiona was full of questions, so Lucy described the first half of the evening as blandly as she could. She didn't want to talk about the second half – if nobody knew about it, she could convince herself it had never happened. 'Pleasant enough, but not worth a rerun,' was the verdict she gave her inquisitive roommate.

She hardly dared to admit, even to herself, that she hoped Guy would contact her. It had been a lovely evening; she couldn't remember ever having enjoyed one more. The bit at the end was unfortunate, but perhaps it was just a misunderstanding. Perhaps she'd given out the wrong signals. Guy had really seemed to like her, before what happened, so she hoped everything would turn out all right. A lot of the books she'd read were like that. The path of true love never did run smooth.

Over the next few days, she jumped every time the communal phone on the corridor rang, willing it to be Guy. She found herself walking along the street where he lived in case she bumped into him, and in the library she was conscious of anyone moving near her, hoping it was him. Perhaps he'd approach her while she was studying, like the first time.

After about ten days, she realised he wasn't going to contact her. She'd seen him once, on the other side of the Old Quad, but he'd quickly run in the opposite direction and disappeared through the arch to North Street. She was filled with misery. What a fool she'd been! Fiona was right – she was so naive. She'd thought Guy liked her, really liked her, but something had gone wrong. Maybe he was disappointed with her lack of experience. Or maybe she was too boring.

It was only a few weeks to the final exams so she spent even longer than usual in the library, trying to forget what had happened, making sure she got the first class degree her tutors predicted. The soreness wore off and the evening with Guy Montgomery was like a bad dream. Now if she saw him in the distance, she was the one to dive down a side street or into a shop doorway to avoid him. She'd been stupid and she didn't want to be reminded of it. If nobody else knew about it, it would be as if it had never happened.

She'd loved her time at St Andrews – the ancient ivy-clad buildings full of history, the exploration of languages she loved, the windy walk along The Scores, the smell of the stacks in the library – but now she wanted to leave. She'd been accepted to do teacher training at Moray House College in Edinburgh and because she was tipped to be first in her year, her tutor had managed to get a scholarship to cover her year's course. He'd wanted her to do a Masters or a PhD but her parents had said it was time she started proper training so that this fancy education would be worth something.

The written exam in the Younger Hall, and then the oral exam, when she knew she'd charmed her examiner, went well. She'd spent so many hours in the library, she sometimes felt a bit weak and sick, and, for the first time ever, was looking forward to going to Scarborough for the holidays, to the safety of her old life.

Chapter 13

A penthouse in Zug

Wildenwil – Tuesday 26 January, 2016

Olivia drove down the narrow road to Wildenwil. There had been flurries of snow all day and although it wasn't settling on the roads, the fields were white. On the dark road through the woods, her headlights caught the snowflakes as they swirled in the cold wind. It was as if she were the only driver in the world. Once she was through the village, there were other cars on the wider road down to Zug and the night didn't seem quite so creepy.

Christian had tried to dissuade her from driving because heavy snow was forecast and the way back could be difficult, but Olivia had insisted. She'd been so keen to meet this mysterious Patrick, and now she had the chance, she wasn't going to miss it. She'd asked Christian to come back from work early to look after Marc and Lara, but he'd arrived home in a foul mood, complaining that Julian hadn't been at school, at an institution where regular attendance was taken very seriously.

As she reached the outskirts of Zug, Olivia felt strange. She never went out much, but this was the first time she'd been out in the evening since Sandra had disappeared. These ten weeks seemed to have been forever, but at the same time had passed in a numb blur.

Arriving in the town, she passed the station and drove towards the old town, catching sight of the lights reflected on the dark lake between the timbered buildings. After a short distance, she turned left up a steep, narrow street. When Julian had texted her Patrick's address, she'd recognised it as one of the most prestigious in Zug, on the small hill looking over the old town and the lake. She parked in front of the modern apartment block and then took the lift up to the penthouse flat.

The lift opened straight into a large open-plan room. It had floor-to-ceiling windows on two sides, leading out onto a balcony, and was decorated in a stylish way, with tall large-leafed plants and bold modern-art pictures. It looked like something from a glossy magazine or a film set. As the lift door opened, Julian stood up from a long low sofa and came towards her. His eyes were shining. 'Mum, I've got some wonderful news.'

Olivia hugged him, pleased to see him looking so happy. Julian looked to his left and Olivia saw a figure was silhouetted against the bright lights of the kitchen area. This must be Patrick.

The figure turned and moved towards her, carrying a glass in each hand. As he moved into the living area, the glow from the low lighting hit his face. Olivia gasped. It was…it couldn't be… She wasn't sure at first but as he came closer, she knew for certain.

It was Guy Montgomery. She hadn't seen him since a chance meeting in Edinburgh in 2004. He'd been very curious about her young son then, but she'd never told him she was pregnant and was determined he'd never find out about Julian. Getting far away from him was one of the reasons she'd come to Switzerland.

Guy put the two tall glasses onto the glass-topped table. Olivia stared at him and then at her son. They were so similar; it looked as if Julian had been cloned from the older man.

'Lucy, how lovely to see you again. Thank you so much for coming. You've arrived just at the right time for a drink. What would you like? Gin? Wine?'

Olivia was shaking, unable to speak. This was unbelievable. How had he found her, after she'd thought she'd hidden herself away so well?

When she found her voice, it came out strangely cracked. 'I'm Olivia now.'

Guy smiled, the same charming smile that had melted her all those years before. 'I'm aware of that, my dear. Your name change made it very difficult for me to find you. But now I have, I'm so glad. You're just as beautiful as ever. And although it was very naughty of you to hide my son from me for so many years, now I've met him I must forgive you.'

Olivia began to protest: 'But he's not your—'

Guy interrupted her. 'Oh, but he is. One only has to look at him to see that, but just to be certain, I took the precaution of taking a saliva sample from his coffee cup when we first met. A DNA test confirmed that he is indeed my son.'

Guy walked towards the kitchen again. 'It's lovely that you're here. What can I offer you to drink?'

'I'll just have some water, please.' Olivia was still standing in the same position as when she'd first come in. Julian was sipping his gin, watching her carefully without saying anything as Guy brought a glass of sparkling mineral water with ice and lemon and led her to the other part of the L-shaped sofa.

He raised his glass to Olivia and their eyes met as they chinked glasses. 'I must congratulate you for raising such a fine boy.' Guy paused. 'To our wonderful son.'

'How did you find us?'

'It's taken a long time. You did an excellent job of disappearing, especially with your name change. I wasted a lot of time searching in Germany because after I traced you to your school, they suggested you'd gone off with the German assistant, which I, or rather my investigator, took too literally.'

'You hired an investigator?'

'Of course. Mike Brady is one of the best in the business – ex-police. Although it was very important to me to find you and our son, I do have a business to run. One which has turned out quite successfully, as you see.' He waved his arm round the room with a self-deprecating smile.

Olivia thought of the car following her and the feeling of being watched. 'A few weeks ago, I was sure someone was following me. Was that him?'

Guy shrugged. 'If you noticed him, Mike wasn't as good as he claimed. But he did find you and was very thorough in his search. He knocked on a lot of doors, talked to a lot of people. He discovered many interesting and may I say, unexpected, things about you.'

Olivia froze for a moment. What had he found out?

Guy smiled and took a piece of paper from the table. 'Married Christian Emil Keller October 2004 in Zug, Switzerland. Adopted Julian Robin Keller in January 2005. Marc Magnus Keller born in September 2005 and Lara Akira Keller born in June 2008. I could tell you how much is in your husband's bank account – I notice you don't have one of your own – and the value of your house. I know how much tax your family paid last year, that you haven't been back to Scotland since you left in July 2004, and many other interesting facts. I know everything about you, Lucy Olivia.'

Olivia shuddered. She felt threatened by his confidence and power, fearful of what he could do to her family, terrified of what he might have found out. 'What are you doing here? Why did you tell Julian your name's Patrick?'

Guy picked up a pile of business cards, the same as the one Julian had given her. 'Of course, you know all about using different parts of your name as it suits you. Patrick is actually my first name, but I've always called myself by my second name, Guy. I think it suits me better. My initials are PGM, which I thought would be fun to use in my company, Phoenix Global Management.'

'But what do you want with us? Why are you here in Zug?'

Guy smiled again. 'Obviously I want to get to know my son. I've missed out on so many years and now I want to make sure I'm involved in his life.' He took another sip from his glass. 'When Mike found Julian, I came to Switzerland to take a look at him. I realised then that this was the ideal place to base my business.

Zug provides very favourable tax conditions for international businesses.'

He gestured round the room. 'Then this flat came on the market and it was fate. My dream apartment, so I had to seize the chance.' He stretched out his long legs. 'I've still kept a little pied à terre in London, but I intend to make Switzerland my main home. Having found my son at last, I want to spend as much time as possible with him.'

Olivia looked at Julian. His face was shining with excitement. 'Dad wants me to finish school, but then I can join him in the business. It's so wonderful. After all these years of not knowing my father or who I really am, now we've found each other.'

Olivia gulped. *Dad!* He was calling him that already. She felt a shudder of guilt when she remembered how she'd told Julian his father had died before he was born, and had no relatives. She'd been relieved he hadn't shown much interest in finding out further details and seemed to accept that he was alone with his mother, who also had no family or relatives.

But now he had his future mapped out with this man, who'd just waltzed into his life and was already taking over. Her mind was in turmoil. She didn't know what to say, so she stuck to the easiest question to give herself more time. 'What sort of business is it?'

'We have diversified into many fields of commodities and services. We're a growing company and now we're based in Switzerland, we're planning to expand all over the world.' He turned to Julian again and gave him a proud smile.

Olivia looked at her watch. She'd only been there half an hour but she felt exhausted. She was afraid to say too much because, having seen the way Guy and Julian were together, she was frightened of how Julian might react if there were any conflict. Julian was not always easy, but he was her son.

They'd been so close when he was young. She remembered playing on the beach at Portobello, reading books with him in bed, watching children's television as she made his tea. He'd grown up into a difficult teenager, but perhaps it was because he didn't know his roots, who he really was. She could identify with that, having grown up not knowing her real identity.

Suddenly feeling uncomfortable in this beautiful room, she wanted to leave. Through the high windows the snowflakes were swirling white and fluffy, reflecting the light against the dense darkness of the sky. She looked across at Julian. 'The weather doesn't look very good. I think we'd better be driving up the road before the snow gets too deep.'

Julian shook his head. 'I'll stay here. If the weather's going to be bad, it will be easier to get to school tomorrow.'

Olivia stiffened. 'I hear you didn't go to school today.'

Guy leant towards her. 'I'm sorry. That was my fault. There were some things we had to sort out together, but I promise it won't happen again. I'm a great fan of a good education and the Swiss one seems to be excellent.'

Julian's face slipped back into the familiar sulk for the first time since she'd arrived. 'Yes, I'll go to school, and I'm sure it will get back to you quickly enough if I don't.' His face cleared as he glanced at Guy before looking back at Olivia. 'You know it's my birthday soon. Dad wanted to buy me a car but he didn't know you have to be eighteen to drive in Switzerland.'

Guy looked at him fondly. 'There are still many things I have to learn about life here. However, I will get him a new motorbike. It's important that he has reliable transport to get around with.'

Olivia was just about to reply when her phone rang. Scrabbling through her handbag she managed to find it before it went to voicemail. It was Christian.

'Olivia, where are you? You need to come back as soon as possible.'

Olivia's heart froze. What was wrong? Had something happened to the children? 'What?'

'It's Bella. She seems to be having some kind of fit.'

Olivia's hand was shaking. 'Oh no, we'll be back immediately.' She finished the call and told Julian what had happened. Bella was his dog after all.

Julian looked only vaguely interested. 'That's a shame, but she's old. It was bound to happen one day.'

Olivia looked at him in shock, picked up her coat and, unable to say anything, took the shiny glass lift down to her car.

Chapter 14

Bella

Wildenwil – Thursday 28 January, 2016

There was fresh snow on the ground, but the sun shone in a clear blue sky. It was the föhn, the area of high pressure south of the Alps, which caused the mountains to the south to stand out like cardboard cut-outs on a model railway set. The sun sparkled off the peaks of the Rigi and Pilatus.

Olivia drove up to the foot of the funicular, but didn't go up. The snow would be really deep on top of the ridge and it was where she'd always gone with Bella. She couldn't do this walk alone. Every step would bring back memories of her wonderful dog.

Tears came to her eyes as she remembered what had happened. After she'd raced home from Guy Montgomery's, she'd been shocked to see Bella lying twitching on her bed. She wouldn't drink anything or even take one of her favourite treats, but had looked up at Olivia with beseeching eyes. Lara had been snuggled in one of the comfy chairs, her knees pulled up, clutching a teddy close to her. She'd seemed better in the time since Christmas, but Bella's illness made her revert to baby mode again. Marc was playing a game on his PlayStation, not seeming too concerned.

Christian looked anxious. 'I thought you'd be back sooner than this. Didn't you realise the dog was ill?' Olivia had thought Bella was getting weaker every day but, as she stroked her, was shocked at how thin she was beneath her thick fur.

'So, did you meet the mysterious Patrick? And where is Julian? He can't just stay away from school. His attendance record will look dreadful.'

Olivia whispered she'd tell him later, and chased Lara and Marc off to bed as quickly as she could. She stayed longer reading a story with Lara, smoothing her blonde hair and kissing her soft cheek. Poor little thing. She was only seven and she'd lost her best friend, and now Olivia was sure Bella was going too. Her heart literally ached as she hugged her daughter. She'd tried so hard to give her a happy childhood, unlike the one she'd had, but it was impossible to protect her from everything.

Christian was waiting for Olivia when she came downstairs. She told him what had happened and he didn't seem very surprised. He'd never asked about Julian's father; Olivia had thought he was being sensitive, but perhaps he just didn't care. 'If he wants to pay for him now, he can. I've done it for the last eleven years. Just as long as Julian goes to school and improves his attitude. My colleagues are complaining about his arrogance. It's embarrassing for me, and the height of ingratitude from him.'

Olivia looked at Bella's huge trusting eyes and thought of her children. She'd do anything in the world to protect them, but now she was frightened. Terrified that she was losing Julian.

The next morning, she'd taken Bella to the vet. Olivia had asked the children to say goodbye to their dog before they went to school because she was almost certain she would never come back. Bella still hadn't eaten anything and had difficulty standing, so Olivia had to lift her into the car and onto the table at the vet's.

She'd known Peter, the vet, for years. He spent most of his time up to his armpits in cows, but he still looked after a few pets for the villagers. He examined Bella and took some blood as the old dog lay passively, patient and good-natured as always, but making no attempt to lift her head or look round.

Peter came back and from the look on his face, Olivia knew it was bad news. He patted Olivia on the shoulder and gave Bella a sympathetic stroke on her silky ears. 'It doesn't look good, I'm afraid.

Bella is a very good age for her breed, but the symptoms suggest bone cancer, which these mountain dogs are unfortunately prone to. I can run further tests and send them away to the lab, but it's only likely to confirm the diagnosis. The lack of appetite, joint weakness, the fitting and weight loss are all very strong indicators.' He patted the dog's head again while Bella looked up with her huge, patient eyes. Olivia's whole body shook. This was what she'd been afraid of.

Peter looked at her with sympathetic eyes. 'I think the kindest thing would be to let her go and I'd recommend you do it now. You could take her home, but I can't guarantee she'll survive until tomorrow.'

Olivia gulped and held Bella tight. She could hardly speak, but managed to whisper, 'Now.' She wanted to be with Bella when she died, didn't want her to suffer anymore. The vet fetched his needle and gently injected it. Bella seemed at peace, and Olivia couldn't tell when her breathing had stopped.

'She was almost gone anyway. I hardly needed to give her anything.' Peter patted Bella again and then looked at Olivia kindly. 'What do you want to do? Do you want to take her home or shall I…?'

Olivia could hardly speak for the sobs racking her body. 'Please, you take her.' She gave Bella one last kiss on the soft fur on the top of her head. 'You were the best dog.'

Reliving the moment, Olivia walked away from the car park, her feet crunching through the crisp, soft snow. She missed the gentle pad of Bella's paws beside her, and her hands felt strange without the lead. The view looked like a Christmas card with the snow-tipped trees and the breath-taking panorama in the distance, but the beauty somehow made her emptiness and loneliness even harder to bear.

She followed a track through the trees, not really aware of where she was going, lost in her thoughts. When she looked up, she was surprised to see she'd reached the Wildenbach Falls. There was still a trickle of water snaking down from the top of the ridge, but most of it was a series of spectacular icicles that plunged and twisted their way between the jagged rocks.

In front of her was a high wall, obscuring the hotel Olivia knew stood behind it. Finding a foothold in the stone, she pulled herself up and peeped over the top. She wanted to see what renovations had been done. The building looked as creepy as ever, with its towers and wrought-iron balconies, arches and blank windows looking like dead eyes.

Her head was still above the wall when a garage door in one of the outbuildings swung open and a people carrier drove out. The windows were darkened, but the vehicle stopped and a window was lowered. It was Aurelia. 'Olivia, I knew you would come.'

Olivia felt embarrassed at being caught peering over the wall. 'Oh, hello. I was just going for a walk.'

'And your walk brought you here. This is no coincidence, Olivia. Everything happens for a reason.' Aurelia reversed the car. 'Please, come in.'

'But you were just going out. And I have to be back to collect the children.'

Aurelia smiled. Her all-knowing smile. 'We have time before the school comes out. And you're more important to me than anything else.'

She parked the car in front of the garage and approached Olivia. 'I'm pleased you've come to see our home. It isn't finished yet, but we love it.' Olivia had always wanted to visit the hotel. She was curious about what was inside, and there was an aura of warmth around Aurelia that made Olivia want to be part of her world.

Aurelia directed her through a small gate in the wall and led her towards the front door. It was opened by an old man wearing a traditional orange and burgundy Tibetan gown. Olivia recognised him from the Spar.

'This is Tenzin,' said Aurelia. 'He and his wife are my oldest friends, the original members of our community. My husband and I met them when we were in India, where they were living in exile after being forced to flee Tibet. They joined us, and since then we have always travelled and worked together.' Olivia smiled and Tenzin lowered his head respectfully before disappearing silently through a door at the back of the imposing tiled entrance hall.

Aurelia opened a double doorway to the right. 'This is the old dining room.' Olivia entered the room and blinked. The room was dark, with heavy tapestries covering all the walls except for one, which was filled with books from floor to ceiling. The room was lit by candle chandeliers, which flickered and revealed dark corners, statues and pictures of what Olivia thought looked like Hindu gods and goddesses. The air was heavy with the smell of incense and in the background, Indian music played softly.

Rugs, richly ornate stools and large cushions were scattered over the floor and there were photos everywhere, mostly of a man with dark swept-back hair, a small beard and piercing dark eyes. Aurelia pointed to him. 'This was my husband. Together we founded the community.'

Another large photo was of a couple, a much younger and slimmer Aurelia and her husband, with his arm loosely round her shoulder. There were other photos of him with different women. With his tight-fitting sweaters and jeans and his intense gaze, he oozed sensuality.

One black and white photograph caught Olivia's eye. It showed a strikingly good-looking boy of about sixteen, with long hair, large eyes and a soft sensitive mouth. Olivia moved towards it to see him better.

Aurelia pointed to the chandeliers. 'It's rather difficult to see the pictures clearly in this light, but we keep candlelight in this very special room. This is the vortex of the power, the crossing of the ley lines. You will see that the rest of the hotel has been renovated to the highest modern standards, but here we are going back to the essence, back to our roots.'

She pointed to the picture that had attracted Olivia's interest. 'That's Sebastian. He's been with us since he was fourteen.'

Olivia heard a movement and looked round. A young man in his thirties came in, obviously the one in the photo. He was carrying a wooden inlaid tray with two cups on it. 'And here he is.'

As he came nearer out of the shadows, Olivia could feel an electricity in the air. Sebastian was tall and slim, with long dark hair tied back in a ponytail and startling pale blue eyes. His mouth, which was as soft and sensitive as in the photo, smiled. 'Take this drink. It's a Tibetan tea which is good for the comfort of troubled spirits.' He spoke in a low voice, with an accent Olivia couldn't quite identify. Irish, perhaps. He certainly had a Celtic air about him, with his black hair and bright blue eyes.

The tea was thick and milky. Olivia didn't like tea with milk, but she drank it politely. As she sipped it, Sebastian smiled at her again and although she hoped he would stay, he disappeared between the hanging tapestries.

Aurelia looked at her in an appraising way and took Olivia's hands in hers. 'I feel this is a very special time for you. You are at a turning point in your life, and what you decide now will influence your future forever.'

Olivia didn't know what to say. She looked down at her tea, which she hadn't liked at all – too sweet, but with a bitter aftertaste. The smell of the incense was oppressive and she felt quite lightheaded, blinking in the flickering candlelight. Aurelia's deep melodic voice seemed far in the distance. 'Trust me. Tell me what's troubling you and we can help you.'

Olivia was floating out of her body and her voice seemed to take on a life of its own. She heard herself saying, 'Everything seems to be going wrong at the moment. Two little girls have disappeared and I can't stop thinking about them. My older son only wants to be with his father who's suddenly reappeared, I'm scared of everything, worried my children will be harmed. And my dog has died…' Her voice trailed off and she struggled to hold back her sobs. It was ridiculous that Bella's death affected her so badly, but it just seemed to be the final straw.

Aurelia held Olivia's hands more tightly. 'In everybody's life there comes a time when the planets collide. It's a testing time, but afterwards you will achieve a new clarity.' She pulled Olivia closer. 'It's not an accident we have met. You are living in a time of turmoil. I feel so many suppressed memories in you. You must acknowledge these, Olivia, work with them, come to terms with them, and then you will find your true self. I want to help you because there is greatness in you. You must allow it to flourish.'

Olivia's head was swimming. Aurelia seemed to understand her. There had to be something in her powers. And Aurelia said she had greatness in her. Nobody had ever said that before.

Olivia sat up with a jolt. How long had she been here? She stole a look at her watch. It was time to meet the children from school. Aurelia sensed her concern. 'Of course, my dear. I know your children are very important to you. Do you need a lift home?'

Olivia explained she'd left her car in the car park when she'd set out for her walk and had just come across the hotel by chance. Aurelia gave a knowing smile. 'You may think it's chance, but there are no coincidences. Everything that happens is what is needed at the time. You were meant to come here. Now you have visited us, you can come back whenever you wish. We will always be waiting for you. Sebastian will give you a lift to your car so we're certain you'll be on time.'

Olivia nodded thankfully and moved through the double doors into the hall. As she went outside, she blinked in surprise at the brightness of the day. The sky had misted over and a breeze had sprung up, but in comparison to the gloom of the room, the light reflecting on the snow was dazzling.

Sebastian collected the people carrier and stopped in front of the house. Aurelia hugged Olivia and made her promise to come again soon. It was only a short drive to the car park but Olivia was very conscious of Sebastian's presence beside her as he watched the road ahead. He stopped next to her car and, fixing his brilliant blue eyes on her, spoke softly. 'I hope to see you again very soon, Olivia.'

Olivia felt herself blushing. For a mad moment, she hoped he would put his arms round her and kiss her, but he stayed still, gazing at her. She pulled herself together. She was nearly forty, a wife and mother, but she felt a buzz of excitement inside her she hadn't experienced for years. Opening the door, she mumbled goodbye and stumbled out, giving a little wave to the blacked-out windows as the car drove away.

Chapter 15

Summer in Scarborough

Scarborough – July 1998

It was a terrible summer for Lucy. Everything had started to go wrong at her graduation. Her parents wouldn't come, even though she was awarded a first-class honours degree and a special prize for the best modern linguist of the year. They said it was too expensive and not for the likes of them. She must have been the only one at the graduation ceremony in the Younger Hall who wasn't surrounded by family.

Fiona was supportive as usual and had invited her to a meal with her large sociable family and proud fiancé, but Lucy had felt really off-colour. She'd thought it was nerves when she had to leave the table to throw up in the Ladies, but then the whole journey back to Scarborough on the train, she'd been sick in the cramped toilets, the smell increasing her nausea.

Back at home, the summer got even worse. She constantly felt sick. She tried to pass it off as food poisoning, something she'd eaten at the graduation, and spent her days lying in bed reading. She lost herself in the other worlds of her books, trying to blank out her fears about the real world, only interrupted when her mother came in with cups of tea. Therese seemed secretly pleased Lucy was her dependent little girl again, although she didn't seem particularly well herself, very thin and tiring easily. Frank was also showing his age, becoming even more bent and crotchety.

Lucy's twenty-second birthday passed without any celebration and as the weeks went by and she felt no better, she began to panic.

She didn't eat properly, couldn't face all kinds of foods she used to love, and felt bloated. She went to the library and looked up her symptoms in a medical dictionary. There were several possibilities that she clung on to, trying to ignore the obvious diagnosis.

She couldn't be pregnant. It was only the once and, although she realised it was a myth that you couldn't get pregnant the first time, she couldn't believe anything could result from that awful humiliating evening.

Looking out of her small attic window, she watched holidaymakers going towards Peasholm Park and down to the beach. People walking about normally, people who didn't have the terrible fear hovering over them. She was sure these women had had sex many more times than her, but they weren't pregnant. It wasn't fair.

A small rational voice told her they probably used contraception. She'd never thought about it because she'd been so sure she'd never have sex until she was married. Guy probably thought she was on the pill – every other female student seemed to be. Why had she been such a fool? In the stories she read, everything worked out well in the end, so she lost herself in her books, anything rather than face up to the awful reality that seemed more likely every day.

And there was Fiona's wedding. It was a big affair at Middleton Lodge, a beautiful Georgian country house in the Scottish Borders. The photos in the brochure looked wonderful. When Fiona had first asked Lucy to be one of her bridesmaids, she had protested that she was too shy and couldn't afford it, but Fiona had pushed all her excuses aside. She said Lucy was her best friend at university and knew her better than any of the other bridesmaids, Rob's two sisters and two school friends. She assured Lucy it wouldn't cost a thing as her parents were paying for all the bridesmaids' dresses and their rooms in Middleton Lodge. In the end, Lucy had agreed, had the dresses fitted at a hen weekend in Edinburgh and had really liked the other bridesmaids. She'd never been to a wedding before, so she'd really been looking forward to it.

But she couldn't go to the wedding. She was swelling up and wouldn't fit into the beautiful cerise dress. She also knew she couldn't face Fiona's questions and keep her secret; Fiona knew her better than anyone else and she'd guess something was wrong. Lucy couldn't talk about her fears of pregnancy. If she talked about it, it would become real, and she couldn't cope with that.

So, Lucy had disappointed Fiona, the best friend she'd ever had. Three days before the wedding, she'd sent a message saying she was ill and couldn't come. Fiona had immediately phoned, pleading with Lucy, saying she needed her to be there. Lucy had insisted she was too ill. Afterwards, she was overcome with shame. How could she have been so ungrateful, unfeeling and thoughtless to the kindest person she'd ever known?

It almost made it worse that Fiona was so understanding. She contacted Lucy after the wedding, sending photos and a piece of cake, inviting her to come and stay with them after their honeymoon in Greece, but Lucy had put her off, saying her illness was getting worse. This awful secret stopped her from being able to talk to anyone.

She put her face in her hands. What was she going to do? She couldn't tell her parents – she'd rather die than do that. They'd be so disappointed. All their sacrifices were wasted and all their warnings and allusions to bad blood would be confirmed.

She couldn't wait to go back to Scotland. She'd been allocated a bedsit in Edinburgh through Moray House College where she was doing her teacher training. She had to get out of Scarborough, out of this fetid atmosphere of dislike and disappointment. Frank barely spoke to her and Therese tiptoed around, trying to keep the peace, full of suffocating love for Marie, as she still always called her. Lucy knew she had to escape before anybody guessed what had happened. And when she arrived in Edinburgh, she would look for a doctor.

Chapter 16

Carnival

Olivia took the roast chicken out of the oven and increased the heat to crisp the potatoes. It was Schmutziger Donnerstag, Fat Thursday, one of the main days of celebration in Fasnacht, the carnival festival before Lent. They were having a special meal before the fasting time and the kitchen was filled with the delicious smell of chicken.

Fasnacht was very early this year because Easter was at the end of March. In Central Switzerland it was an important time of year, especially in Lucerne, where there was a huge parade with bands of Guggamusik, all dressed in extravagant multi-coloured costumes, playing their distinctive discordant music. Even the most respectable citizens dressed in masks and fancy dress, letting their hair down once a year.

The children rushed into the kitchen. Christian had left school earlier than usual and picked them up on his way home. Today all the children had gone to school in their carnival costumes. Lara was wearing a ladybird outfit and Marc was a red devil, complete with a grotesque mask.

They sat down at the table, starving as usual, and Olivia served the food. The low light over the table cast a warm glow over their faces as the children described the different costumes.

'Even Frau Fisch got dressed up,' said Lara, suppressing giggles.

Marc joined in the laughter. 'She was Pippi Longstocking, with a short skirt and stripy tights.'

Because it was a small country school, the classes contained different age groups, something Olivia thought an excellent idea. Lara was small and sensitive, so it was good for her to have her big brother in the same classroom. Frau Fisch was a young teacher, straight out of college, but she had excellent ideas and maintained a good atmosphere in the class. Olivia admired the way she'd handled Sandra's disappearance, still mentioning her, but not being melodramatic about it.

Olivia smiled. 'I bet she looked good. Did she have her hair in sticky-out pigtails?' Olivia could imagine their teacher's red hair suiting the storybook character.

'Yes, she put wire in them,' said Lara.

'But she did look a bit fat,' added Marc, with a snigger.

'Marc, you shouldn't make comments about people's body size,' Olivia said, feeling she had to say something, although she was enjoying hearing laughter round the table again.

Lara shot her mother a cheeky look. 'Yes, she should have gone as a big fish.'

'No, she should have gone as a whale,' added Marc, and both the children collapsed in giggles. Even Christian was smiling, although he attempted to hide it.

'Marc.' Olivia tried to keep her face straight too, but it was too late.

Lara waved her arms in the air, hardly able to speak for laughing. 'She should have gone as an octopus.'

Marc stood up and shook his short, sturdy body. 'No, she should have gone as a big wobbly jellyfish.' He and Lara screamed with laughter.

'And you two should have gone as cheeky monkeys,' Olivia said. The children laughed even louder at this. 'Poor Frau Fisch, having you two in her class! Now, who wants ice-cream?' Olivia stood up and moved towards the fridge.

'Me, me, me!' they both shouted, and Frau Fisch was forgotten.

Julian had sent a text message to say he was '*eating with Dad*', and although Olivia couldn't help cringing when she saw Guy referred to as that, in some ways she was relieved Julian wasn't there. His sulking presence and Christian's gibes often made mealtimes a strain, and the atmosphere was easier when he wasn't around.

When they'd finished eating, the children went into the bath and Christian kept an eye on them while Olivia cleared the kitchen. After the excitement of the day, the children were exhausted. Olivia went up to read to them, but Lara fell asleep almost immediately. Olivia smoothed her daughter's hair from her forehead, and seeing her long lashes on her cheek, her heart nearly burst with love. She kissed her daughter tenderly and moved gently out of the room, closing the door quietly behind her.

Marc had his headphones on, listening to one of his audio books. She gave him a kiss too as he waved her towards the door. He was such a self-sufficient child, 'easy-care' as they said in Switzerland, very like his father, and so different from Julian.

Julian. It was his seventeenth birthday a week on Sunday, and she'd invited Marlene, Sibylle and Rolf to lunch. She'd asked Julian if he wanted to invite any of his friends but he'd said he'd go out and celebrate with them on the Saturday night.

That had been a few weeks ago, before Guy had come back on the scene, and she didn't know what was happening now. Perhaps she should invite Guy as well. The thought only entered her mind for a moment and then she dismissed it immediately. That wasn't going to happen.

When she went downstairs, Christian was sitting by the fire, holding two glasses of wine. 'Come and sit down.' He patted the sofa next to him and Olivia took the offered glass and sat beside him.

Christian raised his glass. 'Cheers,' he said and leant over to her, kissing her on the lips. 'That was nice. It's great to have the family being normal again.'

'Yes,' Olivia nodded. 'But we do have to talk about Julian.'

Christian's face fell. 'Trust that boy to spoil the atmosphere even when he isn't here. Can't we just relax this evening and think about him later?' His words sounded like a joke, but Olivia could feel the strength of feeling beneath them.

'It's his birthday on the fourteenth. He's seventeen so we're having a special lunch for him.'

Christian looked blank.

'I told you about it. I've invited Marlene and Sibylle and, of course, they're coming.' Marlene had replied immediately saying they'd both be delighted, and Olivia was relieved. It was always fun when they were around. They could defuse the most awkward situations with their quick wit, and Julian liked them. 'But I'm a bit worried about Rolf. I sent him a text message but he didn't reply. I worry about him stuck in that godforsaken place. Nobody else would be mad enough to attempt to live there in the winter.'

Christian shrugged. 'Look, he's survived deserts, tropical jungles and the slums of Asia, so I think he'll be able to cope with a Swiss winter. Don't worry about him. He's used to looking after himself. I don't know what happened on his last posting, but he needs this time to get over it. He'll be fine.'

'Have you heard anything from him since Christmas?'

'Not a thing.'

'Aren't you worried? There have been several really heavy snowfalls since the New Year, so how's he managing? He could be lying there, frozen to death.'

Christian leant over and gave her a kiss. 'Don't worry. I know he stocked up with food and he has a phone for emergencies. He's devoting himself to those sheep and I don't really think family birthday parties are his thing at the moment.'

Christian moved closer to her. 'And we have to get back to normal too. Why don't we get a babysitter and go out to the Masked Ball on Saturday?' Olivia had to stop herself from laughing. The name Masked Ball was a bit of an exaggeration for the annual drunken dance in the school gym organised by the village sports club.

Every Wednesday, Christian went to the men's gym group, mainly made up of people he'd known from his school days, and it constituted most of his social life. Although he was a high school teacher, he was a country boy at heart, and despite his university education, still felt most comfortable with his old village friends. After the session in the school gym, the group always went for a drink in the Ochsen Bar in the village.

Olivia didn't think she could face the forced gaiety of the ball, with Sandra still being missing, but she didn't want to annoy Christian by mentioning her. She quickly looked around for an excuse not to go. 'It'll be really difficult to get a babysitter on Saturday. Everybody will be going out – it's a special night for the village.' She gave him a smile, which she hoped combined disappointment, but not too much, and encouragement. 'You go, you'll have fun with your friends. I won't know anybody.'

Christian looked disappointed. 'You'll know lots of people – all the other mothers from kindergarten and school. You really should join the women's gym group though. You'd love it.'

Olivia shook her head. 'I don't like exercising inside. I prefer going for a walk in the countryside.' She swallowed hard as she thought of Bella, and blinked back tears.

She tried to hide them but Christian noticed. 'Look, Olivia, I know you miss Bella, but she was old and ill, and it's better she's at peace now. Get another dog and cheer up. You've been drooping around like a wet weekend for ages.' Christian gave a smile. Olivia knew he prided himself on his colloquial English. 'And you really should get more friends in the village. Now that you don't have Zita to look after, you're by yourself too much and that makes you brood on things.'

'I've met a new friend,' Olivia said, and told him about meeting Aurelia and visiting the Grand Wildenbach Hotel. She described the strange candlelit room, but added that Aurelia had described the rest as being modern. She didn't say anything about Sebastian.

Christian put his glass down. 'Don't get mixed up with people like that. They sound like some kind of cult or sect. You should do more in the village. You used to be so well integrated, I was proud of you, but you're becoming too isolated. If you don't feel ready to do some teaching, what about doing some voluntary work?'

Olivia shook her head. 'I can't take anything on at the moment. I have to make sure the children are safe.'

Christian put his hand over Olivia's. 'I know you were very upset by Sandra's disappearance, but you have to get over it. Please try to draw a line under what's happened and get back to being the Livy I know.'

Christian's mouth softened. He pulled her towards him. 'I know it's been a hard time for all of us, but we have to get back to normal for the sake of the children. They're beginning to get over it and we have to be strong for them.' His voice thickened. 'Olivia, I haven't put any pressure on you, but how many weeks has it been since we made love?' He kissed her and Olivia tried not to stiffen. She wanted to respond, to be normal, but she didn't feel anything.

Christian took her hand and led her towards the stairs. 'I've missed you.' Olivia followed him upstairs. He was her husband, and he was a good one, and she wanted to be a good wife.

As they lay in bed, she felt nothing, until Sebastian's blue eyes and glossy long black hair came into her mind. She felt her body respond.

Afterwards, Christian lay back, smiling. 'We both needed that,' he said, before rolling over and falling asleep immediately. Olivia lay looking at the wooden beams on the ceiling and saw the face of Sebastian. It was ridiculous. She'd only seen him for a few minutes but he seemed to have cast a spell over her.

Chapter 17

At the doctor's

Edinburgh, Scotland – September 1998

The doctor's waiting room looked like something out of the seventies, no gleaming health centre here. Lucy had chosen the cramped practice halfway down the Canongate, the lower part of Edinburgh's famous Royal Mile, just because it did look dingy and rundown. She had to see a doctor, but she wanted to be anonymous. The furniture was worn, as were the other inhabitants: a wheezing old man and an old-before-her-time mother reading a gossip magazine with one hand and reaching out to wipe her toddler's runny nose with the other. Lucy picked up one of the grubby magazines and flipped through it, just to have something to do with her hands.

Moray House College of Education was just a short walk away. Today had been her first day, but although she should have been excited, she'd only felt apprehension. Everything should have been perfect; her dream of being a teacher was in her reach. She'd always wanted that, to be able to inspire other girls as she'd been inspired by her teachers.

Now she was sure it was all ruined. The doctor came to the door and called her name. He was a world-weary older man in a crumpled suit. She could smell cigarettes on his breath. Were there really still doctors who smoked?

'Now, what can I do for you?' he asked, with a distinctive Edinburgh burr. Lucy looked up and saw his eyes were kind behind the glasses. She pulled at the skin on her hands.

'I'm afraid, I think, I may be pregnant?'

'And what makes you think that?'

'I did a pregnancy test and...'

The doctor picked up his pencil and took notes. 'They can be unreliable. When was your last period?'

'I've had periods, sort of regularly, but now I'm afraid they might not have been complete.'

'Do you have any other symptoms?'

'Nausea, which I put down to the stress of my final exams, bloating, tender breasts. And now I can't deny that I'm putting on weight.'

The doctor put down his glasses and led her to a couch. Lucy lay down, holding her breath, hoping there would be a simple explanation. He felt her stomach, pressing and manipulating the flesh. 'We'll need to do further tests, but from my examination, I would say you are pregnant in the fourth month.'

Lucy gasped. 'I can't be. I just can't be. I've started at Moray House...' Tears welled up and rolled down her cheeks.

'My dear, accidents can happen in the best-ordered lives. Courses can be postponed. But tell me, is this the first time you've visited a doctor for this?'

Lucy nodded, unable to speak for the sobs racking her body.

The doctor went back to his desk and wrote notes. 'You need to have a hospital appointment and a scan as soon as possible. And seeing as this seems to be unplanned, you need to discuss this with your partner.'

Lucy sobbed even louder. She couldn't tell this kind doctor what had happened, what a fool she'd been. She couldn't tell anybody. What was she going to do?

The doctor stood up and reached for his phone. He spoke quickly. Lucy felt too distraught to listen. He finished his call and handed her a piece of paper. 'I've made you an appointment at the Simpson Maternity Unit at the Royal Infirmary. You know where it is?'

Lucy nodded. She'd find it. Taking the paper, she tried to thank the doctor between sobs.

'Come and see me on Friday, or earlier if you have any worries. I can see this has come as a shock for you, but think of it as a wonderful blessing. A new life is forming in you.' The doctor patted her hand and then turned to his notes.

Lucy stumbled out of the surgery, blinded by tears. She almost fell on the cobbles as the cold autumn air hit her and the wind whistled between the grey buildings. Clutching the piece of paper, she walked up the hill, her legs moving automatically as she tried to come to terms with what the doctor had said.

When she reached her bedsit, she stared out of the window. The view from her room in an old converted school building was spectacular, looking out over Holyrood Park and with the bulk of Arthur's Seat looming above her. She'd been so relieved when she'd arrived, away from the claustrophobia of the flat in Scarborough, but wasn't able to relax, the unspoken fear of pregnancy dominating her thoughts.

And now it was certain. She was pregnant. What could she do? Was abortion the answer? She could do it secretly and nobody would ever know she'd even been pregnant. But, although she was filled with terror, she knew she could never do that. She was going to have a baby, somebody related to her. She'd had nobody in the world and now she was going to have a relative.

That reminded her of something. She took the file containing all her certificates and official documents down from the shelf. Her birth certificate was there, with her mother's name: Geraldine Elizabeth Sheridan. Her mother had been in the same situation as her. She would understand. Lucy made a decision. She was going to look for her birth mother.

Chapter 18

Rolf

Wildenwil – Friday 5 February, 2016

There was a fresh sprinkling of snow and the sky was blank white. Low cloud surrounded the house and only the nearest trees could be seen from the kitchen window. Christian got up in a good mood, singing as he prepared the breakfast and took Marc and Lara to school on his way to work.

Olivia cleared the kitchen and sat down for another cup of coffee. When she went outside with the rubbish, the trees were encrusted with rime and the temperature was still below freezing. Despite the cold, she wanted to get out of the house and purge herself with the freezing air. Oh, how she missed Bella. She even missed Zita's grumbling and complaining. She always felt better when she was doing something to help other people.

Olivia knew what she was going to do. She put some bread, milk, eggs and cheese in a basket and drove up the hill, past the entrance to the Grand Wildenbach Hotel. She felt tempted to drive in, but made herself carry on further up the road until she saw the collection of farm buildings where Rolf was spending the winter.

The road hadn't been cleared of snow up here so she parked as close as she could and struggled through the deep, crisp snow towards the stone buildings. There was smoke coming from the chimney of one of them and the snow was trodden down between the outbuildings. Rolf was alive.

Olivia knocked at the door of the main building, her hands numb with cold despite her thermal gloves. The front of her hair was frosted with icicles where it had escaped her hat and her nose was freezing. There was no reply to her knock, but she could smell wood burning and thought she could hear some movement inside. 'Rolf,' she shouted, and hammered on the door. 'Rolf, it's Olivia, please let me in. I'm freezing.' She was stamping her feet in an attempt to thaw them out when the door of one of the outbuildings opened a fraction.

'Olivia, what are you doing here?' Rolf was wearing a large waterproof jacket, a woollen hat pulled low over his face and a huge scarf. His face looked grey and pinched. A warm animal smell emanated from behind him.

'Rolf, what's the matter. Are you ill?'

'No, I'm fine, but I have some pregnant ewes in here. They're very susceptible to infection and I don't want to risk miscarriage. I've already lost three foetuses.'

'I'm sorry to hear that, but I'm freezing, Rolf. Please let me in for a moment to warm up.' Olivia held up the basket, feeling like Little Red Riding Hood visiting her grandmother. 'I've brought you some food. I was wondering how you're managing in this weather.'

Rolf's hand shot out and took the basket. 'That's very kind of you, Olivia, but I'm fine, really. I bought a lot of supplies before the snow started.' There was a plaintive bleat from behind him. 'I'm going to have to go. Thanks so much.'

He was just about to close the door when Olivia put her foot in the gap. 'Rolf, I can see you're busy, but I hope you'll be able to come to lunch next Sunday. It's Julian's birthday. Marlene and Sibylle are coming and it would be great if you could come too.'

Rolf nodded. 'I'll certainly try.' His voice became more animated. 'It really depends on the condition of my ewes. It's very difficult to keep them healthy through the winter. These beautiful sheep are dying out so it's essential we keep the line going and deliver lambs this spring.'

Olivia realised she was not going to be invited in for a steaming hot drink, which was what she wanted, so she smiled and said,

'Do come if you can,' and walked back to her car as quickly as she could.

She got into her car and turned up the heating. There was a moment of panic when the wheels spun round in the deep snow, but to her relief, the car jolted forward and she began the precarious drive down the icy road.

She was driving down in a dream, thinking about the very unsatisfactory meeting with Rolf, when a police car, driven at speed up the narrow lane, forced her into the side of the road. She'd just steered her car back onto the track when she had to swerve off again as another two cars came racing over the brow of the hill, followed by an ambulance.

It was so rare to encounter vehicles on this road in winter, never mind an ambulance, that she nearly turned back to follow them. The thought crossed her mind that it could be something to do with Rolf, but she dismissed it immediately. She'd just left and the cars must have set off from Zug much earlier. She was curious, but she could hardly pretend she was just passing, and didn't want to be like one of those ghouls craning their necks at autobahn accidents.

She looked at her watch. She still had plenty of time before collecting the kids from school, so she could just pop into the hotel. It was on her way and she might see Sebastian. She shook her head. *Grow up. You're forty in a couple of months. You're a wife and mother.*

She straightened her shoulders and drove down to the Spar, where she didn't meet anyone interesting, and bought some wholesome vegetables for lunch.

As she was taking the children back to school in the afternoon, a helicopter flew overhead in the direction of the ridge. What was going on up there? Could it have anything to do with Sandra? The missing girl was rarely far from her thoughts.

That afternoon she moped round the house in a restless way, haunted by images of Sandra and Ruth, wondering if the helicopter could have anything to do with them. The local radio station was playing in the background, wall-to-wall Euro pop, but this stopped when the news came on.

The first item was about a body found near the Wildenberg Peaks. The police stated that it was a young female but, at this time, were not confirming any link to the November disappearance of Sandra Kolb from the nearby village of Wildenwil.

Chapter 19

Register House

Edinburgh – September 1998

Lucy walked over the North Bridge, looking down at Waverley Station and across to the castle. The skyline of Edinburgh was so impressive, but she couldn't enjoy the beauty. She was pregnant. The sickness and fear overshadowed every moment of every day.

Passing the impressive hulk of the Balmoral Hotel, its huge clock always three minutes fast so travellers wouldn't miss their train, she crossed Princes Street. Feeling for her birth certificate in her pocket, she wondered what she'd be able to find out about her birth mother. She'd never thought she wanted to meet her, but being pregnant made her feel an affinity with her. Her mother must have been desperate to have decided to give up her baby.

Register House was near the Café Royal, where Lucy had been for a drink on that memorable hen weekend with Fiona and the other bridesmaids. First, she went into the imposing neoclassical Register House building, but was directed round the side to New Register House, where certificates for all the births, marriages and deaths in Scotland were held.

Approaching the desk nervously, she wondered if she'd be able to access the information she sought, but ironically, the fact that she hadn't been officially adopted made tracking her mother down much easier. The staff were helpful, explaining that she couldn't see original documents stored in the beautiful Dome library, but she could search for microfiche copies.

Putting in the details she had, she quickly found Geraldine Elizabeth Sheridan's birth certificate. She'd been born at the Western General Hospital on 15 June 1960. That meant her mother was only just sixteen when she had her. Pregnant at fifteen. No wonder she'd been desperate. Lucy felt unable to cope and she was twenty-two.

What had happened to Geraldine after she'd given up her baby? Half in trepidation, Lucy made a search for her name in the deaths section, but was relieved to find nothing.

Perhaps she had married? She put in her mother's details and quickly came across a marriage certificate. Geraldine Elizabeth Sheridan married James William Lindsay on 26 July 1986 in St Mary's Cathedral, the biggest Catholic church in Edinburgh. That was the first surprise, and when she saw the home addresses she got another shock. Therese and Frank had come from Leith, the rundown docklands of Edinburgh, so she'd imagined her mother as a deprived waif. However, Geraldine's address was in Trinity, a posh area near Leith, and her husband was from Cramond, part of Edinburgh Lucy knew was really expensive.

She paid for copies of the certificates and walked out into the afternoon air, thinking about what she'd found out. The lights were coming on and there was a cold wind blowing up Leith Walk. She was surprised how easily she'd found the information. She could have done it years earlier, as soon as she'd found out she was adopted.

She'd promised Therese and Frank she'd never try to contact her birth mother, but this deceit paled into insignificance compared to the huge betrayal she was carrying around with her. Her pregnancy meant that all Therese's warnings, the prayers, the emotional blackmail, the desperate attempts to keep her from the real world, had come to nothing.

Lucy walked home, her mind whirring. The information she'd discovered meant it may well be possible to find her mother, something she'd assumed would be difficult. But she wasn't sure if she really wanted to.

There were so many immediate problems facing her. She couldn't complete her teacher training because the baby would be born in February. Even if she managed the theoretical parts, the teaching practice would be impossible. What would happen to her scholarship then? And there was Christmas coming up. She couldn't let her parents see her like this. But what reason could she find for not going home to Scarborough?

It was dark before she reached her little bedsit. Although she hadn't done much to personalise it, just a few pictures and throws, she loved it. She wished she could hide away here until after the baby was born. But what would she do for money? And she couldn't hurt Therese like that.

She had to make a plan. Taking a piece of paper, she wrote a list. First, she would see the social welfare officer at college. There she'd get some guidance about the options in her situation. Secondly, she'd go to the antenatal clinic to find out exactly what she had to do. Thirdly, and she had a big question mark in her head as she wrote it, she'd find her mother. The thought frightened her.

Downstairs there was a communal phone booth with a telephone directory. She looked up Lindsay, James William. There was a long list of Lindsays, including a few named James, but no James W. Then she saw it: J. W. Lindsay, with an address in Dick Place. She wasn't sure where it was, but when she looked at her map, she saw it was one of the most expensive and desirable addresses in the Grange area of Edinburgh. She couldn't resist it. She had to look at the house.

The next morning, she missed her lecture again and walked up Dalkeith Road, clutching the map in her hand. When she reached the address, she found a handsome, free-standing, grey stone Victorian villa, surrounded by a neat walled garden. Lucy couldn't believe it. This magnificent house didn't correspond to the picture of her mother she'd carried through the past years, of a desperate young girl having to give up her child because of poverty.

For the next few hours, Lucy kept her eye on the door, walking up and down so as not to look too obvious. At any moment, her mother might come out, or draw up in a car. She didn't want to speak to her; she just wanted to look at her, to understand where she'd come from.

As it got nearer lunchtime, Lucy was sure someone would arrive, but the windows remained blank and the doors unopened. The afternoon dragged on and as it grew darker, her legs were weary, she was hungry, and she was sure the curtains were twitching even more often in a neighbouring house. She looked sadly back at her mother's house as she walked away, and caught a bus back to her bedsit.

As the darkness fell, she went into the sanctuary of her warm lair. She pulled a blanket round her and thought she wanted to escape from the world and stay there forever.

Chapter 20

Ruth

Wildenwil – Friday 5 February, 2016

After hearing the news report about the body on the ridge, Olivia was worried about how it might affect the children, but when she went to collect Marc and Lara she was relieved the news hadn't filtered through to the school yet. There was no confirmation the body was Sandra's, so Olivia didn't want to say anything without knowing all the facts. If it was bad news, Christian would be able to give that in a better, far less emotional way.

She was sitting at the kitchen table playing a game with Marc and Lara when Christian's car drew up. The door opened and she was surprised to see it was Julian who came in first, looking pale and tired and carrying a sports bag. She stood up and gave him a hug. She hadn't been happy about him staying at Guy's, but Christian had convinced her it was better to say nothing and keep the peace. She also knew Christian was secretly pleased when Julian wasn't around.

During the evening meal, Julian was subdued and said he was going to bed early. Olivia followed him up the stairs and caught his arm, wanting to talk to him, but he just answered in monosyllables. When she asked him what his plans were for the weekend, he reminded her he was going out with some of his friends from the village on Saturday, but would be home to sleep. He turned away, and Olivia could see sadness in his eyes. She hated to see him upset but, in one way, hoped Guy had shown his true colours.

After the children had gone to bed, Christian sat at the table with the newspaper while she turned on the television. There was some international news, but then the scene switched to a reporter up on the ridge. He said the body of a young female found by a snow-clearing team had been identified as Ruth Frick, the eleven-year-old who had disappeared from her foster home on Christmas Eve. Forensic tests were continuing on the body and the area was being searched by a specialist team with sniffer dogs.

Olivia turned to Christian, her feelings in turmoil. In some ways it was a relief the body wasn't Sandra's, but the area was still being searched. 'They're looking to see if Sandra is there too.' The tears slid down her cheeks. The thought of Sandra's sturdy little body frozen in the snow was unbearable.

Christian looked up from his newspaper. 'Of course, they have to cover all eventualities, but from what I've heard, the police don't believe the cases are connected. The Frick girl probably just ran away and got caught in a snowstorm. Very sad, but by all accounts, she was a very disturbed child.'

'Ruth, her name was Ruth, not the Frick girl!' Olivia felt the tension that had been building up in her burst out with her words. 'She was a little girl, somebody's daughter. With her whole life ahead of her.'

Christian put the paper down and pushed his glasses up on his nose. 'Livy, don't be so melodramatic. Accidents happen, children die every day. You can't worry about all of them. I know you were upset by Sandra's disappearance, but we can't let it dominate our lives forever. Life goes on and you must pull yourself together. The happiness of our family must come first.'

'But I can't forget Sandra. And I can't stop thinking about that little frozen body…' Olivia's voice broke as the image imprinted itself on her mind.

Christian stood up and kissed her on the cheek. 'I'm going down to the Ochsen. There's a meeting about the sports festival we're arranging. I wasn't going to go because I was hoping we'd spend a nice Friday evening together, watch a film, have a glass of wine, like we used to, but I can see you're not in the mood.'

He looked over his shoulder as he moved towards the door. 'Get a good night's sleep and I'm sure you'll feel better in the morning. It's the Fasnacht parade down in Zug tomorrow and the children are looking forward to it. We can all go and have some fun.'

He closed the door. Olivia watched him go, feeling let down and resentful. Christian didn't seem to understand her at all. She wouldn't have a good night's sleep. She hadn't for months, her nights disturbed by nightmares about her children being snatched, mixed with events from her past she'd tried to forget. And now Christian had walked out on her on this night when they'd heard this terrible news.

She picked up her Kindle and went to bed, trying to lose herself in a fictional world, but echoes of the past kept forcing themselves into her thoughts.

Chapter 21

A walk in the woods

Wildenwil – Saturday 6 February, 2016

The next morning she woke up, the aftermath of her dreams hanging over her like a cloud. Christian was in the kitchen, frying bacon, and in full 'good old Daddy' mode. Olivia went slowly downstairs, rubbing her eyes. Marc and Lara were at the table, already in their carnival costumes, and even Christian was dressed in the knight's tabard he hauled out every year.

'Wakey, wakey, sleepyhead. Get into your costume because we'll have to get down early to get a parking place. The town will be mobbed.'

'I'm sorry, I'm not coming. I've got a headache.' Olivia couldn't bear the thought of the crowds, the confetti throwing, the discordant music, the forced jollity. She usually went along to the parade with the family, but it made her feel like an outsider; although she'd been in Switzerland for more than ten years, the carnival was not her culture and made her realise she didn't belong.

Christian just raised his eyebrows and ushered the children out to the car, telling them what fun they were going to have, while Olivia poured another cup of coffee. She felt scratchy and claustrophobic. She should have gone, but the thought of the crowd of marching bands, the floats and the screaming masked people terrified her.

She had to get out of the house. Without knowing where she was going, she got into the car and drove up the hill. When she got to the deserted car park by the funicular, she parked and wondered what to do next. She felt as if she were alone in the world, without even Bella for company. How she missed her!

She looked around the silent forests. The Grand Wildenbach Hotel was in one direction, but she made herself walk in the other direction. She was afraid of the magnetic pull the hotel had for her.

The track through the forest was mostly in gloomy shade, although the sun occasionally shafted through the branches. Deep in her thoughts, she was walking on the crisp snow when she heard the distant swish of footsteps. She stopped in fear and automatically looked round for Bella.

But, of course, she was alone, and suddenly felt vulnerable. Although Bella had been the friendliest dog imaginable, she was also an excellent judge of character, and Olivia had felt safer with her around.

Ahead, she could make out a shadowy figure. Her heart pounded. Should she run back to the car?

The figure moved into the sunlight and she realised it was limping. Her natural desire to help others kicked in. She couldn't abandon someone who was in trouble and she was sure she'd be able to outrun this shuffling figure. As she walked nearer, the figure stopped, silhouetted against the sunlight sparkling on the frost-laden branches.

'Olivia? Olivia, is that you?'

She recognised the voice immediately and her heart rate returned to normal. It was Stevie Dawber, dressed in black Lycra jogging trousers and a black waterproof jacket, with a purple beanie hat pulled deep over his head. He was carrying two bulging white plastic carrier bags with the Spar logo on them.

Olivia ran up to him. 'What are you doing here? Are you all right?'

Stevie stopped and supported himself on a tree trunk, all his weight on one foot. 'Olivia, I'm so pleased to see you.' Despite a look of pain, he gave his famous lopsided smile. 'I have to apologise for standing you up the other day.'

'Don't worry about that. What's happened to you?'

'Not really cut out for this jogging lark. I think I've twisted my ankle,' he grimaced. 'And just when I need it for once, I realise I've come out without my phone. Stuck in the pocket of my other trousers.'

'My car isn't far away. If you can make it there, I'll drive you home.' Olivia wanted to help, but also thought it might be a chance to get a closer look at Stevie's house, which had intrigued her for a while. Taking out her own phone, she asked, 'Or do you need an ambulance?'

Stevie waved his hands in horror. 'No, it's not that bad, and I don't want any fuss.' He passed his bags over to Olivia. 'If you could just carry these, I'll manage.' He pointed to a branch at the side of the road. 'Ah, a trusty staff. If you could just pass that over, I'll be fine and dandy.'

Olivia fetched it and they made their way slowly back to the car, Stevie wincing every time he had to put his foot down.

'I'm so sorry I didn't meet you in the café. I just couldn't get out of the house at all last week. It was when the Lola Lee thing broke and reporters were camped outside the house, hounding me for a comment.'

Lola Lee. Olivia remembered reading about her. The tabloids had been full of articles about a memoir she'd written, or had ghosted, called *The Wild Girls*. It was about a group of middle-class schoolgirls in the seventies who'd gone to rock concerts and had a competition to see who could bed the most rock stars, giving their performance marks out of ten.

Olivia hadn't paid much attention because her mind had always been on the missing girls, but she knew the newspapers had all been trying to dig up the dirt on any rock stars from that era. She hadn't been aware of any extra reporters in the village but since Sandra's disappearance, she was so used to seeing strangers everywhere she probably hadn't noticed.

She couldn't help feeling curious. 'Are you in the book?'

'Not in the most incriminating sections, thank goodness, but Rocky Parker was. He was the wildest of the Tarantulas, but

Lola Lee exaggerated the stories about him.' Stevie gave another grimace. 'At least I hope she did.'

Olivia thought of the pictures of the Tarantulas she'd found online. Stevie, the pretty-boy front man with his long blond hair and his winning smile, had interested her most, but she remembered Rocky Parker. He'd been the drummer, a wild glowering figure in the background, with flailing arms and long, tangled black hair. He'd been notorious for trashing hotel rooms, and since Lola's book, for the sexual indignities he'd put the young fans through. He'd died in the eighties after a wild night of drink and drugs.

'But you were in the same band. You must have known what was going on?'

'The seventies are a bit of a blur for me. We had such a killing schedule, playing a different town every night, driving in the van during the day, with only a few hours' sleep in a hotel room. The only way I could come down after the adrenaline of the performance was to have a few joints. And there were girls everywhere, hiding in cupboards, bribing the roadies to let them into the dressing rooms.'

'So Rocky took advantage of them?'

Stevie gave her a rueful smile. 'We all did, I suppose. It's what they wanted. It's just this woman says Rocky was violent and abusive too.'

'But wasn't the point that she was only fifteen when all this happened?'

'Who knows how old they were. We didn't ask for birth certificates.' Olivia was appalled and felt a revulsion that must have shown on her face.

Stevie looked at her. 'Please don't hate me for this. I'm certainly not proud of what happened, but we were teenagers too, small-town boys who suddenly found fame and had girls literally throwing themselves at us. It's how I met my first wife, and it's what every girl dreamed of. She thought she'd hit the jackpot with me. Until she went off with Ray Baines...'

Stevie gave his lopsided grin again, looking like the young star he'd once been. Olivia thought back to what she'd read on the Internet when she'd searched for Stevie's details. There were photos of him and the beautiful leggy young girl he'd met on tour and then married. They'd had a child together, before she'd gone off with the legendary guitarist of an even more famous group. After that, Stevie had written one of his best-known songs, 'The Emptiness Without You'.

They reached the car and Olivia put the bags into the boot. She had a quick look inside them; they seemed to be filled with packets of sweets and biscuits. Helping Stevie edge into the passenger seat, she asked for directions. She'd seen his house from above, but she'd never driven past it.

They went along the foot of the peaks and then up a gated drive. The house was in a magnificent position on a sunny ledge, with a panoramic view over the Alps to the south. Stevie pointed to a parking place by a side entrance.

'We'll go in through the kitchens. I want to hide my bags before PP sees them.'

'PP?'

'Ah, Princess Priska, my lovely wife.' He looked ashamed. 'I hope I didn't sound sarcastic. She is wonderful, but I'm afraid I don't come up to her high standards and she would be especially disapproving of my Spar shopping.' As he opened the kitchen door, he whispered, 'I even have to pretend to jog to get to the shops to buy my illicit stash.'

The kitchen was a huge sparkling area with floor-to-ceiling units, an enormous American fridge and a large island in the centre of the room. A short woman with black curly hair stood at the island cutting vegetables. Stevie hid the bags behind his back before limping over to the woman, who had looked up from her chopping board when he came in.

Stevie gave her a hug. 'Concetta, this is Olivia. My knightess in shining armour. She's just saved me from a frozen death in the woods.' Concetta nodded towards Olivia with a little smile. 'And

Concetta saves me every day with her lovely husband, Luigi. They look after us so well.' Concetta's smile widened as she looked up at the old pop star with adoration. 'Olivia and I are going to sit in the winter garden so could you bring us up a pot of coffee?'

He led Olivia out of the kitchen and, looking around carefully, took a key out of his pocket and surreptitiously opened a metal door on his left. Raising his finger to his lips, he stuffed the bags in and locked the door again. 'Just putting supplies into my recording studio,' he whispered.

He hobbled up some stairs into an imposing two-storey winter garden, filled with huge plants. There were white leather loungers and sofas with glass-topped tables between the giant green leaves of the plants. Stevie indicated the seats. 'Please take a seat and I'll go and slip into something more comfortable.'

'What about your ankle? Shouldn't you put ice on it or something?'

'I'll have a look at the damage when I get these wet socks off. It's actually feeling a lot better now. I should warn you, I have a long history of hypochondria.'

Stevie limped out of the room and Olivia sat down, admiring the view. The sky was grey, but the silvery light coming through the clouds gave it an ethereal beauty. Concetta came in and put down a tray of coffee, together with a plate of homemade biscuits.

Olivia was just wondering whether to help herself when a small slim woman wearing a bright pink leotard and white legwarmers came into the room. Priska. She was a very beautiful woman, as befitted a former Miss Switzerland, but she looked even better than in her beauty queen days. Her blonde hair was cut short, in a style that flattered her elfin features, and her body was slim and toned. She looked like a teenager, although Olivia thought she must be well into her forties.

Priska walked over with an icy smile and extended her hand. 'I hear that thanks are in order. I'm Priska Dawber. My husband is very accident-prone and really shouldn't go out alone. We have a gym here and an indoor swimming pool, but he claims he needs the fresh air.'

Olivia took her hand and introduced herself, saying she was glad to help. Priska picked up the plate of biscuits and offered it to Olivia. 'Please take one before my husband comes back. Concetta is an excellent cook but she should be aware by now that sweet things are a definite no-no for him.'

Olivia took one, feeling uncomfortable. Priska was very polite, but Olivia could sense dislike emanating from her in waves. And she was always suspicious of women who called their husbands 'my husband' all the time.

A door opened and Stevie hobbled in. He was wearing a grey lounging suit and had a white bandage round his ankle. His limp seemed considerably worse than before.

He sat down and poured a cup of coffee, looking hopefully at the biscuit plate. Priska whisked it away. 'I'm afraid I have to leave you because my reflexologist is due any minute. It was nice meeting you, Frau Keller, and thank you once again for your help. My husband should rest now because he has work to do recording his new album in his studio.' She shot a stern glance at Stevie. 'So we need not detain you any longer. I'm sure you also have many things to do.' She swept out of the room.

Olivia raised her eyebrows. 'That's me told.' She stood up and looked round, wondering if she had to go back through the kitchen or if there was another entrance.

Stevie took her hand. 'I'm sorry about that. She doesn't mean to be rude.'

Olivia felt her voice getting tight. 'It doesn't matter. I have to go shopping anyway.'

'Don't be like that. I want to talk to you again. I miss English conversation.' He grimaced. 'I mean, I can only speak English and Priska is really very kind but…' He coughed. 'I'd better stop before I dig myself into a deeper hole, but please give me your mobile number. I'm going to be a bit restricted on the jogging front for a while and it would be great to have a longer chat…' He laughed.

'And perhaps you'd be kind enough to help me out with a little shopping?'

Olivia felt herself relax. She nodded and gave him her number, which he tapped into his phone. She enjoyed his company and knew exactly what he meant about English conversation. Olivia spoke English with Christian and the children, but it was so refreshing to talk to someone with the same background and sense of humour.

Stevie led her towards the high glass doors leading onto a terrace. 'You can go out this way.' He leant forward and kissed her on the cheek. 'See you again soon.'

As she drove away, Olivia looked at her phone. No message from Christian. She was suddenly overcome with a feeling of panic. She should have gone to the parade with the children. With such a crowd of people, how could Christian keep his eyes on them all the time? Crowds like that were dangerous. A child had gone missing at a local festival not far away a few years ago.

She drove home as quickly as she could, praying they'd come home soon. She took a deep breath, trying to calm herself. She had to trust her husband, believe her children were safe, but the fear lingered on. Would things ever be normal again?

Chapter 22

Geraldine

Edinburgh – November 1998

Lucy opened the door of the café and looked around. There was a pleasant atmosphere, with wooden tables and comfy mismatched chairs. She was early because she hadn't been sure she'd be able to find it, tucked away in a side street in Bruntsfield. The only other customer, an older man sitting in the window seat, was reading a book and didn't look up when she came in. Lucy picked the table furthest from him, sure that Geraldine had chosen this place to avoid meeting anyone she knew.

A waitress approached for her order. Lucy asked for a glass of water, saying she was waiting for somebody. She felt sick with apprehension. Looking towards the door, she wondered what Geraldine would be like, willing the door to open but scared at the same time.

Since the meeting had been arranged, Lucy had gone through different scenarios in her head: Geraldine would be thrilled to find her lost daughter and would support her through the pregnancy; she would reject her and want nothing to do with her; they would meet but have nothing to say to each other; they would find out they were soulmates and Lucy would have the relationship with her she'd never had with Therese. She wondered which of these would be true.

She'd gone to the address in Dick Place several times but had never seen anyone who could be her mother. People didn't often walk anywhere in that area, which made her conspicuous to nosy neighbours. Cars had emerged from the garage from time to time, but she'd never been able to identify the occupants.

She'd thought about phoning, but after once plucking up the courage to dial the number, she'd panicked as soon as it was answered and had replaced the handset immediately. It would be too much of a shock to make contact that way, so in the end she'd written a letter.

She'd redrafted it many times, feeling as nervous writing the words as if she were saying it face to face. In the end, she kept it very simple. She gave her birth details and simply said she believed Geraldine was her mother and hoped they could meet. Even after she'd sealed the letter, she'd carried it around for several days before plucking up the courage to post it, her hand shaking as she slid the letter into the letterbox.

After that, she'd hardly been able to leave the house because she wanted to check the mail as soon as it arrived. Day after day she waited, but nothing. Silence. Did that mean the woman didn't want to see her? Perhaps the letter hadn't arrived? It couldn't have. Even if her mother didn't want to see her, she would reply, surely.

Three weeks later, an envelope arrived. In it was the name of the café, a date and time. Nothing more. Perhaps Geraldine just didn't know what to write and was waiting until they met. At least Lucy was going to meet her.

She'd tried to get on with things, but her life seemed to be on hold. The hospital appointment had been better than she'd expected and everything was fine with the baby. She looked at the scans, but felt a sense of detachment. Half the time she couldn't believe there was anything inside her, and if she wore baggy clothes nobody would guess.

Margaret McCulloch, the welfare officer at Moray House, had been really helpful. There was a crèche in the college and it would be possible to spread the course over two years. Mrs McCulloch was so kind and matter-of-fact that Lucy had felt confident about the future while speaking to her, but when she was sitting alone in her room, watching the evening sky darken over Arthur's Seat, she was overcome with fear. She couldn't do this. What was she going to do about Therese and Frank? She still thought of them as her parents, but she couldn't imagine telling them about her pregnancy.

The door of the café opened and a slight blonde figure walked in. There could be no doubt it was Geraldine; they looked so similar. Lucy was shocked how young Geraldine looked. Thinking of a mother, she thought of a worn grey-haired woman like Therese, but then she remembered Geraldine wasn't yet forty.

Her mother moved towards the table. Her clothes looked expensive, her hair was in an elegant twist, but her face was white and drawn. She sat down opposite Lucy, ordered a latte, and gave Lucy a cool appraising look. 'Yes, you are my daughter. I can see it in your face.'

Lucy didn't know what to say. There was no smile, no warmth. She hadn't exactly expected her mother to hug her like she'd seen on television programmes, but this coldness was disconcerting.

Geraldine laid an expensive-looking bag on the table. 'What do you want?'

Lucy blushed. What did she actually want? 'I just wanted to see you.'

'You've seen me now. Anything else?'

Lucy froze inside. She hadn't realised how much hope she'd invested in this meeting. She'd thought that at last she'd find someone who'd understand her, someone she could talk to at this frightening time. Tears pricked the back of her eyes, but she blinked them back. She was determined not to let Geraldine see her cry.

The older woman looked at her and seemed to soften slightly. 'I wasn't going to reply to your letter. You are part of my life I've put behind me and tried to forget.' She took a lace-trimmed hanky out of her bag. Perhaps she was softer than her brittle exterior suggested. Twisting it in her hands, she carried on. 'When I was fifteen, I went through a very bad patch. I mixed with a wild crowd, staying out all night. When my parents tried to control me, I ran away from home and went to live in a squat. I did it all

– drugs, sleeping around. Thought I was living a great life, being a free spirit and all that, rejecting the bourgeois ways of my parents. I was so out of it I didn't realise I was pregnant until it was too late for an abortion, and then all I wanted was to get rid of the baby as soon as possible and pretend it hadn't happened.'

Lucy nodded. She could identify with that reaction, trying to pretend it hadn't happened. She looked across at her mother, but her eyes were lowered, staring at the twisted handkerchief.

Geraldine carried on in a dull voice. 'I looked into getting you adopted but they insisted I told my parents because I was so young. I couldn't have told them. Then one day, I was in a churchyard down in Leith, off my head on drugs, thinking of killing myself, when I met this old couple. They were a bit creepy, but when they heard I was pregnant, they said they would take the baby, no formalities, no questions asked, and take it far away. They gave me all the money they had.'

Geraldine looked up at Lucy. 'That's what they promised. To take you far away so I'd never see you again.' She looked close to tears. 'What's your name?'

'Lucy.'

Geraldine's brow furrowed. 'They promised me they'd change your name.'

Lucy felt she had to defend Frank and Therese. 'They did take me away, to England, and they changed my name to Marie. When I saw my birth certificate, I took the name Lucy, because Marie had never felt right. They tried to stop me coming to university in Scotland, but I felt drawn here, back to my roots.'

Geraldine raised her eyes and looked at Lucy closely, as if for the first time. 'You're at university?'

Lucy nodded. 'I was at St Andrews and graduated last summer. I've come to Edinburgh to do teacher training. I got a first,' she added, and immediately regretted it. It sounded boastful, but she wanted her mother to be proud of her.

Geraldine gave a ghost of a smile. 'You're intelligent, and beautiful.' She breathed deeply. 'I'm relieved. I was worried I might have damaged you with all the drugs I took.' She raised the hanky to her eyes.

Sipping her water, Lucy looked at her mother. She hadn't known what to expect, but it wasn't this. She even began to feel sorry for Geraldine and wondered if she'd noticed she was pregnant. Probably not. She'd been sitting behind the table since her mother came in, and was wearing a coat and baggy jumper.

Taking a deep breath, she asked the question that had always been at the back of her mind. 'Who's my father?'

Geraldine laughed, a slight humourless rasp. 'I've got no idea. I was so stupid I jumped into bed with anyone who seemed interested in me – men in the squat, guys from bands, any freak who would have me. Afterwards I realised I was rebelling against my parents.' She blew her nose. 'When it was all over, I went home and they sent me to therapy for years. They were so smug and middle class, they sent me to be cured. Then, when I became the daughter they wanted, they said it was just a phase I'd gone through and it was never mentioned again.' Geraldine pursed her lips. 'I never told any of them about you. I thought if I didn't talk about you, you wouldn't exist.' Lucy shuddered. She could hear herself saying that.

Geraldine straightened herself. 'I came to see you today because I thought I owed it to you. But we can never meet again. After my years of therapy, I went to university, met a good man, and now have a beautiful home and two wonderful children. Nobody, nobody knows you exist and I can't risk everything I've achieved, everything I've become.'

She opened her bag and took out a thick bundle of notes. 'I brought you this. I thought you might be after money and this was to pay you off.' She paused and looked wistful. 'Actually, I'm surprised how well you've turned out.' She shook herself. 'But I can't ever see you again.'

Lucy looked at the money. It would certainly help her, but she couldn't take it. She was being bought off, just as Geraldine had sold her when she was a baby.

Geraldine seemed to read her thoughts. 'Take it. It's yours. Or rather it belongs to that old couple who took you. A thousand pounds, including generous interest. They didn't give me much, but it was all they had – enough to buy me a few scores.'

Lucy felt her hackles rise. She was going to take the money and use it to help bring up her baby. Lucy wasn't going to be like her mother and was glad Geraldine didn't want to see her again, because she didn't want to see her. Taking the money, she tucked it into her bag. 'Thank you for coming. You've made your position clear and I'll respect it.'

Geraldine stood up and pulled her cashmere coat round her shoulders. 'Oh, by the way, I'm very healthy. No medical conditions. Isn't that what people usually want to know in situations like this?' With that, she turned and walked out of the café, without looking back or saying goodbye.

Lucy watched the door close, feeling numb, empty and confused. There was a sudden kick in her stomach and a wave of love washed over her. She was going to devote her life to her child and never end up like her poor apology for a mother. Who had left without paying. *Never mind*, she thought with a wry smile. *A thousand pounds should cover it.*

Chapter 23

Clues

Wildenwil – Tuesday 9 February, 2016

Olivia weighed some courgettes in the Spar and added them to her basket. She was already buying stuff for the family meal she was cooking for Julian's birthday on Sunday. It gave her something to focus on and she was looking forward to it. Julian seemed to have got over his infatuation with Guy, and Marlene and Sibylle were coming. It was always good fun with them. She hadn't heard anything from Rolf, but she wasn't expecting him. He'd no doubt be too busy tending his lambs and he wasn't much of a party person these days anyway.

She looked hopefully around the aisles, but didn't see anybody interesting. Every time she visited the supermarket, she hoped she might bump into Aurelia again. The older woman fascinated her; the way she seemed to know what she was thinking, the understanding she had of Olivia's past. In fact, Aurelia seemed to know her better than she did herself. The more Olivia thought about it, the more she wanted to talk to Aurelia again.

When she got to the checkout, her eye was caught by some copies of the *Blick*. The familiar picture of Sandra was on the front page of the tabloid newspaper, with the blurred picture of Ruth next to it. Olivia popped it in her basket. Christian said she'd become obsessed with the case, but she couldn't help it. She listened to every broadcast, hoping to hear some good news, and searched the Internet for details of the case and other instances of missing girls.

Walking towards her car, she read the front page of the paper. Was there any more information? As usual, the Swiss paper was short on detail because the privacy laws were much stronger than in Britain. But there was something in this article she hadn't known before. Putting her shopping down, she leant against her car and read the details.

Tests showed Ruth Frick had not died on the night she ran away from the foster home, but at least two weeks later. That corresponded with the first heavy fall of snow in mid-January. There was also a photo of the clothes she was wearing, garments the foster family said they didn't recognise. They were more expensive than anything they'd ever bought her. They were Swiss-made and, although readily available in many shops, not from the cheapest chains. This definitely seemed to suggest she'd been held somewhere before she died.

There was also a picture of a bag found beside Ruth. Something on it caught Olivia's eye. She looked more closely at the picture. A little keyring was attached to the bag's strap. Olivia recognised it. It was a miniature St Bernard, similar to Bella. Lara had one of these keyrings, which they'd bought when they went to the top of Mount Pilatus last summer. And so did Sandra. Lara had bought one for her friend and they'd both attached the keyrings to their school bags.

Olivia leant against the car, the newspaper shaking in her hand, her heart pounding. That had to mean Ruth and Sandra had been held together. She knew the search for Sandra's body in the area where Ruth had been found had drawn a blank. But was Sandra being held somewhere nearby?

Olivia thought about where Ruth's body had been found. As it was up near the pass, she could have been held on either side of the mountain range, or maybe the body had been dumped from a car. She looked up at the Wildenberg Peaks in the distance – so wild and beautiful, but with so many places to hide, with caves and tunnels, shacks and huts used only in the summer, like the ones Rolf was living in. Could Sandra be up there somewhere?

Olivia was so deep in thought that when a shadow fell over her, she started. She looked up from the paper and was surprised to see Guy standing next to her.

'Hello, Lucy,' he smiled.

'I've told you. I'm Olivia.'

'I think Lucy suits you better. Beneath your Olivia super-hausfrau exterior, I can still see Lucy, as beautiful, passionate and impulsive as ever.'

Olivia bristled. 'What are you talking about? You didn't know me then, and you don't know me now.'

Guy smiled and pointed to his car, which was parked nearby. 'I need to talk to you. Come for a short drive with me.'

Olivia shook her head. She remembered vividly the only other drive she'd had with him. 'Sorry, I can't. I've got to collect the children from school for lunch.'

Guy smiled. 'They don't finish school until eleven-fifty today.'

Olivia gasped.

'Remember, I know everything about you.'

Olivia was reluctant to go, but she knew she had to talk about Julian. Her son was obviously unhappy and with his birthday coming up, she wanted to be able to resolve whatever was troubling him.

She sat on the front passenger seat. It was soft leather and the car smelt new and luxurious. Guy started the engine. 'We'll just go for a short drive.'

Olivia nodded. She didn't want any of the other mothers from the village to see her. The car roared off with a surge of power as Guy drove too fast along the narrow mountain roads.

'Slow down,' Olivia couldn't stop herself from saying.

'I've never had an accident,' Guy said, revving the engine faster.

'But there may be a cow on the road, or a child.'

The car slowed. 'You're right. Sorry. There are still a lot of things I have to learn about Switzerland. But I love it here and I'm going to spend as much time as I can in Zug, building up a relationship with Julian.' He paused. 'And you.'

Olivia's hackles rose. 'It's good for Julian to have a relationship with his father. He's at an age where he needs this sense of identity. But you've never had a relationship with me and you never will.'

Guy stopped in the car park by the funicular and turned towards her. 'I can understand how you feel, but I've never forgotten you or our meal together in the Grange.' Olivia shook her head, not trusting a word he said.

Guy lowered his eyes. 'I must apologise for my dreadful behaviour that night. It was inexcusable and I've regretted it ever since.' He took her hand. 'Everything I said that evening was true. I'd been watching you since our first year. I was attracted to your beauty and your fragility.' He swallowed. 'And when I realised I'd taken your virginity, I was so angry with myself. I was frightened by what I'd done, taking away your innocence. I'd never done that before. I was so ashamed, I was afraid to speak to you after that. I thought you'd hate me.'

'You had plenty of chances to speak to me. It would have made me feel much better about myself.'

'I wanted to, but every time I saw you, you dived in the opposite direction. I couldn't understand it…' Guy swallowed. 'I realise now how awful I was when I was twenty-one. I was used to getting any girl I wanted, but you were different from other girls in every way. I thought you hated me and, of course, it never crossed my mind that you could be pregnant.'

He looked and sounded so sincere Olivia didn't know whether to believe him. His voice lowered as he carried on. 'The years that followed are a bit of a blur, although I thought they were wonderful at the time. Through my father, I got a job in a hedge fund and made a lot of money very quickly. I thought that was everything – to have more cash than I knew what to do with, going to all the best parties, film premières, openings of galleries, taking out models and actresses.' Olivia was not surprised. It was exactly the kind of life she'd imagined him having.

Guy paused dramatically. 'And then I discovered I was ill. Hodgkin's lymphoma.'

Olivia sat up straighter. Guy was ill? She'd vaguely heard of the disease, but didn't really know anything about it.

Guy looked out of the window. 'To cut a long story short, I received very good medical care and was cured. I'm fine now. But the treatment affected my fertility and I was told it was very unlikely I'd ever be able to father a child.'

Olivia gasped. It all made sense now. That was why he'd put so much effort into finding them.

'Of course, when I heard this, I remembered the time I saw you and Julian in Edinburgh.' Guy gave a rueful smile. 'Although you denied it at the time, as soon as I looked at Julian, I knew he was mine. After my diagnosis, I had to find him. As I told you, it wasn't easy. You'd hidden yourself away very well, coming to Switzerland and changing your name. But eventually Brady did track you down, and then I found out everything about you.'

Olivia shrank back. Guy had put extra emphasis on the final words 'everything about you' and fixed his dark eyes on hers. She thought of the note. Could he have written it?

Guy smiled again. 'Don't worry. Everything I've found out is safe with me. I don't want to destroy your family or your happiness. I just want to share Julian with you.'

'He doesn't seem to be too keen on spending time with you at the moment. What did you do to upset him? He's been moping around at home the last few days.'

Guy frowned. 'He had a bit of a shock.' Olivia raised an eyebrow and waited for him to give more details.

Guy hesitated and said quietly, 'He found out that one of my employees had died.' Olivia was puzzled. That was unfortunate, but why would it affect Julian? Guy cleared his throat. 'The fact is, the young man committed suicide, very near here, actually.'

'The young Englishman whose body was discovered at the foot of the Wildenberg Peaks?' Olivia remembered the incident. It was shortly after Sandra's disappearance and, at first, the police had thought the suicide was connected with her case. 'Why did he do it? Do we know?'

'He had a lot of issues. A psychoanalyst would say he had personality problems. He'd worked for me in London and was a good conscientious worker, but I suspect he was somewhere on the autistic spectrum. When he moved to Switzerland, he found it very difficult to adjust and also had unresolved sexuality issues.' Guy spoke in a concerned voice, but Olivia had the feeling there was something else behind his words.

'But why should that upset Julian?' Olivia was surprised. Julian didn't usually show much empathy for others.

'He left a note.' Guy looked out of the window again. 'In it he suggested his death was related to one aspect of his work. Nonsense, of course, but I think it gave Julian a bit of a fright.'

'What do you mean? What is your work?'

Guy turned to her again. 'We have a portfolio of products and services in different countries, but I can assure you, there's nothing illegal in what we do. The note was just an excuse, a troubled, unhappy young man trying to justify a stupid and selfish act.' Guy's eyes opened wide. 'He left a widowed mother who is devastated. I went to visit her, but she'll never get over it.'

Olivia had the feeling she was being manipulated and led away from the main topic but, looking at her watch, realised it was time to collect the children from school.

When she told him, Christian put his key in the ignition. 'I'll take you back to the village but remember, Olivia, if that's the name you prefer, I love Julian, and I love you too. I will do anything I can to help you and your family in any way. Never forget that.' He leant forward and kissed her lightly on the cheek before starting the car and driving down the narrow road.

Olivia sat next to him, deep in thought. What aspect of Guy's work would cause a young man to commit suicide? Why was Guy being so nice to her? Was it because he was getting Julian involved in something she wouldn't approve of?

Chapter 24

Christmas in Scarborough

Scarborough – December 1998

Lucy looked out of the train window at the wild Northumberland coast. Although it was nearly Christmas, pale winter sunlight sparkled on the beaches of Alnmouth and the misty shape of Holy Isle. She was full of apprehension as the train sped south.

After the disastrous meeting with her birth mother, she felt more isolated and alone than ever. The only people she had left were Therese and Frank. She felt queasy about telling them about the pregnancy. They'd been so protective, she'd been totally unprepared for relationships with men. Sex had never been mentioned and the television had been switched off in embarrassment if the characters even kissed.

How naive she'd been. She'd been bowled over by Guy Montgomery's flattery and hadn't realised what was happening to her. What a fool she'd been and now she was carrying the consequences. Her parents would be so disappointed in her.

She'd even toyed with the idea of just disappearing from their life forever so they'd never know how she'd let them down. But they had brought her up and she owed it to them to tell them the truth. As she travelled towards Scarborough, she had to hold on to that thought, because she was terrified of what faced her.

She picked up a paperback and attempted to read it, but her eyes scanned the same page over and over again without anything going in. The scene ahead dominated her thoughts, playing itself over and over again in her head.

The train arrived in York, the majestic station she'd passed through so often on her journey up to St Andrews. Although it wasn't a long way to Scarborough, the journey in the ancient diesel went painfully slowly, and all the time she was rehearsing what to say.

She'd tell them she was doing really well in her teacher training, which she'd managed to spread over two years, and that she loved the studies, especially the child psychology. The pregnancy was a mistake, but she was receiving great care at the Simpson Memorial Maternity Unit and good support from the welfare officer at the college. She could spend the next term on maternity leave and start again in September, when she had a place for the baby in the college crèche. She was lucky. She also had the money from Geraldine, but she was going to keep quiet about that and would never say a word about meeting her.

As she caught sight of the sea in Scarborough, Lucy could feel her heart beating more quickly, and when she stepped onto the platform, she was shaking with fear. She nearly turned and took the next train back to Edinburgh, but forced herself into a taxi. She made it stop round the corner from her parents' flat, not wanting them to witness such terrible extravagance.

Her heart was thumping as she climbed the stairs beside the betting shop and opened the door quietly. The flat seemed even smaller and darker than she remembered. A thin artificial tree stood on the sideboard, but otherwise the room looked exactly as it always had. Her parents were sitting in their usual seats, one on each side of the gas fire. They looked round and Lucy gasped with shock. They were both skeletal, especially her mother, and looked years older than the last time she'd seen them.

Her mother held out her thin arms. 'Marie, you've come at last.' Her parents knew she'd changed her name at university but they still called her Marie. She ran over to her mother and hugged her. She felt ashamed. She'd been so absorbed with her own problems that she hadn't thought of her mother. She hadn't seemed well in the summer, but Lucy hadn't thought about it while she'd been in Edinburgh.

She still had her coat and a big scarf on, but was sure her mother must notice her bump. Her father approached her from behind with a third chair. 'Sit down, lass. We've got something we have to tell you.'

Lucy sat down, confused. That was her line. She looked from one sad face to another. Her mother put her head in her hands and her thin shoulders shook with silent tears. Her father's gnarled face was like stone, his mouth in a thin hard line.

'This summer, when your mother wasn't so well, I told her to go to the doctor. You know what she's like, though. Didn't want to bother him. She got thinner and weaker, and when she coughed up blood, I insisted.'

His voice wobbled as he looked towards his wife. 'It's bad news.'

Lucy reached over to her mother and put her arms round her bony shoulders. Therese looked up at her. 'The good Lord has decided it's time for me to go and join Him. I wanted to stay longer, for Frank and for you, but I'm ready if that's His will.'

Frank added in a shaky voice, 'It's the cancer. She left it so long that she's full of it, and she won't have any treatment.'

Therese looked at her husband. 'There's nothing they can do. I can't be cured, the doctor said that, and anything they did would only drag it out.' She raised her hands and put them together. 'In You, my Lord, I put my trust.'

She turned back to Lucy. 'God gave me you. I'd always wanted a child. I'll always be thankful for this wonderful gift. You're such a good girl. I couldn't wish for a better daughter.'

Lucy's mouth dropped open. How self-centred she'd been, obsessed with her own problems and never thinking of her mother's health. She had to tell them about the baby as soon as possible and she hoped Therese would see her baby as another gift from God. Lucy unbuttoned her coat and let it fall open, showing the bump very clearly.

Her mother screamed and clutched her rosary. 'Marie...'

Frank stepped towards Lucy and turned her away from his wife. 'How dare you come here and shock your mother like this.

Get out! I always knew the bad blood in you would come out. Leave this house immediately. You are no longer our daughter and you're upsetting my wife.'

'Dad, please listen to me. I want to stay here. I want to help you with Mum. The baby was a mistake, but I hope you'll see it, as I do, as a blessing for our family.'

'I'm not your dad and I never was. I tolerated you for Therese, to make her happy, but you were always selfish, always wanting your own way.'

Lucy was stunned by what he said. She'd spent her whole childhood trying to make her parents happy. She'd acceded to their wishes in almost everything. It was true, she'd insisted on going abroad and therefore saw her birth certificate. She'd also gone to university, although they hadn't wanted her to go, especially not to Scotland. But apart from that she'd always been the obedient daughter they'd wanted.

She felt a flash of anger at the injustice of it all. She was in this mess because they hadn't allowed her to experience the world, hadn't prepared her for people like Guy Montgomery.

She turned back to her mother and held her. 'Mum, I'm sorry. I love you. I never wanted to hurt you. You're the best mum I could have asked for.' She thought of Geraldine and realised how much Therese had given her.

But Therese didn't answer. She appeared to be in catatonic shock, looking straight ahead with unseeing eyes and clutching the cross to her breast.

Frank dragged Lucy roughly away. 'Get out, you ungrateful slut. Look what you've done to your mother, who gave her whole life for you. I always knew the evil in you would come out one day and now look what you've done to her.'

Lucy looked desperately at her mother, who sat rigid in her chair, papery-thin skin on her expressionless face, a collection of bones in her matted woollen cardigan. She was staring ahead, impervious to the drama. Frank stepped towards Lucy, his fist clenched, his face contorted with hatred.

Lucy stood, rooted to the spot. There was a kick in her stomach and she knew what she must do. Frank had often hit her when she was young, but now she had to protect this innocent child within her.

She picked up her case and blew a kiss to Therese. 'I love you, Mum,' she mouthed, and walked slowly down the stairs.

Chapter 25

Meltdown

Wildenwil – Saturday 13 February, 2016

Olivia was in the kitchen, preparing the meal for the next day. She was determined to make Julian's seventeenth birthday a really special family day, a happy occasion after everything that had been happening recently.

Although it was only mid-afternoon, all the lights were on. The sky was grey and overcast and the rain was lashing against the window. When the phone rang, she answered, hoping it might be the police getting back to her, but it was Marlene, asking to speak to Julian. She called him down from his room and he leant against the doorframe, listening carefully. At first, he looked disappointed, but then started laughing. Marlene had always been able to make him happy.

Ending the call, he turned to his mother. 'They can't come tomorrow because Sibylle's ill. But it isn't so bad because Marlene's invited me to Berne as soon as Sibylle's well again and they're going to have a party for me with all their friends. It'll be great!'

Julian noticed his mother's expression. 'Oh, she says sorry, by the way.' He cleared his throat. 'Actually, Mum, I'm going to cry off too. Dad wants to take me for a meal at L'Escargot. If Marlene and Sibylle aren't coming, it will just be like a normal Sunday here, so I'd like to go.'

Olivia tried to hide her disappointment. L'Escargot was Zug's most famous restaurant. She could understand why Julian wanted to go, but she couldn't help herself saying, 'I thought you'd had some kind of disagreement with him.'

'Oh, that's all sorted. I'd misunderstood something about children being harmed because of his business, but he's explained it all to me.'

'What do you mean, children being harmed?' Olivia looked at him in horror. Was that what Guy was trying to hide?

'It was just something that weirdo wrote in his suicide note. No truth in it, but I overreacted. Dad told me exactly what this branch of his company does and everything's fine now.'

Olivia started to speak but Julian interrupted. 'Leave it, Mum. You don't understand.' He yawned. 'I'd better be going. And I'll stay with Dad tonight, easier than getting a taxi to bring me up here.'

'But it's your birthday…' She thought of the memory book she'd been compiling for the last few weeks, with photos and souvenirs of things they'd done together.

'I'll come back tomorrow evening and see you then.' His phone beeped and he took it out of his pocket. 'Got to go, Mum. The lads are waiting.' He picked up his sports bag and ran out of the door.

Olivia watched him go out into the pouring rain. He had the bag packed ready. He'd never intended to spend the night at the house. And the meal at L'Escargot seemed to be planned too. She wondered if Sibylle really was ill…

Olivia felt sick with disappointment and when she saw Lara's school bag, with the little St Bernard keyring on it, lying where she'd dropped it by the door, she felt anger welling up in her. She'd called the police about the keyring, evidence she knew was important, but they'd ignored it.

When she'd seen the picture of the keyring in the *Blick*, she knew Ruth must have got it from Sandra, which meant they must have been held together. No trace of Sandra's body had been found, despite the huge search, so Olivia was more certain than ever that Sandra must still be alive.

She'd wanted to let the police know this new evidence as quickly as possible, so she'd found the emergency hotline number and called immediately. A woman's voice had answered. Olivia explained about the keyring and the woman listened politely, but didn't seem very interested. 'I could bring it into a police station, or you could come and see it?' Olivia was anxious to be taken seriously.

The woman took her details. 'We appreciate your help and you will be contacted if we require any more information.' The call was ended while Olivia was still trying to emphasise the importance of her information.

She'd waited for a call back, but heard nothing. Olivia was still seething with annoyance about this, and upset because her perfect meal would be wasted, when she heard a commotion from the television room. She went in and saw Marc and Lara wrestling on the sofa. Lara looked up. 'Mummy, Marc won't let me have the iPad.'

Marc stood up, his expression so like his father's. 'She chose the DVD, which I had to sit through. She only plays baby games on the iPad anyway.'

'You weren't watching the film. You were playing on the iPad. It's my turn now.'

'No, you can't have it. I'm in the middle of a game.'

Lara screamed. 'That's not fair.'

Their screams went right through her head. 'Marc, let her have the iPad. You've had it all day.'

'I haven't. I was out playing football. She could have had it then. You always give in to Lara. She's your favourite.'

Olivia reached out for the iPad and snatched it away, shaking with rage. 'Right, nobody will have it then. It's time to go to bed. You can read in your room, proper books.'

Both children turned on her. Lara pouted. 'It isn't time for bed.'

Marc jutted out his jaw. 'Daddy isn't home yet.'

Olivia's voice became shriller. 'I don't know when he'll be back and it's time for you to go to bed. I'm tired.'

'Why should we go to bed if you're tired?' Marc stared at her, looking so like his father.

Even Lara, good-natured biddable Lara, looked at her defiantly. 'That isn't fair.'

Something snapped inside Olivia. The tension that had been building up in her all day exploded. She stepped towards the children and grasped both their arms. 'You're going up to bed.' She pulled them towards the stairs. Marc twisted his body, kicking out and trying to get himself free, and Lara started screaming.

They'd just reached the bottom of the stairs, when the door opened and Christian came in. 'What's going on here?'

They all froze. Olivia went to speak, but Christian pushed past her.

'Daddy, Daddy,' Lara cried out to her father, who bent down and took her into his arms. Marc looked on stoically, until his father noticed and picked him up on his other hip. Ignoring Olivia, he started up the stairs, whispering in his children's ears.

As they reached the top, Lara giggled.

Olivia watched as they went up the stairs and let flow the tears that had been building up in her since the phone call from Marlene. She walked back to the kitchen, full of self-loathing. What had got into her? She never spoke to her children like that. She'd tried so hard to be a good mother, calm and understanding, letting them know how much they were loved and giving them a feeling of self-worth.

She was horrified she'd spoken to them like that. From her childhood, she knew only too well what it was like to feel unloved. She sat down at the table and put her head in her arms. She was a terrible mother. She'd tried so hard to create a wonderful family atmosphere but her perfect life was a sham. Hot tears fell down her cheeks. Perhaps she was incapable of being a good mother because she'd never known a proper family life. She was a failure in everything she did.

Raising her head, she looked round the kitchen at the preparations she'd made for the special meal – the marinades, the vegetables crisping in iced water, the desserts chilling in the fridge. Her hands went tense and she just stopped herself from sweeping everything up and throwing it all in the bin. She felt empty. What was the meaning of her pointless life?

She hardly ever drank alone, but she took a glass from the cupboard and poured a large measure of red wine. Hearing laughter upstairs, she took a gulp and moved into the other room. She sat on the sofa and stared into the flames in the wood-burning stove. Why had she reacted like that with the children she loved so much? They were her reason for living.

Tears welled up in her eyes. Her life was falling apart. Julian only wanted to spend time with 'Dad', Sandra was still missing, she was shouting at her own children, Christian was exasperated with her. And Bella was dead.

And there was the note. She'd tried to convince herself it was a joke, but it was always there, nagging at the back of her mind. If the truth came out, that would be the end of everything. Christian was the only person in Switzerland who'd known her in her Edinburgh days and he didn't know the terrible thing she'd done. Could he have found out? Could the note be from him? She immediately rejected this thought as ridiculous.

It had to be Guy. The note came just when he arrived in Switzerland, and he kept hinting that he knew something about her. Another thought occurred to her. He'd also arrived just before Sandra disappeared. His business seemed to involve children, and was bad enough to cause a young man to commit suicide.

There had to be something behind this, no matter how much Guy could sweet-talk Julian into believing everything was okay. Guy had tried it on with her too – all this stuff about loving her. What was he trying to hide? The police seemed to have given up on Sandra, but what if they were looking in the wrong direction? Their investigations seemed to be centred around the Kolb family, never suspecting a respectable British businessman.

Draining her glass, Olivia went through to the kitchen to refill it. The wine helped to numb the pain, but also fed the suspicions clamouring in her head. What was behind Guy's business and the suicide of his employee? On the Internet, she'd read about aristocratic paedophile rings and their parties. Guy certainly knew that sort of person. Could he have taken Sandra? Was he involved in this dreadful trade? Olivia shuddered. Guy wanted to get close to her family. Did he have his eye on Lara?

She was staring into the flames of the fire, wild suspicions racing through her brain, when Christian came downstairs. He went into the kitchen, returning with a small glass of whisky in his hand.

He sat down opposite her. 'Livy, this is going to have to stop.'

Olivia stiffened. 'What do you mean? What has to stop? You don't know what was happening.' She took another sip of wine. 'Thanks for the support, by the way.'

Christian looked at her with sadness in his eyes. 'This is exactly what I mean. You've changed. You never used to react like this.'

'You don't know what's going on. And you don't bother to find out. Firstly, dinner is off tomorrow. Marlene has cancelled because Sibylle is apparently ill, and Julian is going to L'Escargot with his dad.'

Christian's mouth set in a grim line. 'I might have known he'd be at the root of all this. Although I thought he'd fallen out with Wonderdad?'

'It seems it was just a misunderstanding. Something to do with that young Englishman who threw himself off the peaks and the suicide note he left. I bumped into Guy in the village and he explained it.'

Christian leant towards her. 'If that smarmy git comes near you again, I'm going to do something to make him stay away. I don't know if it's him, but something's made you change. I want my old Livy back.'

Olivia felt the anger subside from her. It was true, she had changed, and she couldn't blame Christian for being upset. 'I'm sorry. I just feel so tense. It's as if everything is going wrong. Sandra disappearing, Julian leaving us, Bella dying...' Her voice caught and she blinked back tears. It seemed ridiculous, but Bella's death still made her cry.

Christian paused and took a deep breath before continuing in an even tone. 'Look, you lost Julian long before that creep turned up and there's nothing you can do about Sandra. You have to think of your children, your family.'

Olivia put her head in her hands. It was true, she should concentrate on her own family. But even as she thought this, words spilled out of her mouth, seemingly beyond her control. 'I can't forget Sandra. I won't give up on her, even if everyone else has. I have this feeling she's alive – I can sense it.' Olivia reached into her bag and pulled out the crumpled copy of the *Blick* she'd picked up in the Spar.

'Look. Ruth had new clothes and a bag with this keyring attached. It's Sandra's keyring, the one Lara gave her. I phoned the police but they didn't take me seriously. This is important – it proves Sandra and Ruth were together. Somebody captured them both.'

Christian shook his head. 'Livy, there must be thousands of these keyrings. You can buy them in every souvenir shop. I think we should leave the detection to the police. That's their job.'

'But are they still looking? Everything seems to have gone quiet.'

'Just because they aren't walking the hills, doesn't mean they're not looking. They have sophisticated means of detection we know nothing about.' Christian walked to the kitchen and poured himself another whisky.

'But remember that little girl abducted in Appenzell? Her body was found by a member of the public.'

'You can't do anything, Livy. Leave it to the experts.'

'Somebody has to care.'

'We all care. Just because we're not moping around doesn't mean we don't feel desperately sorry for the family. The best thing we can do is draw a line under it. Life goes on.'

Olivia stood up and just stopped herself from throwing her wine at him. 'I'm finding things very difficult at the moment. I was hoping for a bit of support.'

'I've tried to support you, but seeing your performance this evening, I'm wondering if you need more help than I can give. Have you thought about talking to Dr Bruni about the way you feel? He might give you something to make you feel less uptight.'

'That won't help. The police aren't doing their job. They didn't listen to me. Somebody has to carry on the search and I'm going to do it if they don't.'

Christian stood up. 'You're talking nonsense. What do you think you could find that the police haven't already investigated? It's not like Agatha Christie, you know.' He reached out to her.

Olivia pushed him away. 'You're not taking me seriously. I am upset with good reason and you think I should go to the doctor. We have to do something.'

Christian looked at her sadly. 'I'd like to help you, but you won't let me. You've changed. I remember we used to talk about films and books and have a laugh, but now we just seem to be having the same conversations over and over again.' He walked towards the door. 'There's no point in my staying here if this is the way you're going to be. I'm going down to the Ochsen for a drink with the boys.'

He went out, the second time he'd done that in the last few days. What had happened to the lovely puppy-like Christian who'd adored her? He'd rather go to the village bar and talk to his old school friends than spend time with her.

Olivia felt so alone. She used to feel safe with Christian, which was why she'd married him. After the years on her own with Julian, having to make all the decisions herself, it had been such a relief to have somebody else decide things. She'd thought of Christian as her rock, her best friend. What had happened? Who could she talk to now?

Fiona came into her mind – the only real friend she'd ever had. She wondered what she was doing. Olivia had written to her after Julian was born, trying to apologise for her behaviour. She hadn't said anything about Guy, of course, and Fiona had replied without any questions, full of news about her own little girl and her husband's new job in New York. They'd lost touch after Olivia had moved to Portobello, without giving Fiona her forwarding address. It was her fault they'd lost contact.

Therese was long dead, and probably Frank too, although she'd never heard anything more from him. Geraldine, her own mother, had made it clear she wanted nothing to do with her. And now her husband had gone out and left her. She realised she had nobody in the world she could turn to.

Wiping her eyes, she went through to the kitchen and threw all the preparations for the special meal into the bin. She never wanted to eat any of those things again. Then she scrubbed and polished every corner of the kitchen.

When everything was gleaming clean, she went upstairs and looked into the children's rooms. They were fast asleep, peaceful and contented. She stroked Lara's hair, seeing her long lashes flutter momentarily, and kissed Marc's pink cheek.

She went to their bedroom and sat on the edge of the bed. She was afraid of falling asleep, knowing she'd be sucked into the terrifying vortex of fears, memories and regrets that filled her dreams every night.

Tears of self-pity flowed down her cheeks. She wanted somebody to love her, to hold her. The soft, round face of Aurelia came into her mind. She understood her; she would make her feel safe.

And Sebastian. The image of his blue eyes and his beautiful sensitive mouth flashed in front of her. She knew what she was going to do. She was going to visit them tomorrow.

Chapter 26

Julian

Edinburgh – Sunday 14 February, 1999

'It's a boy!' Lucy heard the cry of the baby, and the pain of the birth disappeared. The midwife wiped the baby and wrapped him in a blanket before laying him on her breast. Looking down, Olivia saw the perfect little face, with dark eyebrows and hair, looking like a little Japanese doll.

He looked up at her with bright, alert eyes and she felt love flooding through her. She'd never known an emotion like it. Now she knew why she was alive. The small vulnerable face in front of her, a perfect tiny finger curling out from the blanket convinced her she'd do everything in her power to make his life as good as it could be.

The midwife reached over and took the baby to be weighed and measured, and Lucy was vaguely aware of being washed and stitched up. She looked around for her little boy, already missing him. She hadn't known if she was expecting a boy or a girl, and had found it difficult to settle on names for either, but as soon as she saw her baby, she knew. He was Julian, a name she'd always liked, not too popular, not too many associations, and perfect for him.

The misery of the last months melted away when she looked at her son. After her disastrous visit to Frank and Therese, she'd spent the strangest of Christmases in Edinburgh, alone in her bedsit. All the other students had gone home. She imagined them standing round the tree, laughing and exchanging presents in the warm glow of candles and decorations in the best Hollywood tradition.

She did nothing to mark the day. She'd discovered the wonderful library on George IV Bridge and read. She worked her way through the classics – Thomas Hardy, Charles Dickens, Raymond Chandler – living in other worlds to compensate for the insubstantiality of her own. Sometimes she began to doubt she existed, the action in the books having far more substance than her life.

She'd sent Therese and Frank a Christmas card, saying she was thinking of them and would always love them, but had received nothing in return. She thought a lot about Therese, who'd invested all her hopes in her. She knew she'd disappointed her. She'd disappointed herself. How stupid she'd been to fall for an arrogant young man's flattery. She'd worked hard at school and university to get good marks, wanting to be the best, but now it all seemed meaningless.

Julian was born in the early hours, and as the morning routine started, he was wheeled into the ward. Lucy propped herself up and gazed at him with wonder. Looking around at the other mothers, with fathers and, in the case of one young girl, a mother as the birth partner, Lucy didn't feel alone anymore. She had Julian. Although the midwives had tried to persuade her to have someone with her at the birth, she couldn't think of anyone to ask. She'd had nobody, but now she had Julian and for the first time ever she had somebody related to her.

The nurses were all particularly kind to her, saying what a handsome little boy Julian was. When she was given help with breastfeeding, her heart swelled with pride when he latched on like a little shark, winning praise from the nurses. *That's my boy,* she thought, as she gazed at his perfect little mouth, eyelashes and ears with wonder.

There was a scurry at the door as a woman came in carrying bunches of flowers, followed by a man with a huge camera. 'We're here to give flowers to the Valentine's Day babies,' she said in a shrill voice. A nurse pointed to Lucy. 'This was our first Valentine's Day mother.'

The woman strode over towards her, followed by the photographer. Lucy grabbed Julian and held him close, covering his face with the blanket. She held up her hand. 'No photos, please.'

'Come on, it'll be a lovely memento of the most romantic day possible,' the woman gushed, waving the cameraman into a good position.

'No. I said I didn't want a photo and I mean it.' She glared at the woman. Looking down at Julian she saw Guy's handsome features reflected in her baby's face. He was not worthy to be the father. She had to keep Julian a secret and never let Guy know of his son's existence.

Chapter 27

Grand Wildenbach Hotel

Wildenwil – Sunday 14 February, 2016

Olivia parked beside the Grand Wildenbach Hotel, which loomed dark beneath the cliffs. She looked around her, nervous about approaching the front door and half inclined to get into her car and drive away again.

But where would she go? She'd stormed out of her house with such a dramatic door-slamming performance she couldn't go back now.

She'd had a terrifying night of black horror and when she woke up, feeling fragile and confused, the other side of the bed was empty. Downstairs, bacon was cooking and the sound of laughter floated up the stairs. When she went into the kitchen, Christian was standing at the stove with the frying pan in his hand. Lara and Marc were sitting at the table watching him.

Lara turned as she came into the room. 'Dad's making us an extra special, super-duper Scottish breakfast.'

'And then we're going out to the Alpamare and I'm going to go down all the biggest slides,' Marc added, with an excited grin. Olivia tried to smile back. Marc had been talking about going to this water park for ages, but Olivia had always put it off. She hated the crowds and she knew it would be mobbed on this rainy Sunday.

'That sounds great,' she said in a tight voice. Without really thinking about what she was doing, she went towards the door, picking up her jacket on the way. 'I hope you all have a wonderful day.' Before anyone had time to say anything, she'd slammed the door behind her.

She'd driven up the road, simmering with rage and misery, past the Kolbs' farm – which looked even more unkempt and rundown than before – through the forest, and between the imposing gates of the Grand Wildenbach Hotel.

She sat in her car with her head in her hands. Why was she behaving like this? She'd been wrong yesterday, and now she was making it worse. What was happening to her?

Except for the roar of the water crashing down from the top of the cliffs, everything was silent. There was no sign of life at the hotel, no movement except for the pine trees gently swaying in the wind. Perhaps nobody was there. She hadn't seen anyone from the hotel in the last few days. She shivered with indecision, alone in the bedraggled landscape, with no sunlight, no colour apart from the last dirty patches of melting snow.

The front door opened and Sebastian stood silhouetted in the doorway. Olivia hesitated, but he beckoned her towards him. She got out of the car and walked towards him, as if she were in a dream, being pulled in. When she reached the door, Sebastian's pale blue eyes and enigmatic smile hit her with a physical force that made her breathless.

'Welcome. We've been waiting for you.' Sebastian spoke softly and smiled as he led her through the double doors into the dimly lit dining room. Candles flickered from the high candelabras, and chandeliers cast shadows over the statues, photographs and the book-lined walls. The air was thick with the smell of sandalwood.

Aurelia stood up from a large, soft chair in the corner and held her arms out towards Olivia. 'Olivia, my dear child, I knew you would come when you needed us.'

Olivia was shaking as Aurelia hugged her more tightly. 'Olivia. I feel a great sadness in you. This must be released. Please sit down and take a tea with us.'

Olivia sank into the cushions beside Aurelia and felt her breathing returning to normal. Sebastian disappeared behind the heavy drapes and returned with the leather-embossed tray holding three cups. They all took one and Olivia forced herself to drink the tea. Like last time, it was too sweet and milky, but she wanted to fit in.

Aurelia was talking in a low sonorous voice. 'Olivia, trust me. Your soul is being blocked by sorrows from the past. Tell me what is troubling you and it will help you to find equilibrium in your life.'

Olivia swallowed. She'd never spoken about her past, even with Fiona, but she felt her inhibitions melting away. She trusted Aurelia, whose warmth and love gave her the confidence to speak. 'I was adopted.'

Aurelia stroked Olivia's arm and looked directly into her eyes. 'I knew we were soulmates. I too was taken from my mother when I was very young and suffered many hardships. And Sebastian was born illegitimate in a country and culture where this was seen as a mortal sin. He was placed in an orphanage and abused by wicked men in the name of religion. He knew no happiness until he joined us.'

Sebastian smiled. 'In this wonderful community, I found safety and love.'

Aurelia took Olivia's hands in hers. 'Is that everything? Adoption is never easy, but I sense there is more to say about that. Please, trust me. The more you talk, the easier it gets.'

After a moment's hesitation, Olivia talked about her childhood in Scarborough. She'd never told anybody about it before and she felt disloyal talking about Therese, who'd done her best for her. As she described what her life had been like, haltingly at first, the words came faster and easier. Memories she had blocked for years came rushing back.

Aurelia nodded. 'My poor dear girl, to grow up in such an atmosphere. You must not be ashamed and you must not blame yourself for anything. Frank was a monster, and Therese was weak. You were denied the truth about your birth, a real family and a carefree childhood. You were deprived of a mother's love.'

Olivia nodded, but when she thought of her real mother, she knew she hadn't missed anything there. She wasn't going to say any more, but without making a conscious decision, the words tumbled out as she described meeting her real mother. 'Of course, I was disappointed, but she was very young and very frightened when I was born.'

Aurelia smiled again. 'You are so sweet, so empathetic, making excuses for everybody.' She enveloped Olivia in a warm hug. 'I felt this. Not all the details, but from the first moment I saw you I knew you had suffered. No wonder you find it difficult to love yourself when your first male influence so belittled you and your own mother rejected you in such a heartless way. You must learn to love yourself. Even the way you tell the story you are making excuses for others, but nothing was your fault. You were blameless. You need to acknowledge this to be free.'

Olivia nodded, a light-headed calm coming over her.

Aurelia continued in her melodic sing-song tones. 'You are beautiful, intelligent and sweet-natured, but you do not love yourself. I feel you have been abused by men.'

Olivia shook her head. She'd never been abused. But then she began to think about it. Perhaps she had. The way Julian had been conceived. How could Aurelia sense things she'd never even acknowledged to herself?

Slowly, Olivia described the night she went out with Guy Montgomery. She spoke in disjointed bursts, pausing sometimes, struggling to verbalise what she'd never put into words before. Aurelia watched her, not saying anything.

When Olivia reached the end of the story, describing how Guy had come to Zug, back into her life and had reclaimed Julian, she felt tears coming to her eyes. 'Now I'm afraid I'm losing my son…' she finished, allowing the words to trail away.

There was a long silence before Aurelia spoke. 'I knew there was more, but I never guessed how bad it was. That man took advantage of your sweetness and innocence. What he did was inexcusable.' She moved round and knelt in front of Olivia. 'You are a remarkable person. You went through all of this alone and you brought up your son yourself. That man treated you abominably then, and now he has the gall to come back into your life and try to steal your son away.' She bent forward and kissed Olivia on the cheek. 'You are a remarkable person, a wonderful mother.'

Olivia snatched her hands away and hung her head. 'I'm not! That's why I'm here. I'm a terrible mother.'

Sobbing and struggling for breath, she spluttered out what had happened the day before – the perfect meal she'd wanted to make, Marlene's phone call, Julian leaving with his bag, losing her cool with Lara and Marc, and Christian coming home.

Aurelia drew Olivia close to her. 'You must be kinder to yourself. You'd had an awful day. Everything you've done is understandable, and forgivable.' She paused for a moment and then held Olivia at arm's length. 'What I do not understand is your relationship with your husband.'

'I'm so lucky with Christian. He's a good husband, a highly respected teacher, a wonderful father…' Olivia's voice trailed away again.

Aurelia gave an enigmatic smile. 'You know the expression, "The lady doth protest too much". Did he support you yesterday when you were understandably upset? I haven't heard anything about your husband that suggests he loves you as he should. As his wife, you should always be his number one priority. Bearing in mind the terrible experiences you have had in the past, does he give you the emotional support you need?'

Olivia lowered her eyes. 'I've never told him anything about it.'

Aurelia shook her head. 'That makes me very worried about him. Does he have no interest in finding out about you and the experiences that have made you the person you are? Does he want a partner or a housewife and mother? Does he really care about you, make you feel cherished and good about yourself, appreciate the wonderful qualities you have? Olivia, you must learn to love yourself, and we are going to help you.' She smiled over at Sebastian. 'I think we all need another cup of tea.'

The room was silent. Olivia thought about what Aurelia had said. The older woman saw everything from a different angle, like the opposite way through a mirror. It was hard for Olivia to put herself first; she always thought everyone else was right, was always looking for approval, thinking she wasn't good enough for them. Looking at things the way Aurelia did was quite new for Olivia.

All her life she'd wanted to be loved. She'd thought Christian was the one, which was why she'd married him. But the seed of doubt planted by Aurelia began to grow. Did Christian really love her or did he just want to control her?

Sebastian came back into the room with more tea. Olivia sipped it. She was getting used to the spicy aftertaste, so she drained it and lay back on the cushions. Her head felt heavy.

Sebastian took her hand. 'Lie down,' he whispered. 'I'm going to give you a massage to help you relax.'

Olivia felt floppy, her limbs like jelly. She allowed Sebastian to lead her to a soft flat surface. He laid her gently on her front and held her left hand between his. With strong fingers, he massaged her wrist, the back and palm of her hand, pulling her fingers. Olivia felt tingles travelling up her arm and, as he moved on to the other hand and gradually up to the elbow, she was floating.

When he'd finished with the arms, he moved to her feet, and as he worked his way up her legs, she felt an electric surge pass through her. How far up was he going? His strong fingers moved onto her thighs and she felt the excitement increasing.

As he moved to her shoulders and neck, he smoothed and pressed, his thumbs rotating, and the tension ebbed away from her clenched muscles. She felt as if she was melting, excited and aroused. She wanted his hands everywhere and didn't want him to stop.

Eventually, Sebastian smoothed his hands gently down her back and kissed her tenderly on the top of her head. 'Relax, Olivia.' She felt her eyes close and she floated into a wonderful sleep.

Olivia opened her eyes. Where was she? As her eyes adjusted to the flickering light and familiar smell of incense, she remembered.

She was here in the Grand Hotel. Raising herself up, she stretched. Her limbs felt silky, and she felt calm yet invigorated.

'I hope you feel better, Olivia?' Aurelia's voice brought her back to reality.

'I do.' Olivia felt amazing. 'That was incredible. Thank you so much.' She reached for her bag. 'How long was I asleep?'

'Only for a short while. It wasn't really a sleep, just an intense relaxation as your mind absorbed what you've discovered today. Remember, Olivia, you are a wonderful person. You are important. You don't always have to do what other people want in order to be loved. Follow your own instincts, your own dreams, and great things will happen.'

Olivia smiled. 'I'll try.' In the warm, comforting presence of Aurelia, everything seemed possible. Olivia looked at her watch. It was already after five and usually she would be worried about being away from home for so long, but she felt completely calm. The children were at the Alpamare and Julian wasn't coming home until the evening, so she didn't have to worry.

Aurelia hugged her and Sebastian walked with her to her car. It was already dark outside, the thick impenetrable blackness of an overcast February night, but Olivia felt light and free as she opened the door and the internal light sprang on. Sebastian leant over. 'Stay safe and see you again very soon,' he whispered, as his lips brushed hers. Olivia felt them tingling as he turned and walked back to the house.

She hadn't thought about her phone all day until she saw it lying on the passenger seat. The light was flashing. She picked it up. Seven missed calls.

Chapter 28

L'Escargot

Wildenwil – Sunday 14 February, 2016

Her hand shaking, Olivia looked at the messages. Two were from Julian and five from Christian. Julian had left a voicemail the second time. 'Mum, where are you? Came up to see you.' Olivia smiled. That was nice to hear.

Christian had also left a couple of messages. That was more serious. He hardly ever used his mobile phone, thinking it was responsible for the decline of the younger generation. Olivia found herself suppressing a giggle. Nothing seemed to be able to dispel her good mood.

She listened to the voicemails. The first one must have been left not long after she left. 'Olivia. Julian's turned up. He wants to apologise. Come back at once.' The second one was left about half an hour later. 'Couldn't wait any longer. We're all going to the Alpamare.'

That's nice that they're all spending the day together, Olivia thought as she drove down the road, nothing capable of shaking her feeling of well-being.

When she arrived at the house, she was surprised to see another car next to Christian's. In the house the lights were all on, making it a gleaming lighthouse in the darkness.

As soon as she opened the car door, Lara came running into her arms. 'Mummy, I missed you.'

Olivia lifted Lara and buried her face in her daughter's hair. 'I missed you too, darling.' She looked over her daughter's head and saw Marc and Julian standing together, and behind them,

Christian and... and Guy. She almost dropped Lara in shock, but remained calm. She could do this.

Putting Lara down, she walked over to Julian. He was now more than a head taller than her so it was difficult to give him a kiss, but she reached up and hugged him. 'Happy birthday, darling.' She looked over his shoulder at Guy, who was looking completely at home.

'Thanks, Mum. I'm sorry about yesterday. When Dad heard what had happened, he insisted we came up here.' He shrugged. 'We were a bit surprised you weren't here, but then we heard about the trip to the Alpamare so we all went together.'

Marc, who had been trying to look cool, couldn't contain his excitement any longer. 'It was great. Jules came down all the big slides with me. They're *so* scary.' Olivia leant over to hug him, although as usual he tried to wriggle away.

Guy stepped forward, suave as ever. 'Olivia, I'm glad you're back. I've changed the booking at L'Escargot and we can all dine there this evening.'

'The children too?' Olivia had never been to L'Escargot, the classiest restaurant in Zug, but she couldn't imagine it being very child-friendly.

'Everybody is welcome there with me,' he smiled. 'Seriously, having met your children I'd be proud to take them anywhere. What delightful, well-mannered youngsters they are.'

Lara and Marc grinned, enjoying the praise, and even Christian seemed to be looking at Guy appreciatively.

'That's great. Thank you.' She looked down at her jeans and the children's tracksuits. 'We'll just pop in and change into something more suitable.' She looked at Guy, smart but casual in a beautifully cut jacket and a silk shirt. Julian was wearing something similar, new clothes obviously bought by Guy.

Olivia went upstairs and helped Lara and Marc choose their favourite clothes and then leapt quickly into the shower.

Christian was waiting for her when she came out. He'd changed into his suit. 'We'll talk later about your irresponsible behaviour, disappearing for the whole day, not answering your phone.' His tone was even. 'I want this evening to be a success. I must say, I was pleasantly surprised by Guy Montgomery. He's acted with a great deal of integrity, when you were the one who deprived him of the chance to be a father to his son.'

Olivia's mouth fell open. The injustice of it. She remembered what Aurelia had said that afternoon and took strength from it. She smiled sweetly. 'You've only heard one side of the story. As you said, we'll discuss this later.'

She turned to the wardrobe and took out her only flimsy low-cut dress, one Christian had persuaded her to buy for a village event years ago, which she'd never worn since. She put it on, combed her hair quickly, put on a bit of make-up and was spraying on her favourite perfume when she caught sight of Christian's face. It was a strange mixture of jealousy and lust.

'It's a long time since I've seen you dress up like that. Is that for his benefit?'

She smiled even more sweetly. 'I've never been to L'Escargot. You have to dress up to go there.' She flounced out of the room, feeling better than she had for ages. She didn't know if it was talking to Aurelia, or Sebastian's massage, but she felt a confidence she'd never known before, and she enjoyed seeing the shocked expression on Christian's pink face.

The meal went surprisingly well. They had the best table in the restaurant in a bay window overlooking the lake. Lights glittered on the dark water, the tablecloth was the finest cotton, and the glasses sparkled. A beautiful arrangement of flowers stood in the centre of the table. Guy was the perfect host, suggesting delicious food, including perfect mini burgers for the children, and keeping the conversation light and witty.

Olivia looked round the wood-lined room and saw the other guests watching them. They were mostly couples out for a Valentine's Day meal, and Olivia felt pleased to be the object of their interest. Usually she hated being watched, but this evening she felt proud to be surrounded by her beautiful family, with everybody laughing. Even Christian seemed to be captivated by Guy's charm.

In the break between the main course and dessert, Guy stood up. He didn't speak loudly, but a hush fell over the rest of the room. 'We're here tonight to celebrate the seventeenth birthday of my wonderful son, Julian. I am so proud of you.' He took an envelope out of his pocket. 'You have already chosen the most powerful motorbike you're allowed at your age, and we'll arrange driving lessons so you can have a car as soon as you're eighteen. Here is another present. The key to our flat. It is your home whenever you want to be there.'

Olivia felt a surge of annoyance. Julian was her son and his home was with them. How dare Guy make this public announcement without discussing it with her. She was wondering how to react when Guy turned to her. He lifted the vase of flowers. 'It's also Valentine's Day and these are for you, dear Olivia. For your beauty and grace, and for being such a wonderful mother to Julian, and to Lara and Marc.' He turned to the children, who were gazing at him with adoration, and with his eyes fixed on Olivia, he presented her with the flowers. She blushed, unsure of the right way to respond. Out of the corner of her eye, she saw Christian's face, expressionless as a statue.

Guy turned to the rest of the room and gave a little bow. In dreadful, but just understandable, German, he thanked them for their patience and offered them all a drink so they could share this very special day with him. He nodded to the waiters, who appeared like magic with bottles of champagne and flutes. An appreciative ripple of applause ran round the room.

The rest of the evening passed in a blur. Olivia drank far more than she usually did, but loved the feeling of lightness, watching Lara and Marc eating their exotic desserts, seeing Julian with a genuine smile on his face. After the trough she'd been in the day before, it was wonderful to feel appreciated. Christian sat looking puzzled, especially when diners came up to congratulate Guy and Olivia, obviously seeing them as the couple.

Guy had organised a taxi to take them back up the road, and although Julian had taken out his key and said he wanted to use it, Guy had persuaded him to go home. Julian owed it to his mother, he said.

There was not much conversation as they drove up the hill. Christian sat in the front next to the driver, Lara fell asleep, and Marc's eyes were drooping. Julian's eyes were fixed on his iPhone. 'Some great photos from last night, and over fifty birthday messages on Facebook,' he said, with a smile of satisfaction.

When the car drew up in front of the farmhouse, Olivia noticed something white sticking out of the letterbox. Probably a birthday card for Julian. Christian picked up the sleeping Lara and carried her to the door, with Julian and Marc following him. Julian still had his eyes on his phone, and Marc looked as if he were just about to fall asleep too.

Olivia went to the letterbox and drew out the paper. She froze. It was the same writing as the last one. She'd almost forgotten about that note, but this time there was more. *How can you look in the mirror in your lovely house with your perfect family after what you've done? I know what you did.'*

Chapter 29

Bill

Portobello, Edinburgh – May 2004

Lucy sat down at her desk as the last of her pupils crashed out of the classroom. Thank goodness that was the end of the day. She'd been so thrilled when she'd got a job at Brunstane High, which, despite its name, was a large comprehensive secondary school in Portobello, the seaside suburb of Edinburgh.

She'd thought that being a single mother with a very young son would count against her, but when the job interviews came up at the end of her two years at Moray House, she'd been surprised how supportive people were. The fact that she'd got a distinction in her theoretical subjects probably helped, and she and Bill Munro, the charismatic head of Brunstane High, had hit it off from the outset.

But teaching was not as she'd imagined. The exam classes were great. She enjoyed working with small groups of students who loved German as much as she did, but the lower mixed-ability classes were a nightmare. She hadn't been so naive as to think that every student would love languages, but no teaching practice had prepared her for the total lack of interest, the prejudice against German, 'a Nazi language', and, she had to admit, her own inability to control the class. She'd started off too nice, she realised now, and although she still had a small group of fans in every class who wanted to learn, the majority made their lack of interest only too clear. However hard she tried, she couldn't get the attention of the group of boys at the back, more interested in farting and trying to find suggestive innuendos in everything she said than learning.

The door opened and Christian Keller, the German language assistant, came in. He picked up some of the paper scattered over the floor and put the chairs back in place. 'I thought I'd come into this class tomorrow and tell them something about Switzerland. I have some slides.'

Lucy smiled at him gratefully.

Christian was short and stocky, with thick light-brown hair and a wide pleasant face. He was doing his year out from studying English at Zürich University, working as a language assistant at Brunstane High, and had been a wonderful support for Lucy. He was only supposed to take small groups out for conversation practice, but he often came into her classes, doing much more than his required twelve lessons. He made it much easier for her because, although he was always smiling, he had a hidden strength the students seemed to respect.

'Can you get a babysitter at the weekend? Perhaps we could go out for a meal or to the cinema?'

'I'm sorry, I don't think I can. My babysitter's away on a school field trip.'

'Or we could go out with Julian, perhaps to the Dalkeith Country Park?'

Lucy nodded. Christian was really good with Julian, climbing rocks and trees and doing exciting things with him, like going on the Flying Fox at the forest adventure playground. 'Thanks, that would be lovely. And afterwards you could have some lasagne with us.' She liked having Christian around, but she didn't want to encourage him too much. The other teachers laughed, calling him 'Lucy's little puppy' because he followed her around with soulful eyes. She liked him, but she didn't fancy him, and was glad she could always put off any of his advances by suggesting that Julian might wake up. Her son was a restless sleeper, so this excuse was half-genuine.

'Have you got time for a coffee before you go to collect Julian?' asked Christian, as he finished cleaning the board.

Lucy blushed. 'Sorry, no. I have to go up to see Bill. But if you could come in tomorrow morning, I'd be so grateful. Thanks for all your help. And looking forward to Sunday.' Christian gave a broad smile that made her feel guilty as he opened the door for her to go out.

Lucy went up to the second floor where Bill Munro's office was. She passed the staffroom, which was nearly empty. Most teachers stayed working in their rooms or escaped from the building as quickly as possible at the end of the day. She tapped at the door of the headmaster's room, where the light showed green, meaning he was free for visitors.

The door opened and she stepped into the room. Without a word, Bill embraced her, locking the door and flicking the light to red.

'Lucy, I've been longing for this moment all day.' He was kissing her and pulling her clothes down as he pushed her to the table.

Lucy's body was aflame as she drew him towards her. When she'd first been interviewed by Bill, she'd felt the attraction between them, but ever since the first time she'd been alone with him in his room, when she'd cried into his arms after her first disciplinary disaster, she'd been in love with him.

He was everything she could wish for in a man: tall, classically handsome with chiselled features, thick dark hair with distinguished greying temples. He dressed beautifully, with well-cut suits and shirts that looked brand new every day. He was sophisticated, intelligent, well-travelled. He was also married.

After the first time in his office, Lucy had been filled with guilt. Since her only other experience of sex, with Guy, she'd kept away from men. When she was at Moray House, some of the other students had invited her out, but she'd always refused, saying she had to look after Julian. That was true, but she was also afraid of getting too close to anyone, especially a man.

But Bill had opened a floodgate of emotion in her. All the years of supressed feelings and loneliness were washed away by the power of presence. He made her feel loveable and attractive and she was obsessed with him. She chose her clothes according to what he liked, went the long way round to her classroom, hoping she'd bump into him. For the first time in her life, she felt attractive and loved.

In moments of self-awareness, she knew she was such a cliché – falling for the hero of one of the novels she read – but she couldn't help it. Fiona had told her girls liked bad boys, and this seemed to be true of her. She'd been attracted to Guy, despite his reputation, and was disappointed when he dumped her, but Bill responded to her and gave her the attention and excitement she craved. She was mesmerised by him. He had opened up her sexuality, had lit a flame in her she couldn't quench.

Sometimes the voice of Therese forced its way into her consciousness, but she pushed it aside. She'd lived by Therese's rules and it hadn't done her much good.

After a short time, their passion was spent. Bill gave her a final kiss, his voice husky. 'There's a governors' meeting on Tuesday. Can I come round to you afterwards?' Lucy nodded, already excited at the thought of him in her bed. She always fitted in with his plans, pleased when he could spend an hour at her home.

Lucy knew their affair was risky, but none of the staff seemed to have guessed what was happening, and the secret element made it more exciting. The fact that Bill was risking his career to be with her made her realise how important she was to him. She didn't want to think about his wife, but Lucy realised that she couldn't be the right person for him because of the way Bill acted with her. She imagined a very good housewife – his shirts were always beautifully ironed – but perhaps his wife didn't understand what it was like being a teacher, and Lucy and Bill had more in common intellectually.

She straightened her clothes and smoothed her hair. Time to go and pick up Julian from the after-school club.

Chapter 30

Paternity

'What's this?' Christian's voice interrupted a nightmare where Sandra and Bella had been running through a meadow towards a cliff. Olivia had been chasing after them but she couldn't reach them, couldn't save them from falling over. Her cheeks were wet with tears.

Olivia blinked and looked at the clock. It was only seven o'clock. Christian was standing by the window, holding a piece of paper. She had a sudden feeling of dread and hoped it wasn't the note she'd found in the letterbox the night before. She'd stuffed it in her pocket, hoping nobody had noticed, and although Christian had wanted to talk when they got into bed, she'd said she was tired. In the end, he'd turned over, muttering that there were still many things to be discussed.

She sat up in bed, feeling fragile. She'd drunk too much and her high of the day before had vanished. Christian held up the paper in the weak morning light. *'How can you look in the mirror in your lovely house with your perfect family after what you've done? I know what you did,'* he read in a slow deliberate voice. 'Livy, what's the meaning of this? What have you done?'

'I've got no idea, Christian. It must just be a stupid joke.'

'Who would write something like that? It's in English, too.' Christian came towards her and sat on the edge of the bed. 'Livy, what's going on? I knew something was wrong. You've been acting so strangely, I hardly recognise you anymore. You've changed so much. Where were you yesterday?'

Olivia hesitated. She hadn't been going to tell Christian what she'd done, but decided that honesty was best. Aurelia had told her she didn't always have to do what other people wanted. She was her own person and didn't need to be controlled by Christian. She drew herself up defiantly. 'I was up at the Grand Wildenbach Hotel.'

Christian took a sharp intake of breath. 'What, with those weirdos? I told you to keep away from them. What did you do? Is that what this note is about?'

'Nothing happened, Chris. I just talked to Aurelia. She's wonderful. She really understands me. We've got so much in common, because she was adopted like me. She's like the mother I never had.'

Christian shook his head. 'They're dangerous people. Don't let yourself be influenced too much by them.' He was staring at the note. 'This is threatening. I'm going to speak to Wiesli about it. People can't go sending notes like this.'

Olivia tried to grab the paper. 'There's no need to involve the police. They've got enough to worry about without unimportant things like this. They should be out looking for Sandra.'

Christian looked up sharply and Olivia realised she'd said the wrong thing. 'Has this got something to do with Sandra?' He took Olivia's hand. 'Livy, you've been weird since she disappeared. I knew your reaction wasn't normal. What do you know about it?' He held her hand more tightly. 'Look, you can talk to me. What's going on?'

Olivia pulled her hand back. 'Of course, I don't know anything about that. And anyway, the other note came before...'

'Other note?' Christian stared at her. 'What do you mean?'

Olivia's lip trembled. 'There was another note. Just before Sandra was taken. I thought it was a joke at first and then I thought it was Guy. I felt I was being watched and discovered that Guy had sent a private investigator to check up on me and find Julian.'

'How many other things have you not been telling me? There's something very strange going on. I'm going to have to get ready for work now, but I want you to think carefully about what's happening and be prepared to tell me everything this evening.'

Olivia bristled. He was speaking to her as if she was one of his students. Aurelia had suggested that Christian didn't really love her. Olivia just didn't know what to think anymore. She thought of Aurelia and wanted to be back in her comforting arms.

After everybody had left the house, Olivia sat down with another cup of coffee. Her head was in a whirl. Was Christian being concerned or controlling? She didn't know who to believe or who to trust anymore.

She walked over to the window. The weather was brighter than the day before, with the sun shafting weakly through the silvery clouds. Oh, how she missed Bella. She felt so lonely, so isolated. She wished she could go out with her dog, feeling the frosty air in her lungs and the wind through her hair.

She looked around the kitchen. Because of her super-clean on Saturday, there was not much to be done and she didn't feel like housework anyway. She picked up her Kindle and thought about reading, but even that didn't appeal.

Going upstairs to shower, she noticed her phone lying by the bed. It was blinking. Missed call. It wasn't a number she knew so she called back.

A low voice answered the phone. She didn't recognise it at first and felt a shiver of fear. Who had her number and was phoning her? Then she heard her name and realised it was Stevie. The day immediately seemed brighter. She'd forgotten she'd given him her number, but now she was certain there was nobody she'd rather speak to. 'I can't talk too loud now, but PP's going out today. Could you come round?'

'Of course. When?'

'As soon as possible.'

'I'll be there in half an hour.' Olivia ended the call and found herself humming as she showered. She should be a nervous wreck considering the events of the last couple of days, but she felt happy, and was looking forward to seeing Stevie.

She drew up at the automatic gates of Stevie's house and was looking around for a bell when she heard his voice. 'Can you park beside the road and then I'll let you in?'

She did as he asked and then waited while he hobbled to the gate and opened it manually. He leant forward and kissed her on the cheek. 'Thanks, pal. Sorry I couldn't let you in, but I haven't quite mastered the technology yet – I don't get many visitors.' He shrugged. 'I don't get any actually – you're it! My visitor!'

He led her into the winter garden with the magnificent view down to Lake Zug where they'd sat before. 'So,' he said. 'What's new?'

Olivia was going to say something bland, but looking at his comfortable, wrinkled face and his kind caramel-brown eyes, her story poured out. Without going into detail, she described how Guy had come back into her life and had claimed Julian, and how she'd gone to the Grand Hotel and found a mother figure in Aurelia. Stevie sat watching her, nodding but not saying anything. There was something about him that made Olivia trust him. She was surprising herself. She hadn't opened up to anybody about personal things for years, ever really, but being with Aurelia seemed to have dislodged a block and now her feelings were pouring out.

When she finished, Stevie smiled. 'It'll all work out okay, Oli. Just keep cool. And if all else fails, you can come and adopt me. I need to be taken in hand.'

'Oli' – nobody had ever called her that before, and she wasn't sure if she liked it. But from Stevie she did. His special name for her. She looked at him more carefully. There was something familiar about him; those pale brown eyes were so similar to hers. A thought began in the back of her mind. Could he possibly be…?

He was the right age and her mother had said her father could be a rock star. No, she was being ridiculous. Just because she'd found a mother figure in Aurelia, she was beginning to see parents all over the place. She coughed and changed the subject. 'I've been talking all the time. What's happening with you? Any more journalists around?'

'No, I think they've gone on to a more interesting story. They can't have found any dirt on me.' Stevie gave a rueful smile. 'I must only have met girls with more discretion. Or very bad memories…'

'When exactly were you touring?' Olivia asked, as casually as she could.

'Most of the seventies. I joined the band in seventy-four. The Tarantulas had been formed a few years before by the others who were all at school together. Their singer left so they advertised for a new one. I auditioned and got the job. And that was it. I was seventeen.' He gave another rueful laugh. 'They led me astray and that was the start of my life of music, travelling and debauchery.'

'Where did you travel? Just in Britain or all over the world?' Olivia was pleased with her subtlety.

'We just started off with small local gigs, universities, but when we got a recording contract we went all over the UK, Europe, America. At least I think so. The seventies are a bit of a blur to me actually.'

'Did you ever go to Edinburgh?'

'Lots of times. One of my favourite places.' Stevie looked at her. 'What's all this? Are you an undercover journalist? Have you got a recording machine in your pocket?' He laughed.

'I'm just interested. I would have had a picture of you in my room when I was a teenager, if I'd been allowed to stick things on the walls.' Olivia laughed too, lightening the tone, but she was excited. Nothing Stevie had said made it impossible. Perhaps he really was her father. 'Tell me about the music you're writing now. Priska said you're recording an album?'

Stevie cleared his throat and looked sheepish. 'Er, yes. I'm supposed to be doing something, but I've got a bit of musician's block.'

'What sort of thing are you trying to do? I know you were the singer, but do you play an instrument too? Is there anything I could do to help?' Olivia felt this was something she'd love to be involved with.

Stevie looked down, not responding.

Olivia persisted. 'I mean I'm not really very musical, but I could hold your sheet of music or something.'

Stevie looked up. 'Look, that's really nice of you, but it's, er, not really at that stage yet.'

'Do you have any backing musicians or is it electronic?' Olivia didn't know anything about recording, but it sounded interesting. 'I'd love to see your recording studio. I've never been in one.'

Stevie still looked uncomfortable. 'Actually, nobody's allowed in, not even Concetta. To say it's a bit of a mess is an understatement. And to be honest, I haven't really achieved much yet.' He gave a smile. 'But don't let PP know, because hiding there is the only chance I have of escaping her relentless improvement programme.'

Olivia felt disappointed, but she could understand. She knew what a strain it could be living up to other people's expectations all the time. She could escape into her books, and Stevie obviously needed a private place too.

He gave her an appealing smile. 'Speaking of which, if I give you a shopping list, could you get me a few essentials that don't pass my dear wife's scrutiny?'

Olivia looked at her watch. 'Of course, I'll need to be going soon to collect the kids, but I could drop them in this afternoon if the coast is still clear?'

'That'll be perfect.' Stevie stood up and gave her a hug. 'You know, you've inspired me. I've got an idea for a song now. And to be honest, I haven't written anything for quite a long time. Oli, you're my muse!'

Olivia's heart gave a leap. Stevie could feel it too, the connection. And she had an idea about how she could find out the truth.

After the children had eaten their lunch and were doing their homework at the kitchen table, Olivia took out her laptop. Making sure the children weren't looking to see what she was searching for, she googled 'paternity testing'.

There were lists of labs, but the more she read, the more complicated it became. From reading crime novels, she'd thought it would be a simple matter of taking a cup or a hair and sending it off to be analysed, but reading the information, it seemed you needed kits and buccal swabs from the inside of cheeks and, worst of all, consent forms.

She was just reading about secondary sources, like toothbrushes, used tissues or cigarette butts when Marc's voice interrupted her. 'Mum, we have to set off now or we'll be late.'

Olivia looked up and saw Marc and Lara both standing with their jackets on and school bags on their backs. As usual, the time had flown while she was following links on the Internet.

She dropped them off at school and watched until they were safely in the door, before popping into the Spar and buying the list of sweets and biscuits Stevie had given her. She looked hopefully along the aisles; it was only the day before that she'd seen Aurelia and Sebastian, but she still hoped one of them might be shopping. A surge of excitement ran through her, just thinking of the touch of Sebastian's hands, but she pushed that thought aside. She had another project to investigate.

Driving up the road to Stevie's beautiful house, she had an idea. The perfect person to help her would be Guy. After all, he had secured a swab from Julian without him knowing and certainly without getting his permission. Guy knew about this sort of thing and, ironically, Olivia trusted him and didn't mind sharing her secret thoughts with him. The person she didn't want to know was Christian.

She was in a dream, driving automatically, when she became aware of another vehicle on the normally deserted road. It was a rusting tractor pulling a trailer laden with turnips, winter feed for cattle. As it drew closer, she saw Hans Kolb was driving it.

She was shocked; he looked so much older, his thin face was even greyer and more pinched than before. She gave him a wave as she moved to the side of the narrow road to let him past, but he didn't acknowledge it and continued to stare straight ahead.

She didn't know whether it was deliberate or if he was just functioning like an automaton. She was sure that was what she would do in his situation. How could he bear it? She shivered. She realised she hadn't thought about Sandra all day. Usually she was on her mind every minute, but perhaps Christian was right. Perhaps they did just have to move on and think about those who were still here and not the poor little girl who had disappeared. Olivia hated herself as she thought it, but maybe it was the only sane way to exist.

As she approached Stevie's beautiful villa, she saw him waiting for her outside the winter garden smoking one of his roll-ups. He stubbed it out as she approached and put the butt into a matchbox, which he slipped it into the pocket of his crumpled denim jacket.

He kissed her on the cheek and led her into the winter garden. Taking off his jacket, he threw it onto one of the white sofas, indicating Olivia should sit down. 'It's hot as hell in here. The temperature is all geared to these plants, rather than a northern lad used to unheated bedrooms. I'll take these into my den before they melt away.'

Lifting up the plastic bags, he took a key out of his trouser pocket and went towards the cellar. He opened the door and when Olivia heard him going down the steps, she reached over to his jacket, took the matchbox with the cigarette stub out of the pocket and popped it into her handbag before Stevie came back.

She looked as casual as she could and was quite relieved when he seemed to want to get rid of her. 'Thanks so much, Oli. You've saved my life.' He coughed. 'I'm sure you've got loads to do, and there are a couple of things I must do before PP gets back.'

Olivia leapt up. 'I quite understand. I've always got lots of things to do.' She waved as she moved towards the door, eager to put her plan into action.

Chapter 31

DNA

Olivia drove down the road towards Wildenwil. She had a couple of hours before the children came out of school so she stopped at the side of the road and took out her mobile phone. Guy might be busy, but it would be good if she could see him during the day when Julian was at school.

Her hand shook as she found his number and pressed ring. She was surprised at herself; a couple of days earlier she would never have done this, but since talking to Aurelia, she felt a new confidence.

'Hello,' Guy answered immediately. 'This is a lovely surprise, Lucy.'

Olivia, she thought, but continued in her most confident voice. 'Hi, Guy. I don't want to disturb you, but I just wondered if you'd be free any time in the next few days as I want to ask your advice about something? Nothing to do with Julian,' she added quickly.

'Of course, I'm more than delighted to help you in any way I can. Where are you at the moment? I'm over in your direction and I could meet you very soon.'

Olivia was surprised. What was he doing in her direction? She realised how little she knew about his business interests, or his life, come to that. She remembered her doubts about him. What was his business that was so bad for children it drove a man to suicide? Did he have a secret building in the hills where he hid girls? Where he was hiding Sandra? She shook herself. This was not one of her detective books where everyone was a suspect. There was probably a simple explanation and anyway, she needed Guy's help.

'Actually, I'm just driving home.' She thought quickly. She didn't really want him in her house, but he'd been there the day before when they'd all gone to the Alpamare and it seemed a better option than meeting him in the village, where somebody she knew might see her. 'Would you like to come to the house and have a cup of coffee? It won't take long.'

'I'll be there in ten minutes.'

Olivia drove home quickly and switched on the coffee machine before taking the matchbox out of her bag, and opening it carefully, she checked the cigarette was still in it.

Almost immediately there was the sound of a car outside and a shadow at the window. She opened the door and let Guy in. He leant over and kissed her on the cheek. 'Lucy, you're looking fantastic. Really sparkling.'

'Olivia.' This time she said it out loud.

'Nonsense. You're not hausfrau Olivia today. You're looking like the real person you are, Lucy.'

Olivia should have felt annoyed, she knew, but there was something about Guy's voice and charm that made her feel good about herself.

'Ha ha. Anyway, no time for flattery. I've got a favour to ask.'

'Anything in my power. And I know how to make most things happen.'

Olivia showed him the box with the cigarette end and explained. At first, she started off by claiming she was asking for a friend, but seeing the sceptical look on Guy's face, she told the truth, and then it all came pouring out. She was shocked. After years of keeping everything secret, she now seemed to be gushing her whole story to everybody she met.

It was liberating in a way. The new people she'd come into contact with were ones she felt she could be herself with, not having to keep up the perfect façade she'd spent the last eleven years erecting. As she finished the story, she looked at Guy. 'After all these years of never knowing who I am, who my father is, at last I feel I may have found him.'

Guy sat silently until she finally stopped talking, when he reached out and put his arms round her. 'My poor, dear girl. I never knew about your background. This makes the way I treated you even worse. I was so young and thoughtless. Because you'd had a boyfriend, and you were so beautiful and adorable, it never occurred to me...' His voice trailed away and he lowered his eyes. 'I feel so ashamed. Things could have, should have, worked out so differently. When I look at Julian, I so regret the years of his life I've missed...' Guy cupped her face in his hands and kissed her lightly on the lips.

Olivia pulled herself away. 'Guy, this isn't right. This isn't why I wanted to meet you. I need help, and I thought you'd be able to give it to me.'

Guy stepped back. 'You know I'll do anything I can. You asked if it's possible to extract DNA from the cigarette end. It is, providing it hasn't become too contaminated. You also have to provide a sample of your own for comparison.'

He paused. 'But I have to warn you, I think this is a long shot. You've gone through a very emotional time recently, and it seems to me you're just clutching at straws.' Olivia opened her mouth to protest, but Guy put his finger up to her mouth and carried on. 'I mean, what are the chances of your father turning up here in the same small Swiss village? If this happened in a novel, readers would be raising their eyebrows at the incredible coincidence.'

'But all I know about my father is that he could have been a rock star. My mother admitted she was one of those groupies who had sex with as many rock stars as she could. And he said he'd been to Edinburgh. And we've got the same eyes, and we've got a connection...'

Guy was shaking his head gently. 'I'll take the cigarette stub and drop off a testing kit to you as soon as possible.' He sat down opposite her and held both her hands. 'Looking at Julian, I can see how important it was for him to find me. You've never known your father and I can understand why you are searching for roots, for identity. But please don't invest all your hopes in this. I don't want you to be disappointed.'

Olivia tried to pull away, but Guy held her hand. 'Listen to me, Lucy. You can always depend on me and I will give you anything you want. Julian is very loyal, but he's told me a little bit about what life is like here – how you do everything to make sure Christian is not displeased, revolve your life around his wishes. I don't know if it's meeting Stevie Dawber, or me coming back into your life, but you've changed. You're vibrant and sparkling…'

'No, you've got it wrong. I love my husband, and my family and my house…' As the image of Sebastian and the memory of his touch flashed into her mind, she realised she had changed, but it was nothing to do with Guy.

'I think the lady doth protest too much.'

Olivia started. Exactly what Aurelia had said. Guy stood up and moved towards the door, putting the matchbox with the cigarette stub in his pocket. 'Think about what I've said and remember, if you're ever in trouble, there's always a place for you with me, a safe haven.'

He closed the door behind him and left Olivia sitting at the kitchen table, her coffee getting cold in front of her. What was all that about? She thought of the note again. It had appeared just as Guy came back, and his last remark suggested he thought she might be in danger. She remembered how he'd looked when he'd said, 'I know everything about you.' What did he know? Was it that she'd kept his son from him? Or was it something more? Although she'd been blurting out secrets in the last couple of days, there was one secret she'd never tell anybody. Could Guy have found out about that?

Looking at her watch, she moved automatically to her car and drove slowly through the low mist, the gloom of the weather reflecting her mood. As she approached the school, the clock on the bell tower showed she was too early, so she parked outside and thought about the last few days. Her normal, well-ordered, boring life had been turned upside down. Everything seemed to be fractured, changing, and she didn't know what to believe, who to trust. She didn't even recognise herself, so different from the person she'd carefully constructed over the last few years. But she did feel alive, almost frenetic.

A knock at the window interrupted her thoughts. Marc's face was pressed up against the glass and Lara was jumping up and down next to him. As they clambered into the back of the car, she turned round and kissed them. They looked a bit surprised, as she didn't usually greet them so effusively, but she needed this contact with them, to feel the softness of their cheeks.

Chapter 32

Ski week

Back at the house, Olivia saw something sticking out of the letterbox. Her first thought was that it was another note but, as she got closer, she was relieved to see it was the DNA kit. Wow, that was quick. She put it in her pocket, determined to get it back to Guy as soon as possible. The sooner he sent it off, the sooner she'd get the result.

She followed the children into the house and they were just having a snack when she heard a vehicle draw up outside. Looking out of the window, she saw a large yellow DHL lorry. That was odd, she hadn't ordered anything, but maybe Christian had. Opening the door, she saw the delivery man staggering towards the door with a large box.

'Frau Keller?'

Olivia nodded.

'Can you take this in? It's for Herr Rolf Keller, but the road up there is still blocked.'

Olivia took the sheet and signed it, surprised the snow was still so deep up by her brother-in-law's settlement. Although the fields around her house were still covered with snow and the trees were heavy with frost every morning, the roads were usually well cleared.

The driver shoved the box into her kitchen and drove away as quickly as possible. Olivia looked at the box and saw it was from Zalando, the clothes firm. That was a surprise; she'd assumed it would be some kind of equipment for rearing sheep.

Not long afterwards, she heard Christian's car draw up and he came in with a briefcase and a bundle of papers. That was unusual because he usually stayed at school working and didn't like bringing teaching stuff home. 'I have to get all these marked before the ski holiday so I'll be busy the next few nights.'

'The ski holiday?' Olivia was surprised. Each region had a different week for the annual ski break, so the resorts wouldn't get too overcrowded, and their area always took the third week in February. She hadn't realised it was so close. 'Have we booked somewhere?'

'Of course, our place in Stoos.' Since the children were small, they'd always gone to the same chalet in Stoos, a ski resort on the plateau top of a mountain nearby. It was a lovely place for families as the pistes were gentle and because the only way to reach it was by funicular railway, it was car-free. But the previous year she was sure Christian had said it was getting a bit boring because the children were getting so much better at skiing.

'I thought you said you wanted to try somewhere new?' she said quietly, certain the booking had never been discussed.

'We thought about it, but it really is perfect for us there so I booked the same chalet again. I told you. Are you okay, Livy? You don't seem to know what's going on anymore.'

'I'm sure I'd have remembered if we'd discussed it. As it is, I've made other plans for next week, so you can go with the children.' Olivia was shocked herself as the words came out of her mouth. Lara and Marc looked up from the table in amazement, and Christian's face simmered with silent fury. 'We'll talk about this later.'

Olivia looked at him defiantly. 'Actually, I think it's a very good thing if you go away with the children. You're all so much better at skiing than me. I only hold you back and I've got things I have to get on with here.'

Christian's expression softened. 'Maybe it is a good thing if you stay here and have a rest. You've been through a very emotional time and really haven't been yourself. Perhaps you can spend the week training a new dog. I know you miss Bella.'

Marc twisted round on his chair. 'But who'll cook for us?'

Christian put on his 'good old Dad' voice. 'We'll go out, to the fondue restaurant and to the rösti hut in the forest – it'll be great.'

Lara clapped her hands. 'My favourite! Can we go out every night?'

Christian picked her up and swirled her round. 'Of course you can, my little darling.' He ruffled Marc's hair so he wouldn't feel left out. 'We'll have such a great time, and Mummy will feel better when we come back.'

Christian led the children into the other room and they played a game while Olivia cleared the table and made the evening meal. As usual, she felt calmer going through the comforting routine of preparing the meal. She was chopping the onions when she felt a presence beside her.

Christian stood close to her. 'What's got into you? I don't recognise you anymore. You've changed so much.'

Olivia put the knife down. 'You don't know what's got into me? Everything's changed. Sandra is missing, Julian's spending all his time in town, I can't sleep at night for awful nightmares, you're treating me like one of your less intelligent students. And Bella's dead…' Her voice shook and she covered her face with her hands before Christian could see her tears.

'I said you should get another dog.' Christian paused for a moment, before turning her round to face him. 'Look, it's been a hard time for all of us, but we have to put the past behind us and look to the future, think of our children, of our family.'

She shook herself free. 'So, Julian is not counted as our child anymore then?' The tears she'd been holding back rolled down her cheeks. 'And we have to forget about Sandra and just be thankful our children are all right, is that it?' She straightened herself to her full height. 'I can't forget Sandra. I think of her every day, every time I look at Lara, and I have this feeling, this knowledge, that she's still alive and we just have to find her.'

Christian pulled her closer, his voice softening. 'Livy, Livy, one of the things I love about you is your kindness and empathy, but this obsession is getting out of control. I shouldn't really say this, but just to help you get closure, Ruedi Wiesli told me, in total confidence, that the police are almost a hundred per cent certain one of the older brothers was responsible for Sandra's death. There's evidence of a definite culture of incest and abuse in the family, going back over generations. The area round the farm has been searched with sniffer dogs and the latest body-seeking equipment, but they haven't found her yet. They're convinced she's somewhere on the farm, but there are so many places to hide bodies – fields, barns, slurry pits – and such a pile of animal bones and rotting carcasses, it's making the search nearly impossible.'

Ruedi Wiesli, Christian's old school friend, the local policeman, had been gossiping again.

'So they've just given up on her, have they?'

'Not at all. Wiesli says this is the biggest missing person investigation Switzerland's ever had. They've followed up all sorts of leads – international child smuggling, Internet sites, everything, but they've all come to nothing. There's no evidence she ever left the valley and everything points to her brothers.

'In cases of missing children, it is almost always members of the family, you know. International child abductors do exist, but in the vast majority of cases, the perpetrator is very much closer to home.'

He kissed the top of her head. 'So, we just have to draw a line under this whole unfortunate business and think positively. Think of the wonderful blessing of the two lovely children who are sitting in the other room.' He took her hand. 'And please come on holiday with us. What will you do without us?'

Olivia shook her head. 'You're right, Christian.' She felt tears coming again, but she blinked them away. 'I think I need some time to get my head in order. I feel everything is crumbling around me. All sorts of things from my past have been coming back to me in my dreams, all mixed up with the present, and I do feel a bit strange.'

Christian's voice grew gentler. 'I knew this was just a phase you're going through. It's Montgomery coming back into your life, too. Those notes must have come from him, although I can't believe he'd be so childish. He spoke to me, man to man, at the Alpamare, and said how much he missed seeing his son grow up.

'Just do what you feel is best for you at the moment. We'll miss you in Stoos, but I can see you need some time to recover.' He stroked her cheek. 'I think you really should make an appointment with Dr Bruni. He can at least give you something to help you sleep, and maybe make an appointment with somebody who could help you with your anxiety.'

'What are you suggesting? Do you think I'm crazy? That I need to go to some psychotherapist? I won't go.'

'Livy, it was just a suggestion. I just want to help you. And I really mean it about getting a puppy. This house needs a dog. We could get one tomorrow.'

Olivia wiped her eyes and blew her nose. 'We will get another dog, but I think we should wait until we find the right one. I'll look around next week.'

She put the hanky in her pocket. 'I'd better get on with the meal or it'll be time for the children to go to bed before we eat.'

When the dinner was ready, she called the children through and they chatted as they ate. The children seemed to have accepted they were going on holiday with their dad and that their mum would be left behind.

After the meal, Christian stood up from the table and his leg brushed against the huge box. 'What's this?'

Olivia explained about the delivery man and his tale of snow further up the road. Christian shrugged. 'It was probably that he couldn't be bothered to go all the way up and took the easy way out by leaving it here. What is it anyway?'

'That's the funny thing. It's from Zalando, the clothing firm.'

'It's about time Rolf bought some more clothes. He wears the same old things all the time.'

'But look at the size of the box. And isn't Zalando women's clothing?'

'Livy. It's nothing to do with you. He can have a harem up there or be a secret cross-dresser as far as I'm concerned. It's his business. You can deliver it if you want to, because I won't have time. I've got all this marking to do, and preparing for the ski week.'

'I'll help with that and I'll take the box up next week. Poor Rolf, stuck up there all by himself. Have you heard anything from him recently?'

'Not a word, but I wouldn't expect to. He probably needs time to himself. We still don't know what happened to make him leave the charity so suddenly.' Christian smiled reassuringly. 'He's lived all over the world so he can certainly look after himself here in Switzerland.'

Olivia nodded, but a suspicion was forming in the back of her mind. She was going to visit Rolf, and this time she wouldn't let him push her away from the door. She was going to find out just what was going on up on the Alp and why he was buying so many clothes.

Chapter 33

Princes Street

Edinburgh – May 2004

Lucy smiled at Bill, straightened her clothes and smoothed her hair. It was time to pick Julian up from the after-school club. As it was Thursday, late-night shopping, she'd take him up to Princes Street and get something to eat there. Julian would love it, and after these encounters with Bill, she always felt unsettled.

Julian was excited. 'Can we go to Burger King? Can I get a new toy?' Lucy nodded. She felt so guilty about leaving him longer at the club that she said yes to everything. They caught the bus up to Princes Street and were just crossing Hanover Street when she was vaguely aware of a tall man in a long navy coat, a fedora hat and a white scarf passing in the opposite direction.

'I want a burger,' Julian said, tugging at her hand.

'And you shall have one, young man.'

Lucy looked up in surprise. The man in the fedora hat had turned round and was standing beside them, staring at Julian. Lucy looked up at the man's face and stepped back in shock. Although she hadn't seen him for nearly six years, she recognised him immediately. It was Guy Montgomery.

Clutching Julian's hand more tightly, she pulled him along Princes Street, trying to dodge the crowds of late-night shoppers.

'Lucy.' Guy caught up with them and kept in step. 'Please let me buy you and your little boy something to eat. Whatever you'd like.'

'I like burg–' Julian began, but Lucy interrupted him.

'I'm sorry, we can't come with you.'

Julian looked up at her in surprise. 'Mummy, I'm hungry.'

Guy smiled, his old charm still very evident. 'Lucy, I'd love to be able to chat about university days and catch up on old times. And get to know you, young man.' Guy bent his knees so he was on the same level as Julian and stretched out his hand. 'I'm Guy… and what's your name?'

Julian looked uncertainly at his mother. 'Julian.'

'That's a great name.' Guy looked closely at his face. 'And how old are you?'

Lucy pulled at her son's hand. 'He's four.'

'Ah, you're a big boy for four.'

Lucy looked around and saw a number 26 bus approaching the nearest stop. Grabbing Julian, she raced towards the bus, just managing to get on before it drew off. Guy followed them, but didn't descend to grappling with them at the bus stop. He tipped his hat. 'Bye, Lucy. I'll be in touch.'

Lucy managed to find a seat on the crowded bus and pulled Julian onto her knee. He struggled on her lap. 'Mummy, I'm hungry. I want a burger. Who was that man?' Julian looked round at her with reproachful eyes. 'And why did you say I'm four? I'm a big boy now. I'm five.'

Chapter 34

Suspicions

Wildenwil – Tuesday 16 February, 2016

The next morning, Olivia went down to Zug and popped the DNA swab in Guy's letterbox, as arranged. She gave it a little kiss before she let go of it, and smiled at her own childishness. The thought of finding her father filled her with excitement. She wouldn't be alone anymore. Of course, she had a family round her, but no roots, no ancestry. The strength of her desperation to find her father had taken her by surprise.

Apart from that, the next couple of days passed in relative calm, sorting out the stuff for the week away, getting skis waxed, checking clothes for size, and buying new goggles and gloves. Because of the lack of snow earlier on in the year, the children hadn't been skiing and were excited about getting the chance to ski for a whole week. At school, they were training their muscles in their gym lessons, and by Friday afternoon everything was prepared. The children were in bed, and Olivia and Christian were sitting in front of the fire with a glass of wine.

'We're so lucky,' Christian said, raising his glass for a toast. 'Our beautiful healthy family, a lovely home, and ten days without work.'

Olivia raised her glass too, not trusting herself to mention that she hadn't seen Julian all week. He'd sent a text, prompted by Guy she was sure, and she hoped she'd see him next week when he was off school. She didn't think he was going skiing, but then she realised she didn't actually know what he was doing these days. But he was safe. Not like…

'I wonder what Sandra is doing now.' The words just slipped out. She wasn't even aware she was saying them out loud.

Christian put his glass down. 'Why do you spoil every pleasant moment we have with this obsession? Please let it go, for the sake of your own mental health. Sandra can't still be alive. They'd have found some trace of her.'

'But it happens all the time. That girl in Austria who was kept in a cellar, and the Fritzl family. And wasn't there a case in America just recently of a man who'd kept three girls hidden in his home for years?'

'Are you suggesting some man has captured Sandra and is keeping her hidden? That would be impossible. The police have searched everywhere.'

'But have they looked in all the buildings? What about ones that are only used in summer, like the place where Rolf is?'

Christian looked at her, the flickering flames of the fire reflected on his face, and spoke slowly. 'Livy, I know all of this has affected you badly, but I cannot believe you have just made this suggestion. Rolf, the kindest, most upright and honest person anybody could imagine, somebody who has spent his whole life helping others in the most difficult of circumstances, is the last person who would ever do anything like that.'

'But working in these stressful situations can have terrible effects on people. You know, post-traumatic stress.'

'Livy, I've tried to understand your bizarre reaction to an unfortunate event that really has nothing to do with our family, but to hear you accusing my brother like that is beyond my comprehension.'

'I didn't accuse him. I merely said it was a possibility.'

Christian stood up from his chair. 'Livy, this has got to stop. I don't recognise the person you've become. While we're away, you must make an appointment with Dr Bruni. This can't go on. I want you to go back to being my old Livy and a proper wife and mother.'

Olivia's faced flushed with shock. She stood up, staring at her husband. 'What do you mean? I spend my whole time being a proper wife and mother. Now you're suggesting that I'm not, and that I'm crazy!' This time she did fling the wine into his face and rushed up to her bedroom.

Closing the door behind her, she threw herself onto her bed. What had happened? She was shocked by her own behaviour. How had everything gone so wrong? Christian was right. She wasn't herself. But she didn't want to talk to a doctor; she wanted Aurelia. She was the only one who understood her, and she had warned her about Christian. He was trying to control her again.

She was crying into her pillow when she heard Christian come up the stairs. Without trying the bedroom door, he went into the spare room.

Chapter 35

Eleanor

Portobello – May 2004

Lucy put a bottle of red wine and two glasses on the coffee table and sat down to wait for Bill. She'd got Julian off to bed early and tidied up by throwing her clothes in the wardrobe, excited at the thought of Bill being in her bed.

Her tenement flat in a rundown stair at the top of Bath Street was small, but she'd made it as comfortable as possible, with bright throws over the second-hand sofa, and shelves of books. The best thing about it was it was only five minutes' walk from Portobello beach. Almost every day after school she and Julian walked along the wide promenade, fringed by pubs, cafés and Victorian tenements. Whenever possible they'd go down onto the beach, in every weather, summer and winter. She was always invigorated by the smell of the sea and the view over the Firth of Forth to Fife, as she watched Julian splashing in the waves.

Lucy looked at her watch. Bill said he'd be round after the governors' meeting and, although she didn't know exactly when he'd arrive, she thought he'd be here by now. She picked up a book and tried to concentrate on it, but her mind was buzzing.

She was so looking forward to seeing Bill and escaping from the worries that were haunting her. Ever since she'd seen Guy on Princes Street, she'd been terrified he'd track her down. She remembered how easy it had been to find Geraldine, but hoped she'd be more difficult to find. She was in a rented flat, wasn't on the electoral roll and didn't have an entry in the phone book.

Since last Thursday she'd avoided the centre of town and, even on Portobello prom, she looked round every time she heard footsteps behind her. Guy had seen her get on the 26 bus and might be able to work out where she lived from that.

The only time she'd felt relaxed was when they'd gone to the adventure playground at Dalkeith Country Park with Christian on Sunday. Julian loved Christian climbing on the high walks with him, and pushing him on the Flying Fox. Lucy also enjoyed being with Christian, who was like a big friendly puppy, always enthusiastic and eager to please.

The doorbell rang. Lucy leapt up, plumped the cushions, fluffed her hair in front of the hall mirror and pressed the entry-phone. Standing at the door to the flat, her body tingled with excitement.

She was so full of anticipation that she didn't notice the difference in the footsteps and was surprised when it was not Bill who came round the corner of the stairs, but a woman. Lucy wondered if she was going to the other flat on the landing, but she approached her door.

'Lucy Sheridan?' The woman looked at her in an appraising manner. She was tall and elegant, with beautifully cut short hair and high cheekbones. Lucy nodded.

'I'm Eleanor Munro, Professor of Anthropology at Edinburgh University, and your headmaster's wife.'

Lucy gasped. Bill's wife. Lucy had always imagined her – if she'd thought about her at all – as a homely creature who ironed his pristine shirts. Eleanor had obviously introduced herself with her academic status to make Lucy feel in awe of her. And she succeeded. With her poise and expensive clothes, Eleanor oozed sophistication, which made Lucy feel very young and dowdy.

'May I come in?' The older woman strode through the door and looked round. Suddenly the room felt very small and scruffy.

Lucy showed her to a chair and, feeling she should do something, offered her a drink. 'No, thank you, I won't be staying long.' Eleanor stretched out her long legs, in beautifully cut trousers and expensive-looking leather boots. 'You're very young, and that makes me even more annoyed. My husband has many good qualities, but he has one deplorable weakness for pretty girls. Some of these women may go into affairs with their eyes open, but when I heard how young you are, and being a single mother, I was appalled. He has taken advantage of his position as your head teacher and of your vulnerability. It is disgraceful behaviour and, as it has gone on longer than usual, I've been compelled to intervene. I've told him it must stop, and it will.'

She gave Lucy a cool look. 'I've come here to advise you to find a new job. You can't continue working at that school. It would cause unhappiness for both you and Bill. He will give you an excellent reference and every help in getting a job in another school, but this must be done immediately in order to secure a position before the beginning of the new school year.'

Lucy sat, stunned, not knowing what to say or how to react. Eleanor stood up and walked towards the door. With her hand on the handle, she turned. 'Lucy, you're young and very beautiful, and from what I've heard, a talented linguist. You may find this hard to believe at the moment, but I promise you you'll look back to this and thank me.' She smiled ruefully. 'Bill is weak and I couldn't depend on him to finish it properly himself. However, now you know the situation, I trust you will begin to search for a new job immediately.'

Eleanor closed the door behind her and Lucy heard her boots clacking down the stairs. She leant against the door and cried, not because it was over with Bill, but because she felt so ashamed. How stupid she'd been. She'd been so blinded by love or lust or something, she'd never considered Bill's wife, never thought of her as a person. Because of all the promises Bill had made, the way he'd been with her, she'd thought they would be together one day. What a naive fool she'd been. Just like with Guy Montgomery.

She shuddered when she thought of him and the way he'd looked at Julian. She was never going to let him have anything to do with her son. She was going to see to it that Julian would grow up differently from these men who'd hurt her so much.

Chapter 36

Rolf is missing

Wildenwil – Saturday 20 February, 2016

Olivia woke up underneath the duvet with her clothes still on. Downstairs, she could hear the sounds of breakfast. She washed quickly and put on fresh clothes, before hurrying down with her best smiley face on.

'Mummy, where were you? Daddy said you were sleeping a long time because you weren't feeling well. Are you better now?' Lara ran up and put her thin arms round her mother.

Olivia felt her heart overflow with love. 'I'm fine, darling. I was just a bit tired. Have you got everything you need? Are you going to take Bowie with you to cuddle at night?'

Lara waved her favourite teddy by one arm. 'He's here.'

Marc stood stolidly behind his sister, holding his sledge. 'I'm taking this so we can play in the slope behind the chalet too.'

'Great idea.' Everything seemed so under control. She'd always thought she was the one who held all the domestic arrangements together, but they seemed to be managing very well without her.

Outside, the car was already packed with all their things. Christian fixed the ski box on the roof, and reaching out to Olivia, gave her a stiff hug. 'Have a good week and get well soon. I'll phone you every evening.'

Olivia turned to the children. Lara jumped into her arms. 'We'll miss you, Mummy. Don't miss us too much.' She gave her mother a hug and a kiss.

Then Marc came and hugged her legs. 'I love you, Mummy.' Olivia bent down and caught him in her arms, still holding on to Lara. Marc, her independent self-sufficient little man, loved her enough to say that in front of everybody.

Her heart felt as if it were bursting as she held them tight. 'Have a great time. Love you to the moon and back.'

The children climbed into the car and waved as it slowly turned into the lane. Olivia watched until they were out of sight, shivering in the frosty morning air, and walked slowly back into the kitchen. Since before Julian was born, she'd never been alone like this. She was nearly forty and for the first time in her life she could do what she liked.

She made a cup of coffee and stared out of the window into the white freezing fog. She was going to use this time well and try to answer some of the questions that were bouncing round her head and disturbing her sleep. She was going to visit Rolf and find out why he was ordering women's clothes; she'd spend time with Julian and find out exactly what Guy's business was, and why it had driven a sensitive young man to suicide; she'd visit Stevie, and maybe – her heart gave a little leap of anticipation – just maybe, the results would come back from the DNA testing and be what she secretly hoped for.

And she'd go and visit Aurelia. She was the one person who really understood her, the one she could really talk to, far better than any doctor. Aurelia was the mother she'd always wanted.

And going up to the hotel, she'd see Sebastian again. A tremor of excitement ran through her at the prospect of another massage.

Catching sight of the big box, an idea occurred to her. At the computer, she typed in the name of the children's charity Rolf worked for: Protéger les Petits (PLP) Cambodia. The first items to come up were a Wikipedia page and some historical documents from the PLP, but nothing up to date.

She decided to refine the search by adding 'sacking', and a recent article from an Australian newspaper appeared, entitled Cambodian PLP Scandal. Her eyes opened wide as she read it. It described the alleged cover-up of paedophile activities by members of the PLP, where the charity had simply removed suspect officials from the country rather than carrying out a proper investigation. Olivia shook her head. That couldn't be Rolf. He'd worked with children for years and was dedicated to his job. He wasn't a paedophile.

She was going to visit Rolf immediately. She couldn't believe he had anything to do with Sandra's disappearance, but there was a mystery surrounding him. He'd stopped doing the job he loved, and changed from the life and soul of the party to a recluse.

Putting on her warmest clothes, she struggled to get the box into the boot of her car, checked her snow chains, in case the road was as bad as the delivery driver had suggested, and drove slowly up the lane. The landscape was swathed in low cloud with the pale wraith of the sun shining faintly though the white mist, giving it an ethereal glow.

She didn't see one other vehicle for the whole journey. When she'd driven as close as she could to the dark cluster of buildings, she picked her way over the frozen snow towards them. She left the box of clothes in her car as she'd never be able to carry it alone.

The dark buildings loomed out of the ghostly white mist and, as she approached them, she saw an old wooden sleigh, the sort the farmers used, propped up by the door. This would be the right thing to transport the box.

There was a thin wisp of smoke coming from the chimney, but no sound in the frozen white stillness. She knocked on the door, but there was no reply.

After a moment's hesitation, she pushed the door gently and it swung open. She didn't want to intrude, but was determined to find out what was happening up on this high mountain plateau.

It was dark inside the house. The shutters on the one window were closed, and not much light came through the narrow doorway. The building consisted of a single room with a low-beamed ceiling and dark stone walls. There was an old stove opposite her, but the weak warmth coming from it did nothing to counteract the deep chill of the gloomy room. Inside it seemed almost colder than it was outside. Next to the stove in an inglenook was a lumpy-looking bed with a dark cover pulled over it. In the other corner there was a small table with some papers on it and one chair. Apart from that the room was empty.

Olivia shivered. Despite the stove, the room felt unlived in. 'Rolf,' she called out, but her voice was quickly absorbed into the cold, dark walls. She called again but there was no response, no sign of life.

She shivered. The creepy stillness frightened her. Going back to the light of the doorway, she looked round the snowy yard. There were three outbuildings. The largest was the one where she'd seen Rolf last time she came up, so she followed the footprints to the large double door. It was closed so she tapped on it and, when there was no reply, pushed it open.

Inside, there was a warm musty animal smell, and in the shadows she saw two pairs of bright eyes reflecting the light from the door. There were a couple of bleats, and as her eyes became accustomed to the darkness, she saw the shapes of white fleeces and black faces. Only two sheep; she was sure Rolf had more than this. She felt on the walls for a light switch, but there was nothing. 'Rolf,' she called out again, but there was no response apart from a slight rustle from the sheep.

A low ghostly light shone from the back of the barn. Olivia moved slowly towards it, calling out Rolf's name again, quietly so as not to disturb the sheep. The light was over a straw-filled compartment that seemed to be a nursery area. A few lambs were curled up together at the back, but there was no movement, no sound except for a low restless baa from one of the adult sheep.

She felt uneasy, unable to forget what she'd read on the Internet. Did she know Rolf at all? Could he possibly be keeping Sandra here?

She shook her head. That was impossible, but where was he? She peered into the shadows at the back of the room, but there was nothing to see.

When she stepped outside again, the whole area was enveloped in thick white cloud, without the faintest glimmer of sunlight, giving it the other-worldly atmosphere of a sci-fi film. She shuddered. She wanted to get away, back to the normality of her home and the village, but she had to find Rolf.

Shaking with fear and cold, she looked into the other two buildings. One was filled with hay and sacks of grain with no hiding places. The third one had some pieces of old machinery, churns and general clutter. But no sign of Rolf.

She was sure now he was not around. She couldn't see his bicycle so maybe he'd gone somewhere on it. Or would he use skis? It was difficult to see if there were any tracks on the windswept frozen snow.

After one last look around, when she was sure there was nowhere a girl could be hidden, she began to worry about Rolf. What if something had happened to him? If he had an accident up here, nobody would know about it.

She went back into the living accommodation and searched every corner. She even patted the cover on the bed to check he wasn't there. It was like the Marie Celeste. The fire showed he hadn't been gone for long. She hadn't passed anybody on the road and she was pretty certain there were no other buildings around, nowhere he could go in this snowy white wilderness.

After calling his name a few more times she made her way back to the car. She was about to reverse out of the deep snow when she had an idea. Going back to the main building, she looked at the papers on the table. She hoped there would be some clue as to what had happened, but there was nothing unusual – a bill from a health insurance company and a bank statement.

She found an old envelope and scribbled a quick message, saying she'd called and had a delivery for him in the back of her car. Keeping the tone as light as possible so as to give no indication of her disquiet, she said she'd call around again later and hoped to see him then.

With a last glance round the eerie empty landscape, she made her way back to her car and drove carefully down the road, avoiding the frozen ruts while keeping an eye out for any sign of Rolf.

She was filled with unease. Had Rolf disappeared as well? Had he found out something suspicious about Sandra and been removed? His house wasn't far away from where Ruth Frick's body was found. Or was there another building in the area nobody knew anything about? Was he hiding Sandra and buying her clothes from Zalando? They said Ruth had been found in new clothes the foster family didn't recognise. Olivia felt alone, confused and frightened by what she'd found out.

She looked at her watch. Despite the gloom of the weather, it was still only midday. She knew what she was going to do next. She was going to the only place she felt safe – the Grand Wildenbach Hotel.

Chapter 37

Back to the hotel

Wildenwil – Saturday 20 February, 2016

The hotel was swathed in the same cloud as Rolf's alp, but looked more welcoming. The fir trees and bushes round the building were heavy with snow and glittered in the reflection of the light shining above the main door. Behind the hotel, giant icicles from the frozen waterfall glowed against the stark darkness of the cliffs.

As Olivia parked her car, the door opened wide and Aurelia stood there, enveloped in her usual enormous caftan. She opened her arms wide and a smile lit up her face. 'Olivia. I knew you would come. I've felt disturbances in your aura. You must talk about what is troubling you.'

Olivia rested her head on the older woman's breast and felt a sense of calm flowing through her. The old rational Olivia would have dismissed all this as mumbo-jumbo, but the new Olivia allowed her worries to drain from her body.

Aurelia led her into the old dining room. The walls of books, the heavy curtains and the subdued lighting, together with the spicy smell of joss sticks, created a welcoming atmosphere.

Tenzin appeared silently through the curtains carrying a tray with the usual milky sweet tea. Olivia was getting used to it; it seemed to take all her tensions away, and left her light-headed and relaxed.

Aurelia sat opposite her and held both her hands. Fixing her large brown eyes on Olivia's, she waited for her to speak. Olivia had expected questions, but after a short pause, she talked, slowly at first, but then the words tumbled out. She told Aurelia about the argument with Christian and her ambivalence about the children going on the ski holiday without her.

She felt guilty for talking about her husband in that way. 'Christian's a good man and a good father, but he makes me feel as if I'm doing everything wrong. In the last few months I've felt cracks appearing in everything I know and sometimes it's making me act in a way I don't like. I really don't know who I am anymore.'

'Olivia, you mustn't blame yourself. When I hear about your past, it is understandable you are confused about who you really are. You've had three names, three personas, and we have to find the real you underneath. You're thirty-nine. You're approaching an important time of self-discovery. It's a painful stage, but one you must go through before you can become true to yourself. You must learn to think about your own needs. You've spent your whole life thinking only of others. It's hard, very hard, but for your health, your sanity and your soul you must do this.'

Olivia pulled away. 'I love my family. They're everything to me. Christian is a good man...' She paused, wondering whether she should say more. She had never told anyone in Switzerland the real reason why she'd accepted Christian's proposal of marriage, why she'd had to leave Edinburgh. She swallowed. Aurelia was wonderful, non-judgemental and understanding, but after hiding her secret for so long, Olivia didn't have the words to articulate it.

'It's just a bad phase we're going through. It's been hard with Julian...' Changing the subject, she told Aurelia what had happened since the last time she'd spoken, on Julian's birthday. She described the dinner in the restaurant, and without giving any details, said Guy had been kind and helpful to her.

Aurelia raised her eyebrows. 'Can you trust this man, this man who robbed you of your virginity without asking for your consent? Why is he being nice to you? Does he feel remorse?'

Olivia shook her head. 'I don't think it's that. It was a misunderstanding. He loves his son, and I think he likes me.' She felt a blush spreading over her face.

Aurelia shook her head. 'My dear Olivia. You are so sweet, so trusting, but so naive. Think about this man. He's rich and powerful, and used to getting what he wants. What does he want now? His son, it seems. He's won him over, and what's the only thing standing in his way now? You. I'm sure he does like you, you are a beautiful, lovable person, but you have to question his motives.'

Olivia blushed again. 'You're right. Oh, Aurelia. I'm so confused. Everything secure in my life seems to be falling apart and I feel lost. Lost in myself. I don't know what to feel or believe anymore.' She didn't mention what she'd found out about Rolf. It seemed disloyal.

Aurelia reached out and drew Olivia close to her. She stroked her hair. 'I understand you so well, Olivia, because I was once you. I never knew my mother. I was fostered by a poor farming family who used me as a slave in every way. I was abused, mentally, physically, sexually, and I felt worthless. I did everything they demanded of me, suffered every indignity they put me through because I wanted them to accept me. I was desperate for love.'

Aurelia's brown eyes took on a far-away look. 'Then I had the greatest fortune. I met Erik, the Master, the man who was to become my husband. His love and teaching made me whole again, and he taught me to love myself.' She paused and held Olivia closer. 'Unfortunately, he is no longer with us in body, but his spirit lives on. He saved me as he saved many people. Sebastian was only fourteen when we found him, and we helped him escape from an institution where he was abused, mentally, physically and sexually. The deep hurt caused by these wicked hypocritical men has been healed, and he has found himself and his place.

'We've lived in many different countries over the years, learning the best from other cultures and religions. We were always looking for a permanent home for our community and now we've found the right place, here in this magical part of Switzerland. And I think you will find it is the right place for you too.'

Olivia sat silently for a moment, thinking of Aurelia's words. She felt safe, and Aurelia had already helped her to get things clearer in her mind. With Aurelia's support, Olivia thought she could face up to her past, become stronger and better able to face the future.

As if reading her thoughts, Aurelia spoke again. 'Everything happens for a reason. You are here because you belong here. Nothing happens by chance. You have this week free from your family to be able to think about what you want out of life, to find the real you.' She moved away from Olivia and stood up. 'You have so many old hurts and emotional wounds that need to be healed. We can help you.'

Olivia looked up and saw Sebastian standing next to Aurelia. He was looking at her with his piercing eyes and an enigmatic smile. He took Olivia's hand and led her out of the library and into a small room, beautifully decorated with rich patterned wallpaper, and a couch in the corner piled high with rugs and cushions.

He indicated she should lie down and began to massage her neck and shoulders. His supple hands moved over her skin, spreading a glowing warmth, and Olivia felt her whole body relax. It was as if she were floating, under his control, tingling with desire. She was sure Sebastian must feel it, but he didn't say anything, just continued to stroke and tease her body.

He moved down her arms, out to her fingers, then to her legs and toes. Her whole body felt alive, separate from her mind. It was a sensation unlike anything she'd ever felt before.

Sebastian straightened and spoke in his soft Irish tones. 'You are a beautiful, sensitive woman. You are your own person, and have complete control of your future, your body and your emotions. Don't allow the barriers of the past to stop you from achieving the happiness and fulfilment you deserve.'

Olivia felt rather than heard the words floating through her brain. She imagined making love to him. Her whole body wanted it. Was this what he was offering? Or was he talking in general, saying she should take control of her life?

She wasn't sure and didn't want to do the wrong thing to spoil the moment. She'd never been near another man since she'd married Christian and she'd never felt she wanted to, although he wasn't an exciting lover. She'd felt passion with Bill, but that had led to disaster. She pushed the thought of him away. She just wanted to float and luxuriate in the sensation of the moment. She drifted off to sleep.

When she opened her eyes, she was alone, with a cover over her. As she stirred, Tenzin came into the room, gave her an embroidered Chinese silk robe and led her to a sparkling shower room, with a shelf of gels, perfumes and thick fluffy towels. He walked respectfully away as she stood under the water, spreading the gel over her body, exulting in the memories of what had happened. Drying herself with the soft towel, she was surprised by the luxury of the bathroom and the fittings, and realised she'd only seen a very small part of the rambling old hotel and had no idea what the other rooms were like.

As she opened the door of the bathroom, Tenzin reappeared as if by magic at her side. He led her into the bedroom, where her clothes were all neatly folded. On a tray next to the bed there was more tea and a bowl of fruit.

Her handbag was lying next to the tray so she took out her phone and switched it back on. There were no messages. It was after four, but it didn't matter. Christian would phone in the evening, probably on her landline. She was free, in a parallel universe, where everything was possible.

Opening the bedroom door, she walked along a carpeted corridor. From behind one door she could hear music, so she pushed it open. Aurelia and Sebastian were sitting next to each other, talking. Sebastian gave a smile that made her stomach leap as Aurelia stood up and hugged her.

'My dear, I see the glow in your face and the sparkle in your eyes. Your healing process has started.' She reached over and picked up a book. The piercing eyes of her husband stared out from the cover. 'Take this book with you. I hope you will read it, but only if you want to. Everybody's journey is different. It can take a long time, or it can happen in a flash. What is important is that you have started, so you must come here as often as you wish.' She smiled and looked over at Sebastian. 'We will be waiting for you.'

Olivia hugged her and turned to Sebastian. She knew she'd be back soon. He smiled again and it hit her like a punch in her stomach. Her pulse rate soared, but she managed to walk calmly towards the door. 'Thank you so much, for everything. I'll read the book and I'll come back very soon if I may.'

Aurelia followed her to the door. 'Sleep well, my dear, and you are always welcome here. Think of this as your other home, your real home.'

It was already dark outside, a dense starless blackness because of the mist, but Olivia drove home in a dream.

Christian phoned soon after she arrived home. He described their journey and how good the snow conditions were. The children were settling in fine, although missing their mum, of course. Olivia hoped she gave a convincing performance of a loving mother left behind by her family, but she wasn't sure how good it was. They'd only been gone for twelve hours, but for her they'd already lost their substance, as if they were people she'd read about in a book.

She'd never spent a night alone in the house, and all the normal shadows and creaks of the wooden floorboards seemed sinister. Her heart raced when she saw a white face in the darkness of the window, until she realised it was her own reflection. Closing the shutters, she put the television on to drown out the sounds of the wind in the trees outside, and pulled Shadow onto her knee. His purring made the house seem less empty.

She went to bed early, but so many thoughts jangled in her mind, she couldn't sleep. Aurelia was right – she had to find her true self. She was playing a role; her whole life was keeping up an act and hoping nobody would find out she was an imposter.

When she'd first got married, she'd felt safe in Christian's love but she wasn't sure anymore. He'd decided very quickly to go away alone with the children. And he'd said she should be a proper wife and mother. She'd tried her best and if he thought she was failing, she had nothing left.

In the hotel, she felt relaxed and accepted. The whole place was filled with a warmth and glow that was more than physical. There was a magic there, an aura of peace, calm and love. She wanted to be part of it.

As the night dragged on, her dark dreams showed Sandra, lying alone, cold and frightened in a dark cellar. Olivia felt her presence so strongly, she knew she must be somewhere nearby. She had to find her. In a strange way, she knew doing this would be redemption for the terrible thing she'd done.

But where could she be? What about Rolf's bleak settlement? If a place could have an aura, that collection of cold, dark buildings was the very opposite of the hotel: hopelessness, desperation, sadness. Could Sandra be hidden near there? The mountains were honeycombed with a network of tunnels the military had built. The police said they'd been thoroughly searched, but in such a dark warren it could be easy to miss somebody. Perhaps there were secret entrances near Rolf's settlement that nobody knew about. He couldn't be the kidnapper, could he? He was a kind man, who'd spent his whole life doing good.

But what about Guy? Olivia remembered Aurelia's warnings. Why was Guy being so nice to her? What had caused a young man to kill himself? How did his business cause harm to children? Guy had charm, money and contacts. Where had he got his money from? Was he somehow involved in an international ring, smuggling children for rich clients?

Another image came to her mind that was more comforting, but still scary: Sandra with an adoptive family, playing happily. Or Sandra being abused by rich and powerful men who passed her around. No, it was unbearable. Olivia tried to blank the image from her mind and at last fell into a troubled sleep.

Chapter 38

Home alone

Wildenwil – Sunday 21 February, 2016

The next day dawned crisp and bright, with clear blue skies and sunlight sparkling on the frosty branches. The frightening images of the previous night melted away and seemed unreasonable as the low winter sun filled the kitchen with light. She really did read too many novels. She had to stop her imagination running away with her in this wild way.

She remembered Aurelia's wise words. She had to relax and enjoy this freedom, time for herself, to find herself. It was Sunday, not a good day to visit Julian. She wanted to see him by himself, away from Guy, so she'd go on Monday. She needed to see Guy too, to find out the results of the paternity test, but after Aurelia's warnings she felt wary. Could she trust him? Guy had promised the results next week, saying he knew the company well.

She made a cup of coffee and opened the kitchen door. The air was cold, but the sunshine made it seem warmer. What a beautiful view and what a lovely house! However, despite living here for more than ten years, she felt it had the atmosphere of a beautiful holiday house. Her soul wasn't here. The image of the book-lined room in the hotel came back to her; that was where she felt she belonged.

She remembered the book Aurelia had given her and, finding it in her bag, took it out to read. The print was small and dense, but the thick band of glossy paper in the centre suggested a lot of photos.

The first picture was a black and white one of Aurelia and her husband. She was young and slim, but her smile was the same. How old must she be now? About seventy, Olivia guessed, so the picture must be getting on for fifty years old. The Master stood beside her, tall and charismatic, with magnetic eyes that seemed to spring out of the photograph.

The next picture was the one she'd seen before of Sebastian, a beautiful child with long hair, high cheekbones and full lips. Olivia's heart gave a lurch as she looked at it. She felt a pang of regret she hadn't known him then, a strange nostalgia for a dream life where they would have met earlier.

There were other photos too, many of them with Sebastian and other young people, both boys and girls. The photos seemed to have been taken in different places and countries, many of them outside, of young people smiling as they worked in fields, eating meals at long tables. The Master was in nearly every picture, his arm casually round the shoulders of different women. Aurelia was in fewer but whenever she was, she was gazing adoringly at her husband.

Olivia read the text, wanting to know more about the community, but found it hard going. It was written in a flowery, almost Biblical style, and was about philosophy and theories rather than a narrative. Olivia was disappointed. She wanted to know their story, rather than the ideology. She would ask Aurelia next time she went.

Olivia put the book to one side and picked up her Kindle. She'd just downloaded the latest book in a crime series by one of her favourite authors, but found she was reading the same page over and over again without taking anything in. There was a missing child in the book, but she couldn't lose herself in the plot – her mind kept coming back to the tragedy in her own life. Putting down the Kindle, she walked to the window. It was a beautiful day, like a Christmas card, with a pure blue sky, the sun shining on the snow, and branches of the trees heavy with snow. A perfect day to go for a walk through the forest, to breathe the crisp winter air and see the ice crystals sparkling in the air.

She dressed in her warmest clothes and reached the front door before she realised it wasn't what she wanted to do. She needed a dog, a reason to walk. She'd told Christian she'd look for a dog, but she felt too unsettled to do it; it was too great a commitment.

She stopped in shock. What was she saying? She was committed to her life. She tried to convince herself this was true, but almost without being conscious of it, she walked to her car and set off up the road towards the Grand Wildenbach Hotel. If she'd been honest with herself, she'd have admitted it was always where she was going. Although it was less than twenty-four hours since she'd left the hotel, she was aching to return.

When she parked outside, she saw a white van by one of the outbuildings. She'd seen it before and had assumed it belonged to some tradesmen. Seeing the quality of the workmanship in the bathroom the day before, she knew they must be good.

As usual, the door of the hotel opened as she approached. Now she knew the contents of the hotel were so sophisticated, she wondered if there was some kind of sensor to warn them when people came near. Aurelia stood waiting for her.

Aurelia welcomed her and led her into the dining room. Tenzin appeared as if by magic with a cup of the familiar tea. Olivia drank it, now enjoying the taste and warm sensation of the spices.

Aurelia smiled. 'When you're ready, you can tell me why you came.'

Olivia didn't really know herself. 'I felt restless at home, but I feel calm here. It's the only place I feel safe, truly at home. The life I knew is falling apart. I'm sad Julian is growing away from me so completely, and terrified the same thing will happen with Marc and Lara. I try my best, but I'm beginning to think I don't know how to be a good mother. I didn't have a real mother, and perhaps that has ruined me, and I can't be one myself.'

'Olivia, my dear girl. You are a wonderful mother, but sometimes part of being a good mother is also knowing when to let go. Julian has been with you all his life, but he's a young man, becoming aware of his own identity, and although his father is a flawed person, you cannot stop Julian from seeing him. It's better he finds out himself what his father's really like.'

Aurelia looked thoughtful. 'Your other children are younger and you can still guide them. It's your duty to protect them from what is ugly and wicked in the world around us. That is the greatest gift we can give to them.'

'But it's sometimes so difficult to protect them. Think of Sandra...' Olivia hesitated for a moment and then told Aurelia about her feeling that Sandra was still alive and that she must save her to find herself.

Aurelia looked at her. 'You're very sensitive. Maybe this need to save Sandra is because you are worried about your own daughter. Concentrate on her. This is a difficult world, especially for girls. There are pressures from society, from social media. You read about very young girls concerned about their bodies, their image, who are sexualised by evil men. Do your best for your daughter, allow her to be a child for as long as possible.'

'Lara is still a little girl. Christian says I baby her, but I want her to enjoy her childhood, to have happy memories, not like mine.'

'I know you'll do the right thing for your little girl. I feel her aura very strongly through you, and I know she will grow up to be a wonderful young person. You will help her by discovering the person you are and being true to yourself. She will thrive with your happiness.'

Aurelia stood up. 'I must go now as I have a meeting with some of the other members of our community. I hope when you feel ready, you will be able to join us at our meetings. I know they will help you.'

Olivia nodded. She was disappointed Aurelia was leaving her, and she hadn't seen Sebastian but, as always, she felt invigorated by contact with this remarkable woman. When Aurelia was speaking, she felt strong and certain about the future, and she believed in herself for the first time in her life.

Aurelia showed her to the front door and Olivia was surprised to see it was dark already. The time seemed to go so quickly in the hotel. She drove down the road slowly, seeing the first stars twinkling between the trees.

Chapter 39

Swiss National Day

Wildenwil – Sunday 1 August, 2004

Lucy sat at the long wooden table in front of the Keller farmhouse and looked over the flower-covered meadows to the mountains on the other side of the valley. It was 1 August, Swiss National Day, a holiday when families get together to celebrate the foundation of the Swiss Confederation in 1291. The sun was shining and the sky was pure blue.

She fell in love with Wildenwil that day. Christian had invited Julian and her to spend the summer on the farm with his family and, although she'd only accepted at first to get as far away as possible from what had happened in Edinburgh, it was the best holiday she'd ever had. She could relax with a book in the fresh mountain air, walk up to the impressive peaks or explore the beautiful cobbled streets of Zug Old Town.

The farmhouse was surrounded by meadows with long-lashed Swiss cows, where Julian could run free with the many sons from the neighbouring farm. Christian's father told jokes in the little English he'd acquired working in a hotel in England, and his mother cooked simple but delicious meals from the vegetables she grew in the garden and meat from neighbouring farms.

Christian was sitting proudly between his parents, introducing the young teacher he'd met while he was doing his year as a language assistant in Scotland to his brother and sister. Although some Swiss were suspicious of foreigners, Christian's siblings were educated and well-travelled; his brother Rolf worked for an international children's charity and was on leave from Somalia, his sister Marlene was a lawyer working for the Swiss government in Berne, and the whole family was witty, open-minded and welcoming.

They all sat at the long table on the grass in front of the house, as Christian grilled meat and sausages. His father proposed a toast and they raised a glass of wine for Switzerland's birthday. Lucy looked across at the mountains in the distance and thought she had never been in such a beautiful place. As she watched Julian running in the long grass with the boys from the farm, while she drank red wine and ate steaks from the grill, she felt more at ease than she could ever remember.

That night they watched the glow of the bonfires on the mountain tops and saw fireworks scatter over the dark skies in the distance. Lucy didn't want to leave. So when Christian came shyly to her bedroom and asked her to marry him, she only hesitated for a moment before saying yes. He held her close and sobbed into her shoulder, 'I love you. I love you so much.'

Lucy knew she'd done the right thing. In Edinburgh, she hadn't really appreciated Christian's qualities because of her infatuation with Bill. Here, she felt safe, enveloped by his love, and realised how genuine he was – solid, honourable and dependable. He'd be an excellent father for Julian, and thinking of what she'd left behind in Edinburgh, the security of this ordered Swiss life was seductive. She was determined to make a success of their marriage, because for the first time in her life she felt truly loved.

The next day, Christian proudly told his parents they were going to marry. Although a single parent from Scotland with a five-year-old son could hardly have been their ideal choice of partner for their youngest son, they welcomed her. Christian couldn't take the smile off his face. He beamed as he introduced her to his old school friends, his fellow students at the University of Zürich and his old colleagues from his compulsory military service.

One evening after dinner, Lucy and Christian walked hand in hand up the lane, watching the beautiful azure glow of the dusk behind the dark silhouette of the mountains while the first stars appeared. Christian stopped and drew Lucy close to him. Kissing her tenderly he said, 'I love you so much. You've made me happier than I could ever have dreamed possible.'

Lucy held him close, feeling a happiness she'd never known before.

Christian then stepped back and cleared his throat, looking slightly embarrassed. 'There's just one thing.' He hesitated as if he'd thought better of it and then carried on. 'I don't quite know how to say this...'

Lucy felt a tinge of disquiet. What was he going to say? Was her newfound happiness going to be shattered?

Christian looked solemn. 'The thing is I really don't like the name Lucy.'

Lucy laughed. Was that all? 'Why not?'

'The thing is, I've always hated it, but I never felt I could mention it before. Lussi is a surname in this area and is pronounced in exactly the same way. There was an awful boy in my class at school called Thomas Lussi, a cheat and a bully. Every time I hear your name, I think of him, and I don't want you to be Lucy Keller. Your second name is Olivia. I love that name and think it suits you so much better. May I call you Olivia?'

Lucy smiled and hugged him. Olivia Keller – that was perfect. A new name and a new life. She'd already changed her name once, and now it was time to do it again, to leave all the problems of her old life behind and disappear in Switzerland. She hugged him. 'I love the name Olivia Keller, Christian, and I can't wait for it to be officially mine.'

Christian looked like a little boy who'd just been given a sack full of sweeties. 'I love you, Olivia Keller!' he shouted, and the echo bounced off the cliffs and faded into the distance.

Lucy smiled. It sounded right and it suited her perfectly. The name change would make it impossible for anybody to trace her and she could start a completely new life.

Christian held her in his arms. 'You have made me happier than I could ever have imagined. I can't wait for you to be my wife and live the rest of our lives here.' He took her hand and they floated down the lane towards the warm lights of the farmhouse. Through the window, she saw Julian sitting on the floor playing with the old farm dog and she knew this was the right thing to do.

When they told Julian about the engagement, he was pleased he could stay in Switzerland. The farmer up the hill let him drive his tractor and Julian had become tanned and fit playing outside in the mountain sunshine. The only thing he'd asked for was his own dog. Christian had been pleased to agree and a few weeks later, Bella had arrived, an adorable bundle of black, white and brown fluff.

The new Olivia threw herself into her Swiss life with enthusiasm. She hadn't felt at all guilty about resigning from the job she'd been allocated Edinburgh, in a sink estate comprehensive known mainly for the number of nervous breakdowns suffered by the staff. Christian had driven over with a van to collect her things from her flat while she'd stayed in Switzerland with his parents, learning to cook from his mother. She loved the fact she could spend time with her son, playing with him and being a real mum, after all the years of being a single parent and working full-time. She was tired of that life, being responsible for everything, and the thought of Christian making the decisions and looking after her was very appealing.

As she walked with Bella and watched the leaves on the deciduous trees turn golden brown and red, she was amazed how easy it had been to leave her old life behind and she revelled in her new one.

Chapter 40

Visits

Wildenwil – Monday 22 February, 2016

Olivia woke up after another night of swirling dreams. She'd been taken back to when she first visited Switzerland, when it had seemed like paradise and she was surrounded by Christian's love. Now everything was tainted. Sandra's disappearance overshadowed everything and the notes had still not been explained. The thought that somebody out there knew what had happened in Scotland meant she didn't feel safe anymore.

She shuddered as she remembered the loneliness of her childhood, and the way she'd been rejected by everyone, by her birth mother, by her adoptive parents, and the isolation of being a single mother. Now she was afraid that Christian was growing away from her. He'd taken the children away and she felt abandoned and isolated in a foreign country.

The hotel was the only place she felt safe and, apart from Aurelia, she didn't know who to trust. The pull of Guy's charm was strong, as it had been that first time in St Andrews. But she couldn't trust him. Everything had started to go wrong when he arrived in Switzerland.

There was so much she didn't know about him. Had he sent the notes? He said his investigator had found out everything about her. What was his business that harmed children and had driven a young man to suicide? Sandra had disappeared just when he arrived. Was he involved with that? And Julian was with him. Was he safe?

She suddenly needed to see Julian, know that he was safe. She sent him a text to make sure he was around and alone because she didn't want to see him with Guy there.

When there was no reply, she panicked. Where could he be? Despite what Aurelia had said, she had to contact Guy. He'd know where Julian was.

Guy immediately replied. *'J at home but could be sleeping. I'm in my office. How about lunch in L'Escargot?'*

Overcome with relief, Olivia realised that she was being stupid. Of course, Julian was sleeping. He was a teenager and it was the school holidays. She had to curb her imagination. Being alone with her nightmares was making her lose her grip on reality.

She set off for Zug, stopping in the village to buy some croissants for Julian. Just as she was paying in the bakery, she caught sight of the grey-haired woman standing on the other side of the road, watching her. She didn't look as dishevelled as the previous times, and Olivia wondered again if she was something to do with the hotel. She'd first appeared in the village about the same time as they moved in and Olivia now knew there were more members there than she'd thought at first.

Ignoring the woman, Olivia drove down the hill to Zug. The old town was looking beautiful, with the clear winter sunlight casting shadows in the narrow streets and sparkling on the coloured roof tiles. She was looking forward to speaking to Julian. She was amazed how lonely she felt after being on her own for such a short time.

She found a parking place just outside Guy's building and rang the doorbell with a feeling of optimism. There was no reply. Looking up to the penthouse, she couldn't see any sign of life. She rang again and when there was still no answer, took out her mobile and phoned her son's number. After a pause, there was a sleepy grunt in reply.

'Julian, I need to talk to you. Can you let me in?'

The buzzer sounded and she pushed the door open and went to the lift. It took her up to the top floor where Julian was standing, wearing a t-shirt and boxers and rubbing his eyes. 'I thought I might at least be able to get a lie-in this morning when I don't have to go to school.'

Olivia looked at her watch. 'It's nearly midday. Hardly crack of dawn.'

Julian shrugged. 'Do you want a coffee or something?'

Olivia nodded and held up the bag of croissants. Julian disappeared into the kitchen, there was a whirr from the coffee machine and then he came back with two cups. He handed Olivia one and sat down on the long sofa. 'Haven't you gone away this week? I thought Chris had organised a family ski holiday?'

Olivia explained the others had gone without her, without giving any details. Julian looked puzzled, but didn't ask any questions. Olivia was determined to be positive, avoiding any topic that would cause tension. 'Great you've got a week's holiday. Any plans?'

Julian yawned and picked up his phone. He was staring at the screen as he answered. 'Just going to chill for a couple of days and then I'm going up to Verbier with some of the guys for snowboarding and partying. Ivo's family have a chalet there.'

Olivia nodded. She hadn't heard of Ivo before, but Julian's friends seemed to change every week. Julian tapped on his phone. 'So, how's school going?' she asked, keeping her voice as neutral as possible.

'Fine. A bit of the pressure's off me as I know I can work with Dad full-time when I've done my Matura.' He looked up from his phone. 'Don't worry, I'm definitely going to pass – Dad's seeing to that. It's a lot easier living so close to the school. I don't waste so much time travelling every day.'

Olivia felt hurt that living up in Wildenwil was dismissed so lightly, but she was determined not to show it. 'Are you already working with...' She hesitated. She couldn't bring herself to say 'your dad' but fortunately Julian answered before she had to finish her sentence.

'Yes, mainly with translation at the moment, but it helps to get to know the business. And when I'm finished with school, I'll be able to travel. That's what I'm really looking forward to.'

Olivia wondered how to phrase the next question. She didn't want to antagonise Julian, knowing how easily he flew off the handle, but she had to find out about the business. 'I know you were a bit upset about some of his business practices at one time. About children being harmed?'

Julian flung down his phone. 'There you go again, trying to undermine my happiness.' His face was dark with anger. 'Just get it into your head. I'm living with my dad. He understands me in a way you and Chris never did. He's a wonderful businessman, with different interests all over the world, and he is giving me the chance to be something more than I'd ever be stuck in Wildenwil.'

'But the suicide, the letter…'

'That was some snowflake just trying to cause trouble. A total loser given a chance here in Switzerland, but he couldn't hack it. Nothing to do with the business, everything to do with him.' Julian picked up his phone and moved towards what Olivia guessed was his bedroom door. 'This has got nothing to do with you. I'm tired and I'm on holiday.' As he reached the door, he turned. 'Close the door quietly when you go please.'

That went well, thought Olivia as she went down in the lift. She'd hoped Julian would have grown up being with Guy, but she saw he was just the same grumpy adolescent he'd been before. She reached her car and took out her phone, looking again at the message from Guy. She had to speak to him, find out what he had to do with harming children, but she didn't feel up to it today. She sent a text message: '*Sorry, can't make lunch today, but how about tomorrow? Any idea about when the DNA result will come?*'

Her phone immediately rang. It was Guy. 'Sorry, I can't do tomorrow. Some business out of town. Sure you can't make it today?'

'Sorry.' Olivia got a perverse pleasure putting him off. Guy gave the impression of always getting what he wanted. 'Any idea about the result of the test?'

'I'll put a bit more pressure on them. They owe me a favour so they'll do it quickly.'

'Thanks.'

'But I have to say again, I don't think it's urgent at all. I can't see any chance of this mad fantasy of yours coming true.'

'I know it sounds unlikely, but I feel an affinity with Stevie. He's the right age, he was in the right place at the right time, according to what I was told, and we look like each other.'

'I can understand why you want this to be true, but I just don't want you to be disappointed.'

'That's for me to deal with. So the sooner I know the better. Can you phone me when you know the result and then we can meet up?'

She ended the call, wondering what to do next. Perhaps she could visit Stevie? Finding his number in the contact list she sent a text: '*How are you?*' She didn't write any more in case Priska saw the text. She could see he was kept on a very short leash and didn't want to get him into trouble.

There was no reply. Feeling disappointed, she realised Stevie was who she really wanted to see. Feeling at a loose end, she decided to buy something easy for lunch and have a lazy afternoon.

She was just looking round the Spar when she felt her phone vibrate. A message. Taking her phone out of her bag, she saw it was from Stevie: '*PP's away. Can you come this afternoon and bring goodies?*'

Olivia smiled and added some sweets and biscuits to her basket. It was always fun with Stevie.

She drove up to Stevie's house and pressed the button at the gate. This time it opened automatically and she drove in. Stevie was standing on the terrace in front of the double-decker conservatory.

As she got out of the car and came closer, she was shocked by his appearance. His complexion looked greyer and more wrinkled than she remembered, and his eyes were pink-rimmed and puffy. He held his arms out to hug her.

'Great you could come today. PP is at some trade fair in Italy so I've got time to myself.' Olivia followed him into the winter garden and handed over the plastic bag of sweets and biscuits. He grabbed them and hurried towards the metal door she knew led to his studio. Like last time, he unlocked it and stowed the bag inside.

'Sorry, hospitality might not be up to our normal standards as it's Concetta's day off.' He smiled and a flash of his usual charm showed on his lined face.

'It's quite all right. I've just had lunch,' Olivia answered, her normal politeness kicking in. She smiled. 'But I'd love to see more of the house. Perhaps if there's nobody here I could have a little look round?'

'Of course. But haven't you seen all the glossy mags? I didn't think there was anybody in the land who wasn't familiar with every perfect room. PP did a great publicity job.' He sat down, looking weary. 'She's got an idea about launching a range of interior design fabrics and this house is her main advertisement. There are photos all over Instagram and Facebook. Haven't you seen them?'

Olivia shook her head. 'I don't really get this social media stuff.'

'Neither do I, but PP is a wizard at it. Self-promotion was always her speciality. I sometimes wonder if I am just another way to raise her profile.' He laughed. 'But, unfortunately, I'm a big failure in that regard. That's why she's always on at me to complete my album.'

'How's it getting on?'

'About the same as last time we talked.' He leant towards her and whispered, 'Which means zilch.' He straightened himself up. 'There, I've said it. I haven't admitted it to anybody, but I have no ideas, no creativity left, and mostly no interest. I just go to the studio to get away from the relentless round of fitness and improvement.'

He stood up. 'You wanted to look round the house. Come and see it, the most beautifully designed prison in the land.'

Olivia stood up and followed as Stevie guided her round the building. She had to keep her admiration muted as Stevie so obviously hated it, but she loved it. The rooms were high and airy, and everything was in beautiful taste. The fabrics in the curtains and bed covers were bold and original. Olivia thought if Priska really had designed them herself, she had considerable talent.

They finished the tour with the indoor pool, which was lined in cool-blue tiles, with one wall of glass looking out over the stunning views into the valley. 'It's amazing!' Olivia gasped. How could Stevie not like this?

But then she realised she was the same. She had a beautiful house, not quite on this scale, but comfortable and full of character. She could appreciate it, but she didn't feel it was her home. It must be the same for Stevie. He'd been an ordinary working-class boy from Wigan who'd achieved fame through his music and been catapulted into another world, of beauty queens and designer houses.

'Yes, it is amazing. But to tell you the truth, when I look back to the grotty squats, the dingy hotel rooms we stayed in when we were touring, I wish I were there again.'

He turned to Olivia and she saw the sadness in his eyes. 'Growing old is hell. My body is falling apart, despite all my diets and exercise. I can't sleep because I'm haunted by so many memories, and I'm living a lie here. I don't want to be old, surrounded by old people; I loved being young, surrounded by young girls.' He stared out of the window. 'When I first met Priska I fell for her because she was young, fresh and soft. Now she's hard and sinewy, in body and mind. I don't know how long I can stand it.'

Olivia looked at him, but he seemed to have forgotten she was there. She tried to think of something positive to say, but couldn't think of anything so she changed the subject.

'Can I help you with your music? You said I was your muse. We could work together and produce something. That would make you feel better, and make things easier with Priska. You said before she'd saved your life.'

Stevie shook out of his reverie. 'You're right, Oli. I'm sorry. You've been great, but I'm just not in the mood at the moment.'

'Can I see your recording studio? I used to write poetry when I was young and they said I had a good singing voice. We could work together.' *And, if you are my father, perhaps I've inherited some of your talent.*

'No. Nobody comes into my studio. I told you before,' Stevie said sharply. 'I'm always saying to PP, a man has to have a space to be himself, to be private.'

Stevie stopped himself and turned to Olivia. 'I'm sorry, I'm just on edge. Priska wants me to join her in Milan at this design fair. I really don't want to go. You know I haven't left this house for more than a few hours for months. I need to be here.'

Stevie looked at her, his red-rimmed eyes sad. 'I've just got into a mess here, and I don't know how to extricate myself.'

Olivia moved towards him. 'You know, anything I can do to help I will. Do give me a ring if you need to talk and I'll be here. I have a week off too.'

'Thanks, Oli, my pal. I appreciate that, but I'm the only one who can sort this out.' He gave her a stiff hug. 'Thanks for the sweeties, and sorry I haven't been better company.'

Olivia hugged him back. 'Just remember, I'm here for you.'

She drove away with a feeling of emptiness. What was Stevie so upset about? Why wouldn't he let her in the cellar? Could he be hiding something there?

A picture came to her, of Sandra in the cellar. Olivia shook her head. It was ridiculous. One minute she thought Stevie was her father, the next that he was hiding Sandra in his cellar. Perhaps Christian was right and she was going a bit crazy.

Olivia felt jangled and confused, and without making a conscious decision, felt her car driving towards the hotel. She wanted somewhere to feel safe.

Chapter 41

Lunch with Guy

Wildenwil – Tuesday 23 February, 2016

The next day was bright again. The low winter sun sparkled off the snow and bathed the kitchen with light. It also showed up the dirt on the windows, but Olivia ignored it. The old Olivia would have immediately cleaned them, wanting everything sparkling before Christian returned, but the new Olivia didn't care. She was filled with a mixture of lethargy and restlessness, in a state of suspended animation, waiting for something to happen.

The day before, she'd been comforted by her visit to the hotel as usual. Aurelia listened to what Olivia said about Stevie and explained he was a flawed individual, damaged by the experiences of his youth. She told Olivia not to put her hopes in him as he would hurt her like all the other men in her life. Not all men were like that, she emphasised, but Olivia had to find the right one.

When Aurelia said this, Olivia's thoughts flew to Sebastian. She was disappointed he wasn't around again. Just thinking of him made her heart flutter like a teenager.

She was sitting at the kitchen table with her coffee, flicking through the local paper to see if there was any more news about Sandra, when her phone pinged. It was a message from Guy. *'Plans changed. Can you make L'Escargot at 12.30 today? I need to speak to you.'*

Olivia jumped up. The day suddenly seemed brighter. She needed to talk to Guy and, she had to admit, lunch at L'Escargot wouldn't be bad either. As she looked out her nicest dress to go down to the restaurant, she was shocked at her superficiality. She didn't recognise this person she'd become: excited about going out to lunch in a posh restaurant, worried about her appearance, not the earth mother she imagined herself to be.

When she arrived at L'Escargot, a waiter immediately showed her to the prime table in the curved window looking out over the lake. Guy stood up and kissed her on the cheek before pulling out her chair. He was wearing a beautifully cut dark suit and a crisp white shirt. Olivia had to admit he looked very dashing.

'You're looking beautiful, Olivia. Thank you so much for joining me.'

'You've got my name right at last,' Olivia noticed with pleasure.

'Yes, you're right about your name. I realise you're not the adorable, innocent and naive Lucy, but Olivia – sophisticated, intelligent and self-assured.' Guy smiled over the table, which was laid with a gleaming white tablecloth and sparkling glasses.

Olivia smiled to herself at the exaggeration and, although she'd told herself she must be wary of his charm, she couldn't help feeling a bit flattered. A young waitress appeared with a bottle of white wine in a silver bucket and poured some into Guy's glass for him to taste. He sipped it and nodded, indicating Olivia's glass. She put her hand over it.

'None for me, thanks. I'm driving.'

'One glass won't do you any harm.' He smiled as Olivia uncovered her glass, before adding. 'Or you could drink the bottle and stay with Julian and me. We have plenty of spare bedrooms and you are free of domestic responsibilities for a week.'

Olivia actually considered it for a moment, but then common sense took over. 'I don't think that would be a very good idea.'

He raised his glass. 'I hope this will be the first of many lunches together.'

'I can only do this because the children are away on their ski holiday. Otherwise I always have to be at home at lunchtime.'

Guy smiled confidently. 'I'm sure we can work something out. You deserve a bit of spoiling. You've done such a wonderful job with Julian, and your other two delightful children, but you're still a young woman and must not allow yourself to become old before your time.'

Olivia protested. 'I'm not old before my time, and I'm very happy.'

'With a husband who's trying to push you into a box, making you conform to his rules.'

Olivia bristled. 'You don't know anything about me or my husband.'

'I've seen you two together and there's zero chemistry. And Julian has told me a few things about your marriage.'

'He's a teenage boy. What does he know about relationships?' Olivia felt annoyed on her husband's behalf. 'Christian is a good man, a good father, a wonderful teacher...'

Guy smiled. 'And an exciting husband.' He paused. 'I notice you didn't say that.'

He reached over and put his hand on top of hers. 'I know I behaved very badly when we were young, but I've regretted it ever since. I've said this to you before but I'll say it again because I want you to believe me. I'd been watching you since our first year, and had been entranced by your beauty, modesty and intelligence. The only thing that stopped me asking you out earlier was that I'd heard you had a boyfriend. And you were so beautiful and intelligent – I thought you were too good for me. It was only when I found out the boyfriend was history that I plucked up the courage to ask you out for dinner.'

Olivia took a sip from her glass and watched him. Part of her wanted to believe him.

Guy looked into her eyes. 'I remember everything about that night. You were delightful, sparkling, talked about books, and I fell in love with you. And then we went for a drive.' He paused and raised his glass. 'I was such a boor that night. I really thought you wanted it as much as me. Your body responded and I just got carried away. I am so sorry. When I realised it was your first time, I didn't know how to act. I'd never been with a virgin before. I was a stupid, insensitive fool. If only I could turn back the clock and play that evening so differently.'

Olivia didn't know what to think. He seemed so sincere. Guy lowered his eyes and carried on. 'Afterwards, I thought you hated me, and I was too ashamed to approach you. I was angry at myself for blowing my chance with the sweetest and most beautiful woman I'd ever met. I threw myself into a glitzy superficial life, but I was never really happy. I didn't know it then, but what I wanted was a family. What I wanted was you.'

He looked up at her again. 'When I discovered I had a son, I knew then what I'd been looking for all my life. I want to be with you, to be a family. I'd like your other children to be with us too.'

Olivia stared at him in amazement. 'I was almost fooled for a moment, but then I came to my senses. Are you so arrogant, so insensitive, that you don't realise I have a wonderful family life that I would never jeopardise for your slick platitudes?'

Guy looked apologetic. 'I can understand why you feel like this, Olivia, and I deserve every word of what you're saying. But I really mean it, and I'm going to prove to you I'm sincere. I'm not going away. I'm based here in Switzerland now, and Julian is the most important thing in my life. I have money, more than I know what to do with, and I will give him everything he needs.'

Olivia opened her mouth, but Guy carried on. 'I know what you're going to say. I know I can't buy love. I'm not going to spoil him. He'll have to work, but I'll give him the best financial foundation and he will be wealthy.'

'But what is your business? How do I know it isn't something unethical, immoral or illegal, something I wouldn't like my son involved in? You never give any details, and I know you have at least one man's blood on your hands. How do I know you don't have others? How do I know you're not involved in people trafficking, or something worse?' She felt her voice getting shriller and wondered if she was going too far, but she had to know the truth.

Guy looked genuinely hurt. 'Olivia, you can't think so badly of me. I've explained before that Jeff's unfortunate death was not really anything to do with his work and everything to do with his personal problems. However, I do owe you an explanation. I want you to understand.'

He paused and, looking at the half-empty bottle, picked up the menu. 'We should order some food before we get another bottle of wine. I can highly recommend the salmon trout, fresh from Lake Zug.'

Olivia nodded. She enjoyed this local fish delicacy but thought it typical of Guy that he, who'd only been in Switzerland for a matter of months, was giving her tips on the local specialities.

The waiter took their order and refilled their glasses. Olivia found herself drinking automatically as Guy began his story. 'Have you heard of jatropha?'

When Olivia shook her head, Guy explained it was a plant that had been recognised as a source of biofuel, because oil could be made from the seeds. It was especially attractive because it seemed to thrive on marginal lands unsuitable for cultivation of foodstuffs. 'Jeff was very keen on this and saw it as a chance for poor farmers to grow a crop on their unproductive land and get an income. At the same time, biofuel was seen as the answer to environmental problems with fossil fuel. It also seemed to be a great opportunity for us to make money. Goldman Sachs and many other big players saw it as a sound investment.'

The fish came and Olivia started to eat as Guy continued to give more details about jatropha. The trout was delicious, and she was surprised how hungry she was. She drained her glass automatically and it was quickly filled by the attentive waiter. Guy was still explaining the properties of the plant, including the fact that, as it was poisonous, it was resistant to pests.

He was going into a lot of detail and Olivia wondered where it was leading. 'It all sounds very interesting, but I don't see what this had to do with Jeff.'

'We invested in a project in Indonesia. Jeff visited it for a couple of weeks to conduct the due diligence and encouraged many local families to plant it. Unfortunately, the early projections of success were not fulfilled. The plants took a long time to mature and, unless they were on fertile ground, the yield was very poor. Many families had stopped planting foodstuffs hoping to make more money and were hungry. This was bad enough, but the final tragic event, and what affected Jeff so badly, was that the fruit of the plants are sweet, but highly toxic. A group of school children ate them and although they were immediately taken to hospital, several of them died.'

'How awful!' Olivia gasped.

'It was a tragic accident, but because he'd encouraged families to grow jatropha, Jeff felt responsible. Of course, we immediately withdrew from this venture, but the deaths of the children preyed on Jeff's mind and he took his own life.'

Christian looked down sadly. 'Julian was shocked when he first heard about it, but when he learnt the truth, he was reassured. He has a very fine head on him – a credit to his mother. I hope you understand now what happened.'

Olivia nodded. What a terrible story. Those poor children. She could understand how it could tip a sensitive young man over the edge.

Guy finished his fish and leant towards her. 'I've been talking an awful lot about me. I want to know everything about you. You are so intelligent, one of the star students at St Andrews, and I heard you became an excellent teacher.'

Olivia felt herself blushing. Her teaching career had been less than stellar. She felt uncomfortable. 'I wouldn't say I was very successful as a teacher. But you seem to know an awful lot about me. You didn't ever send me an anonymous note, did you?'

Guy looked genuinely surprised. 'A note, no. Did somebody send you a note?'

'Er, yes, some kind of joke, I think. I just don't know who did it.'

'If it's upsetting you, give it to me. I still have my investigator, very effective, as you've discovered.'

Olivia smiled, feeling reassured that Guy could not have sent the note. 'Useful to know.'

She sipped another glass of wine, and looking out at the lake sparkling in the winter sun, she felt free. On a usual day, she'd be washing up after lunch with the children.

Guy was looking at her. 'Don't push me away because of the past. Please believe me when I say I love you. I'll always be here for you.'

Olivia laughed out loud. The wine was going to her head. Love! Guy was being ridiculous.

Guy waved to the waiter and asked for the dessert menu. Turning back to Olivia, he asked, 'Do you still read as much as you used to?'

Olivia was surprised at the change of subject. 'Yes, I do.'

'Tell me the best book you've read recently.' She hesitated. 'Olivia, we've got a lot of years of catching up to do. I want to find out everything about you.'

The rest of the afternoon passed in a blur. Olivia knew she was talking a lot, but Guy was interested, entertaining and attentive, and didn't make any more extravagant declarations.

As the light darkened over the lake, she realised they'd spent the whole afternoon in the restaurant.

Chapter 42
Lara

Olivia woke up with a headache; she didn't usually drink so much. Trying to piece together what had happened, she remembered she'd gone for lunch with Guy in L'Escargot and drunk far more than she should have. He'd made all sorts of crazy declarations, but she'd enjoyed the afternoon. It was good to feel attractive and interesting, and to eat fish and drink wine in a beautiful restaurant.

She sat up and her head swam. What was she thinking? A feeling of self-loathing washed over her. What was happening to her? She didn't recognise herself.

Guy had wanted her to go back to his flat but she'd refused, so he'd driven her back home. He didn't seem to have drunk nearly as much as her and made sure she was safely in the house before driving away.

Christian had phoned as usual, but she couldn't remember exactly what she'd said. Would he realise she'd been drinking? Her post-alcoholic depression kicked in more intensely. Olivia reached out to Shadow, the cat, who was curled up next to her on the bed. Stroking him, she was glad to feel the warmth of another living body next to her, because this morning she felt vulnerable, stuck in this isolated house without a car.

She saw her phone flashing on the bedside table – a message from Guy. '*Wonderful afternoon! Send a text when you wake and I'll come and get you. Breakfast on the terrace and you can collect your car.*'

Olivia was relieved because she'd felt lost without her car, but felt a little apprehensive about being alone with Guy again. She sent a message saying she'd be ready in half an hour and took a shower, hoping the water would calm her crashing headache.

It turned out to be a lovely morning. After two aspirins, she felt better, and Guy was charming. They sat on the terrace of his flat in the winter sunshine, looking out over the lake at the distant mountains. Julian had gone to Verbier with his friends, and they talked about his schoolwork, what was in the news. It was just like being normal parents, Olivia thought.

As it approached lunchtime, Guy looked at his watch. He had some work he had to do, but asked if she fancied going to the pizzeria on the corner for a quick Italian lunch. The idea of something garlicky did appeal to Olivia, but she didn't want Guy to feel he could organise all her time, so she invented things she had to do, and collecting her car, drove back to the house.

When she got home, she remembered Rolf's box of clothes still in the boot of her car and the note she'd left. Rolf would be expecting her so she should go to the smallholding and deliver it. But she told herself he might not be there again.

She realised she was making excuses because she really didn't want to go. The atmosphere was so creepy and frightening there. She'd wait until Christian came home and he could go.

But maybe Sandra was being kept there? Perhaps this would be her chance to rescue her?

Or was Stevie a more plausible suspect? Olivia's head was in turmoil. She didn't know what was real anymore. Everything was changing like a picture in a kaleidoscope. All the certainties in her life had fractured, her perceptions changing every moment. Like one of the pines in a winter storm, she was bending in all directions.

She didn't want to think badly of Stevie, but what was his mess? Why was he so secretive about his cellar? Who was he buying sweets for? She'd read on the Internet about men who had kept girls secret, hidden in cellars. Stevie wouldn't let anybody into his recording studio, which was certainly soundproofed. He'd admitted he'd been attracted to girls when he was younger, and all the girls he had married were small, slight, childlike. Priska still had a youthful air.

Olivia looked at her Kindle. Maybe she did read too many crime novels. Perhaps she was just unable to accept Sandra was probably dead or far away. Was she clinging on to this feeling Sandra was nearby just because the alternative was too painful to contemplate?

She opened the kitchen door and looked around the beauty of the landscape. Her stomach churned and her head was spinning. Was it still the alcohol she'd drunk the day before or was she becoming delusional? In a state of confusion, she got into her car and drove up to the only place she felt really safe – to Aurelia and the hotel.

The hotel looked much less sinister bathed in the spring sunshine and, as she drove up the drive, she was surprised to see people working in the garden. There were young men and women she'd never seen before clearing dead plants and cutting back overgrown bushes.

One of them was Sebastian. When he saw her, he gave a quick look back to the house and ran to the car. She stopped and rolled down the car window.

'Olivia, I'm so glad to see you. I've missed you.'

Olivia felt her heart pounding. Sebastian looked wonderful in his high boots and green loden jacket, his cheeks flushed with the exertion. 'I've been up here a couple of times. I was disappointed not to see you.'

Sebastian looked back to the house again. 'Actually, Aurelia has been keeping me away. She could see how attracted I was to you, and warned me about getting too close. She said you were in a vulnerable state at the moment.'

Olivia was thrilled to hear him say he was attracted to her – she hadn't been wrong about the chemistry between them – but she felt a surge of annoyance towards Aurelia.

She was wondering how to reply when Sebastian moved away. 'I'd better get back to work.' Olivia looked over at the house and saw the door was open, the first time she'd seen this. Aurelia was standing there, enveloped in her usual caftan and wearing a scarf round her scarlet hair.

As Olivia parked in the normal place, Aurelia walked towards her. Olivia expected her to say something about Sebastian, but she smiled and said, 'This beautiful weather raises our spirits, doesn't it? We've finished the main renovations inside so we're starting to prepare the grounds. By summer, everything should be ready. Come this way. There's something I'd like to show you.'

Olivia followed as Aurelia walked round the barn to a maze of outbuildings. One was a stable, with a splendid roof and balcony. 'In its heyday, guests arrived by horse and carriage so the stables were very important. The coachmen and grooms could sleep up above the stables and keep an eye on their horses.'

Olivia saw a movement and a black head. 'Have you got a horse?'

'Two. Come and have a look.' Aurelia led Olivia to the stables and opened a door. Two Shetland ponies stood looking at her with huge eyes.

'We're going to start a small farm – a couple of cows, some goats and sheep, hens. We are aiming to be self-sufficient as far as we can. I must admit the ponies are a self-indulgence. When I was a child, I always wanted a pony, and now, aged seventy-one, my dream has finally come true.'

Olivia reached over and stroked the silky manes. The ponies were adorable. Aurelia took two apples from her pocket and the ponies ate them with their soft mouths. 'I'm sure your little girl would love these. You can bring her up to see them sometime.'

Olivia looked at Aurelia in surprise. That very thought had just gone through her mind. Perhaps Aurelia really was a mind reader. Aurelia gave her usual knowing smile and led Olivia back to the house.

They went in a back door and through an enormous well-equipped kitchen. Three people she'd never seen before were working there. Olivia realised she'd only ever seen a tiny fraction of the building, which had dozens of bedrooms and other public rooms. She'd no idea how many people were living in the hotel.

Aurelia led her into a bright room looking out over the waterfall, with comfortable easy chairs facing the large windows. Because of the thaw, the icicles were melting and more water was crashing down the rocks. 'Olivia, I've brought you here because I feel it's time for you to learn more about us and meet some of the other members. I know you belong with us. I know the goodness of your soul. Our community is built on love and respect, for other people and for nature. If you want to know more about us, you can come to some of our meetings. It will help you.'

Olivia looked down at her hands. 'Aurelia, I've got something to tell you. I love this place and you. I feel safe here, and you understand me and believe in me in a way I've never known before. But I'm not good. I did a terrible thing. I've never told anybody about it, but I think you'll understand. The reason it's especially worrying me now is because I've been getting notes. I think somebody knows.'

Aurelia held her hands. 'You can tell me. Like you, I was brought up a Catholic and, although there is much I disagree with in this religion, I think confession is a very powerful tool. Like a priest, I do not judge and I will not share.'

Olivia was beginning to tell the story of that night in Edinburgh when her mobile phone rang. She usually put it on silent when she came into the house, but because Aurelia had come out to meet her, she'd forgotten.

She looked at it and saw it was from Christian. 'I'm sorry, can I take this? Chris would only phone during the day if it were really urgent.' She answered. 'Is everything all right?'

'Now don't worry, Livy, but we're in the hospital in Schwyz.'

'What? What's happened?' Olivia felt panic running through her whole body.

'Lara took a tumble and we've just had the X-ray. She's broken her wrist, and they're setting it now. Luckily it seems to be a clean break and she doesn't have to be operated on, but naturally she's a bit upset. She's asking for you.'

Olivia stood up, making her way towards the door as she spoke. 'I'm on my way. I'll be there as soon as possible.'

She looked back and explained to Aurelia what had happened. 'Of course, you must go, my dear. Is there anything I can get you, anything you need for the journey?'

'No, I don't need anything. I'll just go straight to the hospital.'

'Yes, go to your darling girl.'

Olivia ran to her car, found the address of the hospital, which she put in her satnav, and drove there as fast as she could.

Chapter 43

Hospital

Olivia stopped in the car park of the modern hospital and ran into the A&E department. She gave her name to the receptionist and was led into a side room where Lara was lying on a bed, her left arm encased in a plastic sheath. She looked pale but beamed when her mother came in. Christian was sitting at the side of the bed, and Marc was slouching on a plastic chair, playing a game on his iPad.

Olivia ran over and hugged Lara. Christian stood up and gave her a stiff kiss on the cheek. 'You can sit down here and have a chat with Lara. I'll take Marc down to the cafeteria to get something to eat. We missed lunch.'

Olivia was pleased to have some time alone with her daughter. After the boys had gone out, she stroked Lara's hair away from her brow and asked what had happened. Lara seemed remarkably chirpy. Olivia guessed she'd been given some painkillers and now seemed quite excited by the drama of it all.

'I was coming down a big, red slope and going really fast. But then a snowboarder turned in front of me and my skis crossed and I fell on my hand. It was so sore. But, Mummy, they came and collected me on a big sledge and then I went in a helicopter.'

'Wow, a helicopter. You must be really important.'

'They said it's the quickest way to get down the mountain. They were really nice and made me laugh. Said it was good my head hadn't fallen off.' Olivia laughed and felt the tension drain out of her as she realised it was not as bad as she'd feared. She was pleased the paramedics had been kind to Lara.

Lara couldn't stop chattering and told Olivia all about her ski instructor and the other children in the class. Olivia wondered if she realised it was the end of her skiing this season.

A nurse entered the room as Christian and Marc came back, saying she was going to do some checks to make sure Lara was ready to be discharged.

While Marc sat outside the room with his iPad, Christian leant towards his wife and whispered, 'I think you should take Lara back to Wildenwil tonight.'

Olivia was surprised. 'Aren't we all going?'

'I think it would be unfair on Marc if he misses the rest of the holiday. He's showing real promise in downhill racing and could do well in the race on Friday. The best place for Lara is in her own bed, though. And you're probably at a bit of a loose end stuck at home by yourself.'

Olivia's mouth fell open. It was typical of Christian to have made the decision without discussing it with her. 'It'll be late when we get back, and I'm not sure if I've got everything we need at home.'

'What have you been doing with yourself the past few days? I thought you'd have plenty of time to get things in order while we were away.'

Christian's assumption that she had nothing to do except clean the house annoyed her so much she told him what she'd been doing. 'Actually, I've been quite busy. I've had lunch at L'Escargot with Guy and seen Julian, but now he's away in Verbier with friends; I've visited Stevie; I went to Rolf's, but he wasn't there so I still have the box in my car; I've been talking to Aurelia at the hotel…'

Christian had been looking increasingly exasperated as she went through the list, but the mention of Aurelia seemed to particularly incense him. 'I've told you before to keep away from that woman. They're some kind of sect, and you've been peculiar ever since you met them. Do they know you haven't got any money? That's all they're interested in people for, to brainwash them and get them to give them all their money.'

'You don't know anything about them. They've never mentioned money, and anyway, they seem to have plenty. They've modernised the hotel really well. I think Aurelia's late husband was wealthy.'

'And how did he get his money? Olivia, you're not to go there again. They're dangerous people, who are having a terrible influence on you.' Christian's face darkened. 'And that pop star is another waster, hippy-dippy type. I don't know why you want to hang about with these people and won't have anything to do with the really nice young mothers in the village. I'm telling you now, Olivia, I don't want you or my children spending any more time with these unsavoury types.'

Olivia ignored the comment about Aurelia because she didn't want to make any kind of promise about not seeing her. 'But they're my friends.'

'You hardly know them. But I must say, Guy Montgomery seems to be having a good influence on Julian. My colleagues say his marks and attitude have improved recently.'

The nurse approached them, holding Lara's right hand. Her left arm had a bright blue band supporting it. 'Herr Keller. Your daughter is ready to leave now. Fortunately, it was a simple break and was treated quickly.' She handed over a large envelope. 'Please give this to your family doctor. It contains the X-rays and details of the accident and treatment. He will be able to deal with it from now on.'

Olivia thanked the nurse and took the envelope. 'We'll be going now,' she said to Christian coolly. Christian bent down and kissed Lara. 'I'll see you on Saturday. You take care and make sure you don't fall over and break the other arm. You won't be able to eat your dinner.' Lara laughed and moved towards the door.

Christian looked at Olivia. 'You'd better be getting back before it gets too dark. We'll be fine. It'll be good for Marc and me to have some boys' time together. You know what it's like for middle children. They do tend to get left out.'

Olivia gave a forced smile but was seething inside. Marc was in no way neglected, although Christian often suggested she favoured and spoiled Lara. Olivia bent down and gave her son a kiss. He looked up from his screen for a moment, but then his attention returned to his game. Olivia noticed Christian didn't make any move to kiss her so she took Lara's hand and waved before hurrying down to the car.

Chapter 44

A surprise

Thursday was another sunny morning. Olivia found herself singing as she made Lara's breakfast. It was nice to have somebody to look after. She'd been worried Lara wouldn't be able to sleep, but the nurse had given her some painkillers, and Lara had snuggled up with her cuddly toys and fallen asleep immediately.

'What would you like to do today?' Olivia asked, as her daughter drank her hot chocolate.

'I'd really like to go skiing, but I suppose I can't.'

'No, you'll have to wait a while before you can do that again. It'll be nice to play here with your toys and read your books.'

Lara took out her toys and books, but she soon became distracted. 'Mummy, I'm bored. Will you play with me?'

Olivia put down the duster and asked what she'd like to play. Lara chose Eile mit Weile, a board game they often played as a family. With only two players it was soon over, and Lara closed the board. 'It's no fun without the others. I want to play with somebody.'

Olivia wondered what she could do. Because the weather was so lovely, most of the other children in the village would be skiing. Even if they hadn't gone away for a ski week, they'd probably be making day trips to the nearest resorts. She realised she didn't know. After Sandra's disappearance, she'd lost contact with the other families. They'd been living in their own bubble.

'Can I watch a DVD?'

'No, it's lovely weather,' Olivia said automatically. 'Not until it's dark.'

Lara stuck out her bottom lip. 'There's nothing to do. I wish I was in Stoos with Daddy and Marc.'

What could she do? They couldn't go swimming with her arm bandaged. Going to the library probably wouldn't be considered very exciting. She was wracking her brains and then had an idea. Aurelia had said she should bring Lara to see the ponies. She probably didn't expect a visit so soon, but she knew about Lara's accident. They'd call by and if it wasn't convenient, they'd carry on up to Rolf's. Pleased she had a plan, Olivia told Lara they were going on an adventure, a magical mystery tour. Lara cheered up immediately and, after they'd dressed in their winter jackets, they got into the car.

At the hotel, they drove through the gates and saw there were young people working in the garden again. Olivia looked out for Sebastian, but couldn't see him. As they approached the door, Aurelia appeared like magic as usual. Olivia was now certain there was some kind of CCTV system that informed them of all arrivals.

Aurelia opened her arms wide and bent down to Lara's level. Lara looked a little apprehensive at first – Aurelia was certainly larger than life – but the older woman's wide smile and comforting voice soon won Lara over.

'Lara, my dear. I've been wanting to meet you for a long time and I'm so delighted you've come to visit us. How's your arm now?' Lara raised it, and Aurelia looked impressed. 'You've certainly got a lovely coloured bandage and it's great you can lift your arm so well. You must be a very clever girl.'

Aurelia turned to Olivia. 'Thank you so much for bringing her. I knew you would, but I didn't dare hope it would be so soon.' She ushered them into the hall. 'You can leave your bag and jackets here, and then we'll go and see the ponies.'

Lara looked excited as Aurelia led them along the corridors and into the kitchen where she picked up some apples and carrots before going to the stables. The two ponies, with their large liquid eyes peering out from their silky manes, moved towards them as they arrived.

Lara was thrilled to give them the food and when Aurelia asked if she'd like to ride one of them, Lara looked as though she would burst with excitement.

Olivia was worried. 'She's only got one arm. We don't want her to break the other one.'

'Don't worry. These are special child saddles. They don't even need to have one arm for these.' Aurelia called to a young girl who brought over two saddles.

'This one will be fine for you, Lara.'

Olivia didn't have the chance to say anything before Lara excitedly climbed onto the pony and was led round the arena. She was beaming.

'You're a natural. Have you been riding before?' Aurelia asked.

'Only at fairs and things. This is awesome. The pony is so cute.' Lara was delighted and stayed on as long as she could.

'We've got some other animals. They've just arrived.' Aurelia took Lara and Olivia into another stable where a long-haired goat stood patiently as three kids drank from her. The kids noticed them coming in and leapt onto bales of hay, wagging their tiny tails. Lara was entranced. 'Can I touch them?'

Aurelia nodded and Lara ran towards them, patting their fur. 'They're so soft.'

After Lara had played with the goats and helped to groom the horses for what seemed like a long time, a young woman came and whispered something in Aurelia's ear. She turned towards Lara and took her hand. 'Now, who'd like some cake? And I have another surprise for you inside.'

Lara ran alongside the older woman as they went into the building, through the kitchen, down some steps and into a high-vaulted cellar lined with barrels and racks. 'This was the wine cellar in the days when this was one of the finest hotels in Europe.

We don't use it for that nowadays, as we have no need for alcohol here, but we have converted it to another use.'

She pressed a button and a door, which had been invisible before, slid open. On the other side was an area like a wellness room in an exclusive spa. It reminded Olivia of the hotel in Zermatt where she'd gone with Christian for their tenth wedding anniversary. The walls were tiled in sparkling pale blue and lights shone like stars from the ceiling. Tall large-leafed plants stood in the corners and a smell of eucalyptus filled the steamy air.

'We have a sauna here, and a pool. A lovely relaxing atmosphere.' She bent down to Lara. 'You'll be able to try this out when you get your cast off. But just now, I have another lovely surprise for you.'

They followed Aurelia into another room where soft music played in the background. Two women in fluffy white bathrobes lay on loungers talking to Sebastian. Aurelia smiled at them as she took Lara's hand and led her into a wood-lined room. Once again, she pressed a button and a hidden door slid open.

Through the door was another room, bathed in pink light. A young woman with long, black curly hair was sitting on a chair, with a pale yellow puppy on her lap. She had a beautiful profile, but when she turned to face them, Olivia saw the other side of her face was puckered with ugly scarring.

'This is Tina. She's been with us since she was a child. We rescued her from her family, who not only neglected her, allowing her to be scalded by boiling water, but were also cruel and unfeeling.'

Tina smiled and answered in English with an Italian accent. 'Aurelia saved me. This is my family now.'

Aurelia took Lara's hand again and led her round the corner of the L-shaped room. 'And here, Lara, is your special surprise.'

The walls of this part of the room were lined with books and pictures, with toys everywhere. Sitting on the carpet with her back to them was a blonde girl, her head bent over a large picture book. As they approached, the girl looked round.

Olivia's heart stopped. It couldn't be… she could hardly believe her eyes.

It was. It was Sandra. But a slim, healthy Sandra, with clear skin and shining hair.

The little girl leapt up when she saw them approach, running and hugging Aurelia's legs. 'Oh, Mama, hello.'

Then she noticed Lara standing behind Aurelia. She screamed with delight and threw her arms round her. 'Lara, you're here. I asked for you to come so many times. I missed you so much. Come and play with me. We've got so many lovely toys. All I wanted was my friend, I wanted you.'

Aurelia smiled as she watched the girls hug each other excitedly. 'You know, Sandra, I do everything for you. You are my special girl and I will do everything in my power to make all your dreams come true.'

Chapter 45

The Fall

Edinburgh – May 2004

After Eleanor Munro had left the flat, Lucy leant against the door, her heart pounding. What a fool she'd been! When her heart had regained a normal speed, she went through to Julian's room. He was lying with his hands thrown above his head, looking so peaceful and innocent. She leant over, kissed his warm cheek, and brushed his dark hair from his brow. He was the most important thing in the world to her.

Sitting down in the living room, she noticed the wine. She didn't usually drink, but she opened it and poured herself a glass. She was halfway through the bottle when the doorbell rang. Slightly unsteadily, she walked through the hall and opened the door.

Bill was leaning against the doorpost, his head hanging down. He was beautifully dressed as always, but the top button of his shirt was undone and his tie was crooked. He'd obviously been drinking.

'Lucy, my darling.' He leant forward, breathing alcohol fumes over her, and tried to kiss her. She dodged his kiss and pulled him into the hall. She didn't want her neighbours to hear them.

'Bill, I want you to leave immediately. Your wife came to see me. I've been so stupid. It's all been a terrible mistake.'

Bill slurred his words. 'Lucy, I love you. We're meant to be together.' He reached his arms out, swaying slightly. 'You've met my wife. We're not right for each other. She doesn't love me; she just doesn't want the humiliation of a divorce. It's convenient for her to have a husband.'

Lucy stepped back from him. 'Your wife is a beautiful, intelligent woman, and contrary to the cliché, she understands you totally. I'd never really thought about her, but now I've met her I realise how wrong this all is. It has to end.' Even as she said the words, Lucy didn't want to believe them. Bill was the only thing that made teaching bearable, and being with him was the only time she felt right at school. He made her feel special, attractive and intelligent. Nobody had ever done that before.

Bill swayed towards her. 'You don't mean that, Lucy. I'll leave her. I want to be with you.'

'I want you to go, Bill. I'm going to take your wife's advice and leave the school. Please put me in for a transfer immediately.'

Bill lurched in her direction, his mouth slack. 'Don't say that. Life will be nothing without you. I wouldn't be able to work, to live, without you.'

Lucy stepped back from him. 'I'm not that stupid. I know I'm not the only affair you've had, and I'm sure you'll quickly find a replacement for me.' Even as she said this, she felt a pang of jealousy. Bill was drunk, dishevelled and unsteady on his feet, but there was still something about him she found difficult to resist.

She steeled herself. She had to have some self-respect. 'Please go now. I'm serious. I won't be coming to school tomorrow. I'll be ill so you'd better arrange cover.' She opened the door and guided him out onto the landing.

'Lucy, I love you. Don't do this to me.' Bill reached out and, grabbing her breasts, attempted to kiss her on the mouth.

'Get away from me!' Lucy struggled out of his arms and pushed him as hard as she could.

Bill staggered back to the top of the stairs and swayed for a moment, trying to recover his balance. Then, his eyes wide with fear, he fell back.

Lucy watched in horror as he bounced off the banister and twisted, desperately trying to regain his footing. Then he somersaulted before landing with a sickening crack at the foot of the staircase.

Lucy froze for a moment, unable to move. What had she done? The angle of his neck as he lay in a crumpled heap and the contorted grimace on his face made her blood turn to ice. Stepping carefully down the stairs, she lifted his limp wrist, trying to feel a pulse. There was nothing.

She looked down at the body, numb with fear. Above her, she thought she heard a movement and a click, but when she looked up, everything was still. There was no sound except for the faint hum of a television behind one of the closed doors.

Bill was dead, she was sure of that. What could she do? It had been an accident. She hadn't meant him to fall. But like an image from a nightmare, the look of terror on his face when he realised he was falling, flashed before her. And she had pushed him.

Her body began to spasm with shock. What would happen? Would she be sent to prison? Who would look after Julian? Tears were streaming down her cheeks. Julian had nobody without her. She had to be here for him.

She stared round the dingy stairwell. As usual, one of the lights was broken and the steps were worn and uneven. It would be very easy for a drunken man to miss his footing.

She waited. One of the neighbours must have heard and would come out to see what had happened. But all the doors remained firmly closed. She took several deep breaths and stepped over the body. If there were no witnesses, nobody could say it wasn't an accident.

When she phoned the emergency services, she didn't have to pretend to be upset, she was verging on hysteria. And when the police and paramedics arrived, they were very sympathetic, believing her story without question.

Chapter 46

Verdingkinder

Wildenbach – Thursday 25 February, 2016

Olivia looked at Sandra, paralysed with shock. Eventually, she heard her voice, high and squeaky. 'Aurelia, what have you done?'

Aurelia stepped towards Olivia and led her away, while looking back and smiling at the girls. 'Sandra, you can show Lara your toys, and there's cake for you both. Olivia, please come and have a cup of tea with me. Tina will look after the girls.'

Olivia followed Aurelia as if in a dream into a small room with comfortable chairs and a massage table. In a corner, she saw her suitcase, and Lara's favourite elephant bag.

'Olivia, my darling one. I'm so glad you and your dear daughter are joining us. I knew you would. I just didn't dare to hope it would happen so quickly.'

'We're not joining you. Lara and I are getting straight out of here.'

Aurelia bent down and pointed to the suitcases. 'We collected some of your things from your house, and as we speak, your car is being driven to Zürich airport. One of our community members looks enough like you to fool the CCTV cameras. Your car will be parked in the multi-storey car park at the airport and your phone will be left in the car. And then, you and Lara will disappear.'

'You're mad. The police will search for me. Christian will never give up.'

'When they read the note you've left, they'll realise why you had to leave. You couldn't live with the burden of guilt from your terrible secret any longer.'

'I didn't write a note,' Olivia said in a low voice.

'You didn't, but there is a note in your house. An excellent calligrapher in our community imitated your writing. Christian will believe it, because you've been acting so strangely recently. He's seen the notes left for you, and he knows you've been under a great deal of strain. When he finds out exactly what happened that night in Edinburgh, he'll realise how you used him to get away from Scotland and why, now the secret is out, you can't continue to live with him.'

Olivia's mind was racing. This was a nightmare. She couldn't believe what was happening.

Aurelia reached to a tray on a small table. 'Have a cup of tea. It will make you feel better. And then Sebastian will give you a massage.'

'No. I don't know what you put in that tea, but it affects my thinking. I'm not drinking it, and Lara and I will be leaving as soon as possible.'

Olivia attempted to stand up, but felt strong hands on her shoulders. Sebastian was standing behind her. 'Accept this is your destiny, Olivia. When you do, you'll be able to enjoy our wonderful life.'

'You're mad. You can't keep me here. Christian will call the police and they'll come and get me.'

Aurelia looked at her sympathetically. 'The police were here several times during the search for the missing girls and have never found these rooms. We have an excellent relationship with them and, of course, when I tell them about your deep unhappiness, shame and disturbed mental state, they'll understand why you had to run away. You were distraught the last time I saw you, admitting you were responsible for the death of Bill Munro in Edinburgh in 2004.'

Olivia gasped. 'I wasn't responsible. It was an accident.'

'That's what you said at the time, and the police believed you. But now the truth has come out, that you killed your headmaster, so there's no wonder you've been troubled.' Aurelia spoke gently, her smile as understanding as ever.

'You won't get away with this, Aurelia. Christian will never give up looking for me and Lara.'

'You feel upset at the moment, Olivia, but you'll soon realise this is the best place to be. Here, you and your daughter are safe from the evils and dangers of today's world.'

Sebastian began to massage her shoulders. Olivia shook him off. 'What are you doing? Have you been involved in this all the time?'

Sebastian moved in front of her and knelt down. Olivia was vaguely aware of Aurelia leaving the room. 'Olivia, I can understand how you feel deceived and mistrustful. But believe me, I always told the truth. From the first moment we met, I've known you were something special. I've been in this community for more than half my life, but I've never felt a connection like this. Olivia, I've always been waiting for you.'

Olivia looked into his eyes. They were so sincere, but could she believe him? Aurelia had tricked her, lured her into this community. Was Sebastian also part of it?

'I want to go back to Lara and Sandra.'

'Of course, we'll talk again later.'

When she went back into the room, the girls were playing a board game with Tina and a very blonde girl, who looked about fifteen, with pale eyebrows and eyelashes.

The girl stood up and shook hands. 'Hello, I'm Brita.' She had an accent, perhaps Scandinavian. 'I also help to look after the children. There's always one of us with them. I'm so glad Lara has come. Sandra has talked about her a lot and they will have such fun together.'

Olivia felt as if she were in some kind of parallel universe. These people had kidnapped Sandra and imprisoned Lara and her, but they were talking as if it were some kind of holiday camp.

Sandra stood up and walked towards her, followed by Lara like the little shadow she always was. 'Now Lara's here we'll be able to work together. School is great here. I can do all my times tables and I'm really good at mental arithmetic now. I'm reading lots of books, some really difficult ones, and I'm learning English and Italian too. We've got Honey,' she indicated the puppy, a golden Labrador, who jumped off Tina's knee and ran to them, 'and lots of other animals. I help with them every day. We always go outside once a day, even when it's snowing.'

Her eyes shone with excitement. Olivia couldn't get over the difference in the subdued, introverted girl she'd known before. 'And I've learnt to swim. I go swimming in the pool every day.'

Olivia gave a tentative smile. She wanted to ask how Sandra felt about her family; she must miss them so much. On the other hand, perhaps her life had been so unpleasant on the farm she was glad to be at the hotel, so Olivia didn't say anything, not wanting to frighten Lara, who was talking excitedly. 'I can help Sandra with English and I want to learn Italian.' She pointed to a huge map of the world covering one wall. 'Brita's going to tell us about Finland. That's where she comes from. She says there are people in the house from thirteen countries in the world. They're going to come and tell us all about it.'

Olivia forced herself to smile. Lara didn't seem to understand the situation at all. She looked at her watch. Probably nobody had even noticed they were missing yet. Christian would phone that evening. How long would it take him to be worried?

Sandra hugged Lara. 'I always wanted a friend and Aurelia found me one. But she wasn't a good friend. She wouldn't play with me and took all my things. I was pleased when she went. It was always Lara I wanted.'

Olivia's blood ran cold. A friend who disappeared? Could that be Ruth? Olivia had felt angry at being tricked by Aurelia, but now she was gripped with terror. How had Ruth died?

There were so many questions running through her head, but she was afraid to ask them, anxious not to disturb the atmosphere.

If Lara could just carry on thinking she was on a wonderful holiday until they were rescued, that would be the best thing. Olivia hoped Christian would be worried and start a search for them as soon as he couldn't get in touch with her.

She felt a pang of worry. She and Christian hadn't separated on very good terms. Perhaps he would think she was deliberately ignoring him because of their stupid argument. How she missed Christian now; missed his organisation and dependability. She hoped he could sense how much she and Lara needed him, and come and rescue them from this nightmare as soon as possible.

Aurelia appeared at her side. 'Will you come and have a meal with me, Olivia? I'm sure you have a lot of questions. The children will eat with Tina and Brita, who'll then put them to bed.'

Olivia looked at Aurelia, and saw her eyes as warm and sincere as ever, not seeming to realise that what she was doing was so wrong. Olivia followed her. There was nothing else she could do.

Aurelia and Olivia sat together at a round table in a small room decorated in an Oriental style. Tenzin brought each of them a steaming earthenware casserole dish.

Aurelia took a mouthful. 'Do taste this, Olivia. It's delicious.'

Olivia took a small spoonful. She didn't think she'd be able to eat, but the meal was very tasty – meat and vegetables in a spicy sauce. She waited for Aurelia to speak.

'You joined us a little earlier than I'd anticipated, but when you came here with Lara, I knew it was the right moment. I wanted you to choose to come here with your daughter, but it might have taken a long time to convince you this is where you and Lara belong, away from the dangers of the modern world.'

Olivia opened her mouth, but Aurelia waved her hand. 'You haven't yet achieved that level of knowledge, but it will come. Everybody who lives here has come voluntarily, and everybody is free to leave when they want to. I'm afraid I can't allow you that privilege yet, but it will come when you have learnt that this is where you belong.'

'But Sandra. She didn't choose to come here. You kidnapped her.'

'Yes, Sandra is a special case. I noticed her soon after we moved here and I knew I had to save her. Because she is me. She is my young self, the daughter I never had.' Aurelia's eyes were gleaming. 'You've heard of the Verdingkinder?'

Olivia nodded. There had been a lot in the papers in Switzerland in the last few years about these 'contract children', who were forcibly taken away from their parents, often because the mother was unmarried, and sent to live with new families. These were often poor farmers looking for cheap labour, and many of the children were treated like slaves.

Recently some of the victims had written about the physical, psychological and sexual abuse they'd suffered. It had caused a national outrage, forcing the Swiss government to make an official apology and pay compensation to survivors. It had reminded Olivia of the Home Children scheme in Britain, where thousands of poor children had forcibly been sent to Australia and other colonies, where many of them had been abused.

Aurelia looked at her with sad eyes. 'I was one of those children. I was sent to a farm near here when I was eight years old, and endured years of beatings and sexual degradation from the farmer and his son. The wife was terrified of them too and couldn't protect me. I tried to tell a teacher, but I was told I was ungrateful and a fantasist.'

Olivia remembered the famous Swiss film, *Der Verdingbub*, which told the story of a boy and girl fostered on a farm, where they suffered terrible abuse. Olivia had seen it at the cinema in Zug with Christian and had cried all the way home. She could identify so much with the children, although her difficult childhood was nothing compared to what these children had endured.

Aurelia took Olivia's hand. 'When I saw Sandra, I could see in her eyes, in her walk, that she was abused. It took me a little while to get her confidence, but then she told me everything. Her brothers used her as a sexual plaything, passed her around, experimented with her. Her parents knew nothing of it, or if they did, they turned a blind eye.'

Olivia couldn't believe it. She knew those boys, or had done when they were younger. They were coarse and poorly educated, having left school as quickly as they could, but surely no boys could treat their sister like that. Then she remembered a couple of distasteful jokes they'd made about sex and animals. She shivered. She'd read about incest and bestiality in books, but found it hard to believe it had been taking place just up the road from her.

Olivia automatically took another spoonful of food as Aurelia continued. 'You've seen Sandra. You can see how she's thrived here in the proper environment. Do you know she has never once said she misses her family or asked to go back? She spoke far more about Lara and missing her.'

'Sandra talked about another girl who was here. Was that Ruth Frick?'

Aurelia's face sagged. 'That was a mistake, a terrible episode I regret so much. Sandra was so happy but always said she wanted a friend. When I heard about a girl in the canton of Zürich being ill-treated by a foster family, I thought it was the ideal chance to save another girl and make Sandra happy. I saw how Sandra had blossomed and thought I could do the same thing for her. But Ruth was such a damaged girl, had been in so many dysfunctional situations that she couldn't appreciate the chances here. She was cruel to Sandra, teased her relentlessly and stole her things.'

Olivia thought of the little St Bernard keyring.

'And she was sly. One day when they were outside, she ran away.' Aurelia's eyes glistened. 'We looked everywhere for her, sent search parties in every direction, but we couldn't find her. Now I think she must have hidden somewhere very near the house and gone further under cover of dark. She was clever, but so damaged.'

'But she died.'

'The night she ran away was the night the snow eventually came. We think she was trying to go over the mountain pass, back to Zürich where her mother was. She must have been caught out by the snowstorm. Poor girl. I hope she is now at peace.'

Olivia found herself nodding. What a frightening end for the young girl.

Then, an even more terrifying thought came to her that made her blood run cold. What if Ruth's death hadn't been an accident? Would Aurelia ever have allowed Ruth to escape to freedom? She would have told everyone about Sandra, and Aurelia would have been revealed as the kidnapper. Had Ruth been killed to keep her quiet?

No, she couldn't believe that. Aurelia was motivated by kindness, although Olivia couldn't agree with the way she had acted. She didn't want Aurelia to have any inkling of her suspicions – that could be dangerous – but she had to say something. 'You can't just take children away from their families, however good your intentions.'

Aurelia shook her head. 'But many families are damaging their children, making their lives unbearable. In our community we believe in giving love to those who have been mistreated, giving them the chance to live happy and productive lives.'

'What about the way you treated me? Pretending to be my friend but, all the time, you just wanted me to bring Lara as a playmate for Sandra.'

'No, no, Olivia. It wasn't like that. I have an instinct for people and the moment I met you, I recognised something in you, a potential for greatness and happiness that was being strangled by the way you were living. I knew that our community was the right place for you and your daughter.'

Olivia tried to speak but Aurelia waved her hand. 'It was only as I got to know you better that I learnt about the pain of your past, your suffocating childhood, your rejection by all those who should have given you love, the struggle of bringing up a child alone. It is no surprise that you have found the pressures of living in a sham relationship here in a foreign country has brought so much unhappiness.'

Olivia shook her head. This was a distorted view of her life.

Aurelia looked directly into her eyes. 'But then I heard from dear Eleanor Munro that you are also responsible for the death of a man.'

Olivia gasped. 'Eleanor Munro?' Bill's wife. She hadn't thought about her for years, having blocked the memory of that terrible night.

'I met her when she came to Switzerland to find you. She was in a distraught state, very distressed and resentful, convinced you had ruined her life.'

'She came to Switzerland?' Olivia couldn't believe it. She'd been so sure she'd escaped her past. Then she remembered the woman who'd been watching her in the Spar and knew who she was. It was Eleanor.

She'd thought she looked vaguely familiar, but hadn't made the connection. The wild unkempt woman looked so different from the sophisticated university professor who'd visited her that fateful evening. Now she knew where Aurelia had been getting her information. She also realised that it was Eleanor who'd sent the notes.

Aurelia watched as Olivia absorbed this. 'Since she has joined our community, Eleanor has learnt to live with her grief.'

Olivia gasped again. 'She's here?'

'Yes, in fact you passed her in the spa area when you arrived. She was relaxing with Sebastian, and Tammy Sue, another treasured member of our group. I thought about introducing you then, but realised it would be better to wait until a later time.'

Olivia began to shake. 'The death wasn't my fault. Bill fell when he was drunk.'

'That's what you said at the time. And that's what the police chose to believe from a beautiful distraught girl. He had a very high level of alcohol in his body – three times the legal limit – and so it seemed consistent with your story that he overbalanced and fell.'

'That's what happened.'

'And that's what Eleanor believed for all these years. When she learnt the truth, she felt you'd ruined her life.'

'I don't understand.'

'After her husband's death, she tried hard to carry on as normal, but the fact that he'd died in a drunken fall, while visiting his mistress, festered in her consciousness. She tried to cover it up, pretending the visit had been to do with a school matter. She wanted to maintain her position in the university and in Edinburgh society, but it took a terrible toll on her. Her work suffered and eventually she was encouraged to take early retirement.'

Olivia shook her head. 'But why did she come to Switzerland?'

'When she heard the truth about what had really happened, she had a complete breakdown. She blamed you for ruining her happiness and when she heard you were leading a supposedly perfect life in Switzerland, she came here, wanting to make you suffer too.'

'What made her think that I was responsible? How did she find out I was here?'

'You know that Montgomery employed a private eye to find his son. When he was trying to track you down, he spoke to your neighbours in Edinburgh. One of them told him what had really happened that night.'

'But the police interviewed the neighbours. There were no witnesses.'

'This neighbour didn't say anything at the time. He was a petty criminal and no friend of the police. However, when the investigator knocked on his door and offered him money, he told the whole story of what he'd seen that night.'

'But how did Eleanor Munro find out?'

'The investigator had also contacted her when he was looking for you and discovered she was a wealthy widow, still very bitter about the death of her husband. When he found your address in Switzerland, he visited her again and told her the truth about how her husband had died. He also revealed your address in Switzerland, in exchange for a considerable sum of money.'

'So she came to Switzerland, followed me, and left the notes.'

'Yes, I've discussed that with her. A very irrational way to deal with her resentment, but she was so bitter when she saw the way you lived. You had a husband, the children she'd never had and a lovely home. She was in a very bad way when our paths crossed.'

'I can't believe she's here in the hotel.'

Aurelia gave her knowing smile. 'Everything happens for a reason. When we first met, she was distraught, consumed with resentment. Now she's found peace and has realised, as you will, that this is the right place to be.'

Olivia stood up from her chair. 'This is not the right place for Lara and me. You kidnapped us.'

As she said this, Olivia realised it was not the right reaction. She spoke in a softer voice. 'Aurelia, please let Lara and me go. Now I know Sandra is safe and happy, I won't tell anybody. Christian won't have realised that I'm missing yet. Nobody need know.'

Aurelia took her hand. 'Olivia, it will take a little time to get used to, but once you accept this is your destiny, you will realise how wonderful our life is here. Our community is full of artists and writers, craftsmen, gardeners and chefs. Once you embrace life here you will be able to develop your talents. You are full of creativity that has never been allowed to blossom.'

Olivia realised that Aurelia would never let her go, and thinking of Ruth, she was afraid of what might happen to Lara and her if she tried to escape. She was trapped in a nightmare.

'I have to see Lara.'

'Of course. We'll go and see them now.'

Olivia was desperate to see her little girl, to cuddle her, to keep her safe, but as they went to the children's area, Brita stepped forward. 'They're both asleep. I wondered if they'd want to sleep separately, but they insisted on going together.'

Brita led Olivia into a beautiful bedroom, swathed in chiffon and gauze. Sandra and Lara were lying together, both fast asleep. Olivia had thought she'd have to comfort Lara, who often found it difficult to go to sleep in strange places, but her daughter looked totally relaxed.

Brita took her hand and showed her to another comfortable room and said it was hers for as long as she wished. Olivia knew it wouldn't be long. Christian would have phoned now and would know that something was wrong. She and Lara would soon be rescued.

She tried to sleep, but it was impossible. So much had happened that day. She had a feeling of panic when she realised that as soon as Christian got to the house, he would read the note that had been left. The note that said she'd run away because of killing Bill.

In the darkness of the silent night, everything seemed dark and hopeless. Would he believe it? Would he even try to find her? She tossed and turned, trying to find peace for her swirling fears, petrified at the thought of being abandoned. She felt desperate, her head pounding with sleeplessness and terror.

Shaking with fear, she got out of bed and looked into the girls' room. They were sleeping peacefully. By the bedroom door, Brita was on a futon, also fast asleep. Holding her breath, she crept to the door to the sauna area and tried to open it. It was locked.

There was nothing she could do but go back to bed, where the tears she'd been suppressing all day came flooding out.

She'd fallen into a troubled sleep, her pillow damp with tears, when there was gentle tapping at the door. Olivia raised her head as the door opened.

Silhouetted against the pink light outside stood Sebastian. He stepped into the room and took her in his arms. 'Olivia, I shouldn't have come to see you, but I couldn't stay away. I had to know you are all right.'

'Sebastian. You must help me to escape. Lara and I can't stay here.'

He kissed her tenderly and a surge like electricity ran through her. 'Olivia, this is a wonderful place, the right place for you, a place where we can be together as we are destined to be. You are so special, so beautiful,' he whispered, running his hand over her body.

She tried to resist, but she was so tired, so frightened, so alone, so fragile she allowed herself to respond and was carried away on a wave of sensation, reaching peaks she'd never experienced before.

Afterwards, Sebastian kissed her tenderly. 'That was wonderful.' He stroked her hair. 'Please don't tell anybody about this. Aurelia wouldn't approve. Once you are fully a member of our community, I think she will be pleased, but she mustn't know until then.' He kissed her again. 'May I come back tomorrow night?' Olivia nodded, still in the afterglow of passion, and drifted off to sleep.

After a short while, Olivia woke with a start. She was overwhelmed with self-loathing. What had she been thinking? She'd never been unfaithful to Christian. Sebastian was mesmerising, like a drug, but she must have gone crazy to behave like that.

It mustn't happen again. She must stay strong to resist the temptations of this strange world until she and Lara were rescued. Which would happen. Soon. She was sure.

Chapter 47

A parallel world

Grand Wildenbach Hotel – Monday 7 March, 2016

Eleven days had passed and nothing had happened. Olivia had been so sure they'd be found within twenty-four hours, but there'd been no sign of police activity. The hotel would surely be one of the first places they'd check. She'd come here several times in the days before she'd gone missing. But, she thought with a sickening feeling, even if they searched the whole building, it would be easy to miss the secret entrance to their suite. And she knew Aurelia could be very plausible.

Her emotions fluctuated between hope and despair. Maybe nobody was looking near Wildenwil? Perhaps they'd been convinced by the forged note and believed she'd disappeared because of her feeling of guilt about Bill Munro's death? Because her car had been left in the airport, perhaps they were concentrating the search far away? Christian would make sure they never stopped searching for her and Lara.

At least she hoped so. Stuck in the hotel with no contact to the outside world, it was difficult to imagine what was going on in that other universe, which seemed so far away, like a half-remembered dream. And the police had never found Sandra, despite all their efforts.

It was difficult to know what was best for Sandra. She was alive and thriving in this strange environment, completely happy in this new life. And Lara was also happier than Olivia had seen her for months. She spent the days playing with Sandra, thrilled to be reunited with her. Olivia realised how much she'd been missing her friend, even though she'd stopped talking about her.

They spent time with the animals every day, in a secluded paddock behind the house, hidden by rocks and tall trees, and had schooling with Tina and Brita. One of the members of the community was a nurse and checked Lara's injury. Luckily it was a simple break and as it was her left wrist, she was able to do the lessons and craft.

Olivia spent a lot of time with the girls, or swimming, reading and writing. The life was seductive, almost as if she were in a luxury spa, with delicious meals being served and no need to cook or clean. Olivia had never been so pampered in her whole life and sometimes almost forgot she was a prisoner in this parallel universe.

Sebastian was another complication. After the first night she'd vowed she wouldn't allow him to visit her again but, during the day, he was constantly in her thoughts and every evening she burnt with desire, waiting for him to tap at the door. He made her feel loved and fulfilled, forgetting her worries in the magic of his touch.

The only members of the community, apart from Aurelia, that Olivia had spoken to were Eleanor and Tammy Sue. Eleanor had been very cool at first, but then surprised Olivia by sitting down next to her at the pool one day and hugging her. 'I'm sorry for the hate I felt for you, Olivia. I've talked about it for hours with Aurelia and she has made me realise you and I were both victims of Bill, a man who didn't respect women at all. I wasted the best years of my life with a man who was serially unfaithful. I'm sorry for your suffering with him.'

Eleanor smiled, her eyes sparkling, and Olivia saw once again the elegant woman she'd met in Edinburgh. 'In this community I've found my place. My house in Edinburgh has been sold and I'm going to live here permanently. In this atmosphere of love and peace, I have rediscovered my creativity and am writing again.' She gave a beatific smile.

Olivia wondered what had happened to Eleanor's money. Aurelia had said Eleanor was a wealthy widow. Was this why she was so welcome in the community? Olivia pushed these thoughts aside. She was pleased Eleanor had found comfort after what had happened and if she wanted to give some of her money to the community, it was hers to give. After all, she was living here in luxury.

Tammy Sue was an American widow, an attractive blonde, rounded, confident and very talkative. She described how she'd first met members of the community while she was on holiday in Italy. 'My Hank made billions with oil, but did it bring him happiness? No, a massive heart attack at fifty-four and what did it all mean? I was left alone, no children, more money than I knew what to do with and I was so bored. I went on cruises and cultural holidays, surrounded by lots of other bored widows like me, and it meant nothing. I just thank the Lord for the day He brought dear Sebastian and Aurelia into my life. They've made me realise the meaning of love and life. I've discovered my true self, my hidden creativity and spirituality. I've started painting and feel happier than I ever have in my whole life.'

Olivia listened to her, carried away by her enthusiasm. It was lovely that Tammy Sue had found happiness, but Olivia wondered what had happened to her billions. The renovations in the house must have been very expensive and Olivia wondered if, as Christian had suggested, the community may have targeted lonely wealthy women.

The photographs in the book of Aurelia's husband came into her mind. They showed him with many different women, and there was a tangible air of sensuality about him. Had he seduced these women and brought them into the community?

She looked around for ways to escape, but it seemed impossible. She never went outside, except to the paddock, which was surrounded by high cliffs and the stable buildings. When she was there, Tenzin always stood silently beside her, watching her every move. There seemed to be no way out. In any case, taking

Lara with her would make escaping much more difficult, and she could never leave her daughter behind.

And if she was caught trying to escape, what would happen? Would she end up dead on a hillside like Ruth? The thought turned her blood to ice.

Every day, Aurelia talked to Olivia as they drank the sweet tea she'd hated at first. Now she'd begun to like the taste and the calm she felt afterwards. When Aurelia was talking, it was easy to feel her doubts dissolving. The philosophy and ideals of the community were convincing and Aurelia promised that when Olivia was ready, she'd be able to go to meetings with the other members.

'Lara and Sandra are so happy here, and will grow up in a safe and pure environment. You may have noticed Tina and Brita are pregnant so a new generation of children of peace and love will grow up in this magical place.' Olivia was surprised. Both the girls always wore long flowing dresses so she hadn't noticed. She wondered who the fathers were.

'You are still a young woman. You too could have more children to bring youth to our community, a new start in this magical place.' Olivia smiled as an image of holding Sebastian's baby flashed into her mind.

Aurelia touched her arm. 'You have suffered so much with evil men. You deserve happiness, to be given the love you deserve from a genuine and sincere man.'

Olivia wondered if Aurelia was referring to Sebastian. Was she giving her permission to their relationship? The thought was exciting.

Aurelia gave her a sideways look. 'Christian tried to control you, suffocate your true self, and now he has shown himself to be very shallow and unfaithful.'

Olivia started. What did she mean? Wasn't he looking for her and Lara? What was happening in the outside world? Was everyone just carrying on with their lives without them? Christian was always talking about drawing a line under things, but he loved Lara and her, didn't he?

Olivia's head was in turmoil. What about Marc? Surely, he would miss her? She missed him so much she couldn't bear to think about him playing football, or the last affectionate hug he'd given her just before they went skiing. It was too painful.

But Lara was so happy with Sandra and never mentioned her father and brother. Was Marc happy, just getting on with his life with Christian, doing all the boy things he loved together?

Aurelia leant over to her. 'I'm sorry Christian has let you down, as you have been let down by every other man in your life. The founding principle of our community is to save those who are vulnerable, unhappy and abused. When you are fully committed, you can join in our work, creating our haven for good in this troubled world.'

As usual after their talks, Olivia felt convinced by her words and looked forward to becoming a full member of the community. And that evening, when Sebastian slid into her bed and said, 'How wonderful it will be for us to have a baby together,' she believed that everything would work out well.

Chapter 48

Time passes

Wildenwil – Friday 18 March, 2016

Three weeks had gone by. Lara was thriving, becoming more confident, looking after the animals and showing a talent for riding. She'd started to learn Italian, and she and Sandra sang English songs together. Olivia spent time every day reading English books to them, and was pleased to see they were both now reading books alone. Lara seemed to have accepted their life there without question, and never talked about Christian, Marc or her former home.

Olivia thought about Christian and Marc all the time at first, but as the time passed, they seemed to fade away, like a half-remembered dream. They were part of another world, one that seemed insubstantial compared to her new life.

Most of her free time she spent writing. Aurelia had said she should start a memoir, describing the experiences of her other lives, when she'd been Marie and Lucy. Once she started, she wrote frenetically, images from the past coming back to her as the words flooded out, leaving her emotionally drained. She was emptying and renewing herself. Looking back at her three names and three lives, she wondered if she should think of a new name to match this new existence.

She began to avoid Tammy Sue and Eleanor. She'd always been a loner and their constant chatter got on her nerves. They seemed besotted with Aurelia and Sebastian, parroting Aurelia's words and constantly saying how wonderful they were. They especially loved

Sebastian's massages. Olivia smiled when she heard this. She knew his massages were special, but she had something extra from him. She stroked her stomach. Perhaps their child was already growing inside her.

She was in the lounge writing when Aurelia came in with two cups of the usual tea. She sat down beside Olivia and took her hands, staring into her eyes. 'I've read what you wrote yesterday. It is wonderful. You capture the pain and loneliness of your childhood so vividly. Despite all those years of emotional abuse, you have such strength.' She paused. 'I can see you growing spiritually. Soon you will be ready to become a full member of our community. Then you can come into the rest of the house and meet the others who live here.'

Olivia felt the warmth of Aurelia's words and knew that this was her destiny. This was where she belonged.

Aurelia continued in her compelling hypnotic voice. 'You are nearly there, but you must be certain this is what you want. You must be prepared to sever your ties with your old life and devote everything to your new life, to your children.'

Olivia nodded and was about to speak when the door opened. Tenzin came in and whispered in Aurelia's ear. She stood up. 'I must leave you now, my dear. Think about everything we have said, and do write more. Writing it down will help you to erase the unpleasant past from your soul and reach your true potential.'

Olivia began to write again, losing herself in her memories, when she became aware of somebody standing beside her. She looked up and was surprised to see it was Sebastian. She didn't usually see him during the day. Taking her hand, he whispered, 'Come with me.'

He led her through the hidden doorway into the children's area. Everything there seemed peaceful. Lara and Sandra were laughing and playing with the puppy. Tina watched them with a serene smile as the little dog ran between them, trying to catch a ball they threw from one to the other. Lara looked up briefly and smiled to her mother before going back to the game.

Sebastian pulled her hand and took Olivia to her room, closing the door firmly behind him. He kissed her. 'There is danger outside and we must stay here together until it has passed. There are forces trying to destroy our community.' He stroked her body and kissed her more passionately. She resisted at first – Lara was in the next room – but her desire soon took over.

She was floating on a wave of passion when a loud crash reverberated outside, followed by a scream. Olivia tried to stand up, but Sebastian held her down. She struggled to free herself. 'What's happening? I must go to Lara.'

'Stay with me.' Sebastian pulled her closer. She looked up and saw tears in his eyes. 'Whatever happens, remember that this was real.'

Voices sounded outside and the door burst open. Two armed policemen came into the room. 'Stand up and put your hands behind your heads.'

Olivia was paralysed with fear. What was happening? Sebastian stood up, kissing her as he put his hands behind his head. 'I love you.'

She was going to kiss him back, when one of the policemen pulled her away. She gasped and looked back at Sebastian. 'I love you too.'

The policeman marched her outside where she saw Aurelia holding Sandra in her arms, trying to keep her from a policeman. She was screaming, 'Don't take her away from me. She is my life.'

Chapter 49

Therapy

Olivia sat at the large window of her room in a private clinic in Heiden, a small town high on a hill in Appenzell, a mountainous canton in the East of Switzerland. The town centre was beautiful, with Biedermeier houses and a large number of convalescent homes and clinics. The most famous, where Henri Dunant, the founder of the International Red Cross, had spent his final years, was now a museum. Olivia had visited it and was fascinated by the poignant story of his life.

From her window, she saw a magnificent view over the hills down to Lake Constance shimmering in the distance. There was blossom on the fruit trees, sparkling against the blue spring sky. She'd been here since the rescue from the hotel.

That time was a blur. She could only remember being prised away from Sebastian, who'd been handcuffed and led off by two policemen. The heartrending primal screech as a hysterical Sandra had been dragged from Aurelia's arms still rang in Olivia's ears.

When she'd been led outside into the bright sunlight, armed police had been positioned all around, with helicopters circling overhead. Behind a security tape Christian was waiting, holding his arms out as Lara ran to him.

The next thing she remembered was being in an ambulance, and after a check at the local hospital in Zug, which showed she was medically healthy, she was whisked off to Heiden. Christian had persuaded the authorities she'd had a breakdown and needed urgent psychological treatment.

It was peaceful in the clinic and her long conversations with Dr Eva Meyer, a fiercely intelligent psychiatrist, helped her to make sense of what had happened. Christian came regularly, and at Easter he'd brought Marc and Lara for a short visit. They all seemed to be managing well without her. A housekeeper had been hired, paid for by Guy she later found out, and Marlene and Sibylle came from Berne every weekend. Olivia had been very touched when she heard this; usually they spent their weekends in a whirl of art exhibitions, theatre and dinner parties. That they would give this up to look after their brother and his children was unexpected and strangely moving. Even Rolf came down from the settlement occasionally to spend time with the children.

Lara seemed to have taken the whole experience in her stride. Olivia so envied her ability to live in the present, but Olivia was sure she must miss Sandra. She'd heard that Sandra had been placed with a foster family while the police investigated her brothers for child sexual abuse. Olivia hoped she was happy.

Aurelia and Sebastian were being held in a secure psychiatric unit. Olivia wasn't sure what to think about them. Aurelia had undoubtedly done things in the wrong way, but Sandra had been happy and thrived. Was her life better now? Olivia was struggling with ambivalence. Aurelia had the right ideas, but had caused such harm.

And Sebastian. Olivia's heart still somersaulted when she thought of him, but she didn't know whether what happened had been real or not. Had she been special? She remembered his words as they'd been torn apart. She patted her stomach. For a while she'd thought she might be pregnant, but now she was certain she wasn't, she was relieved. The time in the hotel was like a dream, so separate from the reality she'd known before and after, and Sebastian was part of that parallel universe.

Christian was very gentle with her, never asking directly about what had happened while she was inside. It was only after several visits that he talked about the search for her and Lara while they were missing. Contrary to her fears that he'd abandoned her, she could sense the anguish he'd suffered when they'd disappeared, although he played it down. He described instead the huge national and international search operation for Lara and her.

The police had retraced her steps in the days before her disappearance. Guy's apartment had been thoroughly searched, and Stevie Dawber's. 'Poor old Stevie,' said Christian. 'You've got to feel sorry for him really. The police went up to question him and wanted to look round the house. He had a locked cellar that he refused to open so they broke down the door.'

'And what was in it?' Olivia felt foolish for imagining he might have been hiding Sandra.

Christian smiled. 'A cannabis farm. Apparently, his wife made it difficult for him to access any drugs, so he started his own cottage industry.'

'And smoking it gave him the munchies, which was why he was always asking me to buy him sweet things.' Everything was clear to Olivia now. 'But what's happened to him?'

'The poor guy's been thrown out. It seems that it was the last straw for Priska. Or maybe it was just an excuse because she's already been photographed in the glossy magazines with her new lover, an Italian designer.'

For a moment, Olivia felt sorry for Stevie but then realised it was probably for the best. The life in that shiny house was not right for him.

'They also searched the hotel, but found nothing at first. That woman seems to be able to pull the wool over the eyes of everybody she speaks to.' Christian spoke lightly, but Olivia could see the tension on his face. It must have been an awful time for him.

'We were desperate. You just seemed to have disappeared. And, of course, you were international news. All the British newspapers picked the story up, with photos of you and Lara. There were television crews, journalists everywhere.' He rubbed his eyes. 'I tried to keep things normal for Marc, but it was difficult. I didn't know if you and Lara were alive or dead.'

His voice broke but he composed himself. 'You were so well-hidden we still might be looking if it weren't for that American woman.'

Olivia opened her eyes wide. She'd been wondering how the police had discovered the hideout, which was impossible to find without knowing about it. So it was Tammy Sue who'd told them.

'She told the police you and Lara were being held in the hotel, and also said she'd discovered the sect was evil, making young girls pregnant in order to bring up a new generation. She'd felt it was her duty to reveal this and get it stopped.'

He gave a wry smile. 'Ruedi Wiesli told me in confidence, and you mustn't say a word about this to anybody, that she seemed jealous of the young ones. Maybe because she was too old to have children herself. She'd certainly been the queen bee there, hardly surprising as she'd invested more than twenty million dollars in the community. Wiesli also said she'd seemed particularly jealous of you.' He smiled. 'Can't imagine why she was worried though because it's not as if you have any money.'

Olivia thought she knew why Tammy Sue was jealous, but she wasn't going to say anything to Christian. He'd never mentioned Sebastian and she certainly wasn't going to say anything about him.

Christian had been incredibly understanding. Olivia looked back with horror at how she'd behaved. What had she been thinking, jeopardising her family and home like that? She didn't recognise herself in those mad few months. She'd been another person.

All this had made her realise she loved Christian, really loved him. When she'd first married him, he'd been the answer to the difficulties in her life, allowing her to escape from Edinburgh, to be adored and looked after. Now she missed Christian, the loyal, honest person she now recognised he was, and couldn't wait for his visits. She wanted to kiss him, be held by him. She wanted her family life back.

Christian had so many good qualities. Dr Eva had made Olivia realise that Aurelia had brainwashed her, alienating her from Christian by exaggerating his faults and sowing seeds of doubt in her mind about his love and character. And she'd fallen for it. Now she knew how hollow it was. What a fool she'd been to doubt Christian's sincerity.

Guy and Julian had also visited. Julian came in first. He kissed her and lowered his eyes. 'Mum, I really am sorry for the way I behaved. I know I've been a nightmare. I promise you I'll try to be a better son from now on.'

Olivia put her arm round her son. 'It was a bad time for all of us, and we all made mistakes. All I want is for you to be happy.'

'I am, and I'm doing really well at school. The teachers are predicting top marks in the Matura exam.'

'Well done, you.' Olivia drew him closer and hugged him, while Guy came into the room, watching his son with a look full of love and pride. He then told Julian to go for a walk round the garden while he spoke to his mother by himself.

'Olivia, you are looking so well after that awful experience.' Guy sat opposite her. 'I have an apology to make. I've found out that I contributed, without my knowledge, to your distress. I've discovered that Brady, my investigator, was responsible. He told Eleanor Munro what your neighbour had witnessed on the stairs in Edinburgh. In exchange for a considerable sum of money, he also gave her your address here in Switzerland and she was the one who left the notes.'

Olivia nodded but had to voice one of the many fears that still haunted her. 'But what will happen? Will I be charged now?'

Guy shook his head. 'The police have no intention of reopening the case, but if they were to, the neighbour would definitely testify on your behalf. He said you were a,' he signified quotation marks with his fingers, 'nice wee lassie and that drunken bawbag was assaulting you.'

Olivia heaved a sigh of relief. Guy was so supportive. Strangely, she felt no attraction towards him now. She'd found him exciting at first, embodying everything her life was missing: sophistication, flattery, a world of fine restaurants and exotic travel. But now she knew it was just part of her madness. She didn't want that or him. Now, he was more like the brother she'd never had, one she could confide in and know would always be on her side.

Dr Eva had told her that she'd been susceptible to flattery from men like Guy and Bill because of the way she'd been brought up. Frank had constantly belittled her, causing her self-esteem to be non-existent, so Olivia always made excuses for men's bad behaviour, blaming herself. Now, with Dr Eva's help, she was learning to value herself more, to believe in her own judgement and become more assertive.

Guy interrupted her thoughts. 'By the way, I received the results of the DNA test. No match, I'm afraid.'

Olivia felt a momentary sadness. 'I knew it was a long shot. It would have been great to have a dad.' She paused and looked at Guy. 'And talking of dads – you've been wonderful with Julian, and I'm so glad for his sake you found him. I know some of his awful adolescent behaviour came from the fact he didn't know where he came from – something I can identify with.' She swallowed. 'I'm sorry I deprived you of him for so long. I thought I was doing it for the best, but now I realise how wrong I was.'

Guy put his arm round her, a brotherly gesture. 'The important thing is that we're together now, and he, you and your family are my priority now. Don't worry about anything, get well as soon as possible and we all can't wait to have you back home where you belong.'

At last the day came when she could go home. She just had to have a final interview with Dr Eva before the release papers were signed. Olivia had told the psychiatrist everything, feeling she could share her most shocking secrets with her. The doctor was probably not much older than her, but had a calm motherly wisdom that made Olivia trust her completely.

'So, Olivia, do you feel ready to go home?' Dr Eva asked.

'I do, I can't wait, but I'm still so ashamed of the way I've behaved.'

'Do not feel ashamed. You had a complete breakdown and nobody acts rationally then. When I heard about your early childhood, it was almost inevitable that this would happen one day, and, frankly, I'm surprised it didn't occur sooner. For so many years, you'd been suppressing so much pain: you were let down by your adoptive parents, by your real mother, and then had to face a pregnancy and bring up a child alone.

'You coped very well with life in Switzerland for years and then a series of events coincided to precipitate the crash. The approach of forty is a difficult time for many women, and for you this coincided with Sandra's abduction, which affected you particularly intensely because of your childhood and Lara's closeness to her. At the same time, Julian's father entered his life and you felt you were losing your first child. You received threatening notes and had the feeling unpleasant events from the past were catching up with you. The last straw may well have been the death of your dog. Very often the loss of a pet can be the thing that tips people over the edge.'

Olivia nodded again. The loss of Bella, her best friend and daily companion, had been very hard. She still felt tears close to the surface whenever she thought of Bella's patient, devoted eyes.

Dr Eva continued. 'Because of all these factors, your judgement was affected. You began to act irrationally, but you were not aware of what was happening, and neither was anyone else, although your husband suspected that things were not right with you. This fragile emotional state made you vulnerable to brainwashing, which is what that cult did to you. Aurelia skilfully played on your fears and insecurity and poisoned your mind against all the significant people in your life, increasing your dependence on them.' Olivia thought about this. It was true. Aurelia was always telling her how badly Christian, Guy and Stevie were treating her.

Eva continued. 'They also used a drink made from hallucinogenic mushrooms to reduce your self-control and affect your judgement.'

Olivia gulped. She'd known there was something strange about that sweet milky tea.

Dr Eva looked at her with knowing eyes. 'Aurelia, or Ursula Kopf to give her real name, comes across as a caring person, and has definite talents. Many of the remarks she made about the influence of your childhood trauma were very perceptive. Unfortunately, she did not always use this gift in the best way, because of the influence of her husband, Erik Hess. He was a very dangerous man, a prolific sexual predator of both women and men. The sect members are now being given counselling, and several of them have been proved to be his children by different women.'

Olivia gasped again, but could believe it, given the photographs in the book. How could Aurelia have remained so loyal to him all these years? Even after his death she'd carried on his work and the group seemed to be flourishing, particularly because of Tammy Sue's money, of course.

'Erik ruined many lives. These children have never known the real world, and his influence also corrupted many of those he rescued.' She looked carefully at Olivia. 'Women of your age who've been married for some years are often looking for romance and sexual excitement and Aurelia exploited this. And she used Sebastian as an enticement for you and for others.'

Olivia had vowed not to say anything about Sebastian – she didn't want to be accused of being in denial – but she couldn't keep quiet. 'I think what he felt for me was real. Aurelia even tried to stop him seeing me because she could see how genuine his feelings were.'

'I'm afraid Aurelia was manipulating you and him all the time. It's a classic brainwashing technique – to withdraw what is most desired to increase its value.' Dr Eva looked at her sadly. 'I know you felt very close and very special to Sebastian, but he was one of those most damaged by this cult. He's undergoing intensive therapy, but it will be very difficult for him to adjust to the real world. He saw sex as his sole talent, the only way he was valued. This has left him emotionally and intellectually stunted. He's been in this sect since he was fourteen, and had sexual relations with both Erik and Aurelia. From Erik, he learnt to use his sexual power to seduce potential cult members.' Olivia shook her head, not wanting to believe what Dr Eva was saying.

'Sebastian's role was to attract new members, particularly rich widows who would give money to the community, bewitching them with his special massages and sexual expertise. He was under Aurelia's control, and always had a deep emotional and physical relationship with her.' Olivia was shocked. With Aurelia. She didn't want to believe it.

Eva looked Olivia in the eye. 'You must address this topic before you leave. You can't continue to have a romanticised view of your abusers. You'll have heard of Stockholm syndrome, where hostages begin to identify with their captors. You experienced a form of this called captor bonding. You have to accept none of it was real.'

Olivia kept quiet, not trusting herself to say anything. Dr Eva closed her file. 'You're an intelligent woman, still young, and you have choices. You've told me you wish to go home to your husband and family, but you should continue to have counselling once you're there, because you still have unresolved issues and need continuing support.'

Olivia could answer this genuinely. 'I will. I'm so grateful to you, Dr Eva, for making me sane again. When I look back, I can't believe how I behaved.'

'Don't feel guilt or shame. Everything happened for a reason, and now you can understand the reason why, you must forgive yourself. Learn to love yourself.' Olivia nodded.

There was a knock at the door. Christian popped his head round. 'Hello, should I come back later?'

The psychiatrist looked at Olivia. 'Unless you have any further questions…'

Olivia shook her head.

Dr Eva held out her hand. 'In that case, I wish you all the very best, and never hesitate to contact me if you need to speak to me again.'

Olivia stood up and took her hand. 'Thank you for everything. You've helped me so much.'

The doctor smiled and went out of the room, shaking Christian's hand on the way out.

He came in and kissed Olivia. 'Ready?'

Olivia held him close. 'Yes, I'm ready to come home.'

Chapter 50

Whit Sunday

Wildenwil – Sunday 15 May, 2016

It was Pfingstsonntag, Whit Sunday, a crisp sunny day, warm enough to sit outside. The long table, covered with the checked tablecloth which had been used at every family occasion Olivia had been part of since that first one on Swiss National Day in 2004, stood in front of the house.

Marlene and Sibylle sat at the top of the table, with Guy and Julian on their right, facing out over the forest to the distant mountains on the other side of Lake Zug. Marc and Lara sat opposite them. Olivia sat at the end with Rolf on one side and Christian on the other. It was the first time everybody had been together since she'd come out of the clinic and she couldn't help feeling nervous. Christian and his family had been so kind to her, but she still had an unspoken fear they'd all suddenly tell her to go.

In the centre of the table was a raclette grill, where cheese was grilled on little shovels until it was brown and bubbling. Strips of bacon sizzled on top, boiled potatoes were kept hot in a special basket, and there were bowls of gherkins and pickled onions for garnish.

Christian stood up and held up his glass of white wine for a toast. Everybody raised their glasses, including Rolf and the children, who had iced tea. 'This has been a very hard winter for us all, but now with the spring, we can look forward to a brighter future. I want to thank you all for your amazing support of Olivia and me. It makes me realise how lucky I am with my wonderful family…' Christian stopped and swallowed, his voice breaking with emotion. He seemed to be blinking back tears. Olivia hardly recognised him; Christian was rarely one to show his feelings.

Marlene stood up and rescued the situation. 'Here's to us all – the greatest family in Switzerland.' The others also got up from the long benches and clinked glasses as Christian surreptitiously wiped his eyes. Olivia felt her eyes misting too.

Sibylle leant over and kissed Marlene, while Lara jumped up and held out her arms. 'Group hug.' Everyone reached out to the others and there was laughter as they held each other.

The moment over, they all settled back to their food. Marc took it upon himself to be the custodian of the grill and was distributing bacon and reminding everybody when their cheese was ready. Marlene asked about Julian's school results and Christian said how much they'd improved. Guy looked on with pride.

Olivia sat back and watched them, her heart aching with love. She hardly dared to believe how lucky she was. How many men would be as understanding and forgiving as Christian? She shuddered, realising how close she'd been to losing all this.

Rolf turned towards Olivia. 'Can we go for a little walk afterwards? There's something important I have to say to you.' Olivia nodded. She was especially happy Rolf was there – the first time she'd seen him since her spooky visit to the smallholding just before the kidnap.

There was lots of laughter and teasing from Marlene and Sibylle. Marlene asked about Valmira, the housekeeper who'd come to help while Olivia was in hospital. 'I wish you could send her to Berne. Valmira's a wizard.'

'I agree,' said Christian, 'and that's why she's staying with *us*.'

'You're so lucky. We're going to have to come and steal her,' laughed Sibylle.

Christian leant towards Olivia and spoke quietly. 'Yes, Valmira's staying. I realise now how many mistakes I made. You were tied to the house and I didn't appreciate everything you did. From now on, I want you to have more freedom – to write, to get another dog, even teach if you want. With Valmira coming in every day to help with the house, you'll have more time for yourself.'

Olivia was incredibly touched. She didn't deserve this. She was the one who'd behaved so badly. Sitting watching her family as they talked and laughed round the table, she felt wrapped in the warmth of their love. She'd never had a family when she was growing up and she wasn't going to throw away the chance to be a part of such a wonderful one. She was going to do everything in her power to make it work.

After the dessert plates were cleared and the coffee was served, Rolf leant over to Olivia again. 'Can we go for our walk now?' Together they walked towards the forest behind the house, where the sun was shining through the branches, dappling the woodland path.

Rolf cleared his throat. 'I need to talk to somebody and I think you'll understand. I haven't told anybody else, but I've had a terrible few years.'

Olivia nodded. 'We realised something was wrong.'

'It all started in Cambodia. I was very involved with a wonderful orphanage for girls, which started a café to help train young people. Girls learn to cook, serve and clean, and this gives them the skills to get a job afterwards. That had always been the greatest problem for the girls leaving the orphanage.'

He paused. 'Then there was a scandal involving a rogue member of our charity who behaved disgracefully with some young refugees. After this, there was a suggestion I had become too close to the girls.' He turned to Olivia and looked her in the eyes. 'I did want to help them, and there was one girl, Champai, I thought had particular potential. But there was never anything inappropriate between us. She was sixteen, and I was helping her to look for a job when she graduated from the café. But rumours gather dirt, and after what had happened, the charity wanted to avoid a scandal, so I had to go. I had to leave a job I loved and had done without blemish for over thirty years.'

Olivia nodded. This tied in with what she'd read on the Internet. Rolf was shaking. 'I came back to Switzerland, but

I couldn't forget those girls and this wonderful project. I sent money to support them, but discovered it never reached them. It was siphoned off by corrupt officials and none of it arrived at the café.' His face filled with sadness. 'That's when I had the idea of sending clothes, a kind of uniform. That was the box delivered to you.'

'Rolf, how awful. I can't believe you were treated like this. It must have been so hard.' Olivia took his hand. 'But it's wonderful you're still supporting the café. And now you deserve your retirement and can devote yourself to your sheep project.'

Rolf stopped and stared ahead. 'That's another problem. My project failed. The sheep caught a virus and all the lambs either died in utero or within hours of their birth.' Olivia remembered when she visited the smallholding. She'd thought the lambs in the incubator were asleep, but now she knew they were dead.

'The adult sheep became sick too and eventually they all died. I was distraught.' He swallowed. 'And that's when you saved my life. I saw you coming that day, but I was too depressed to speak to you. I hid in the loft. When my last two ewes died, I thought I had nothing left to live for. It seemed everything I touched turned to dust. I prepared a noose in the barn where I was going to hang myself.'

Olivia gulped. The creepy atmosphere in the place, combined with everything that had happened, would make anybody depressed. 'Oh no, Rolf.'

'But it was your note that saved me.' Rolf turned to face her. 'When you said you were going to visit again, I couldn't do it. I couldn't run the risk of you finding me, and maybe even having the children with you.'

Olivia couldn't speak. Rolf had still been thinking of her and the children at that awful time. She reached up and hugged him.

Rolf held her close. 'Thank you for listening. I've got over it now and there is good news from the café. All the girls who finished last year have found jobs, and my clothes arrived.' He smiled. 'And I've bought some more sheep and hope that, if they spend the summer with me on the alp, they will build up resistance and be able to survive the winter better. The numbers of these beautiful animals are falling rapidly so it is more important than ever.'

'But this year please let us help you. Don't isolate yourself. If we all work together, it will help us all.'

'I will. I just felt such a failure. I thought the more I did it alone, the better it would be. I couldn't admit to people that I'd lost my job, but now I'm looking at things differently. I know I'm innocent, and I see this as an opportunity to do other things.'

Olivia reached up to him and kissed him on the cheek. 'I've had to learn this, too. I've spent my whole life feeling guilty, haunted by the past, but now I know I must look ahead. I didn't always appreciate what I had. Now I know how lucky I am to have your brother and his lovely family.'

Rolf smiled. 'And we'll put up with you, even if you are a foreigner.' He nudged her with his shoulder affectionately. Olivia stuck out her tongue, but inside she was jumping with joy. The old Rolf was back. She grabbed his hand and they walked back to the farmhouse.

Marlene and Sibylle were playing hide and seek with Marc and Lara, while Christian sat on the bench watching. Olivia went up to him and sat close to him, her cheek on his. 'Thank you so much for everything. I can't always keep saying I'm sorry, but I'll say it once more and for the last time. I'm sorry. I was mad. I behaved appallingly, but it's made me realise what I really want. It's you and our family.' She turned towards him and kissed him on the lips. 'I love you.'

Christian looked at her and Olivia recognised the puppy-dog look of devotion in his eyes again. 'It wasn't just you, Livy. I was wrapped up in my job and took you for granted. I didn't stop to think how lucky I am and how much I love you. Things are going to be different from now on.'

Olivia put her head close to his as Lara came running over and jumped on them. 'Marlene and Sibylle are cheating. They keep looking.'

Marlene came running up behind her, wiping her brow with a hanky. 'Of course we look. That's life, kids – you have to keep your eyes open.'

Sibylle arrived panting behind her. They were both considerably overweight, living a life of wine, good food and culture rather than sport. 'That's enough for now. It's more exercise than I've had all year. What about a nice quiet game of cards?'

Lara jumped up and down. 'Tschau Sepp. That's my favourite.' She ran into the house to get the cards, followed by Marc and their aunties.

Olivia's eyes followed them. 'I love them so much. Everything I'm going to do now is to make their life as good as it can be. And our life.' She kissed him again.

Her phone vibrated in her pocket. She'd sent Stevie a message to see how he was and saw he'd written a reply. '*Hey Oli. How are things? Everything's great here in Wigan. Playing music with some of my old mates and I've got a girlfriend. What a laugh she is – couldn't be happier! Hope things are okay with you. Come round and have a few sweeties next time you're in the UK. Xx*'

Olivia put her phone back in her pocket. Stevie seemed to be in the right place. And, as she watched the sun setting over Lake Zug, she knew this was her right place. She realised how close she'd come to losing the most important things in her life. Now she knew this was where she belonged, and she was going to do everything in her power to make her family happy.

THE END

Acknowledgments

Many people have helped me with this book. Firstly, my amazing family and friends, John, Alec, Taina, Heather, Rowena and Michael, and my wonderful writer friends, Sarah Ward, Tana Collins, Linda Huber, Louise Mangos and Meredith Wadley-Suter. You were my first readers and your input has made it a much better book - and it would probably still be in a metaphorical drawer if it weren't for your encouragement! Many thanks to you all.

The story is a work of fiction but is set in places I know. Wildenwil and the countryside around it are not actual locations but a composite of Swiss villages and mountains I've visited. The customs and daily life described in the book are ones I've got to know living in this beautiful country.

Scarborough, St Andrews and Edinburgh are also places I've lived in and most of the flats and houses are based on real ones. Other references in the book are usually real facts; for example, the Verdingkinder, whose stories were one of the inspirations for this book.

I'd also like to thank Betsy Reavley and everybody at Bloodhound for all your help and support.

The last word must go to my wonderful grandchildren, Akira, Magnus and Robin, to whom this book is dedicated. You are my inspiration, my hope for the future and my greatest joy.

Printed in Great Britain
by Amazon